Jo Harris, author of  and *Close Relations*, lectures in photography college.

JO HARRIS

Partners

This edition published 1994 by
Diamond Books
77–85 Fulham Palace Road
Hammersmith, London W6 8JB

First published by Grafton Books 1991

A catalogue record for this book
is available from the British Library

ISBN 0 261 66129 9

Set in Times

Made and printed in Great Britain

This book is dedicated to my family and many friends.

Chapter 1

When James had picked the boys up from school, and given them something to drink and a piece of cake each, he sat at the kitchen table with them discussing the events of their day. It was hot. That afternoon the streets around Camden Square had been quiet, the general hum of the city somehow more muted, as though dissipated by the unusual warmth. James had gone out to the shops after lunch. They lived in a big, white house close to the square: James, Wessley, Alexander, and Elizabeth. There were some builders further down the road ripping out the interior of a house, creating clouds of white dust which floated lazily in the still atmosphere. James had looked into the interiors of the houses as he passed by, searching for signs of life, but the wilting sun had driven everyone away. A cat lay dozing under the warm shade of a dusty laurel bush, one paw outstretched on the hot pavement. It didn't stir as James walked past.

Later, before starting work again, James had prepared a salad for their evening meal and scrubbed some new potatoes. He worked methodically, making everything ready. Mrs Reed had been in that morning so the house smelt of polish. James had made them both coffee and sat with Mrs Reed for a while at the kitchen table discussing the minutiae of the day.

Now he turned his attention to the boys. Wessley, the eldest, was fourteen with a breaking voice and a face that was turning towards handsomeness, away from his child-hood beauty. Both boys favoured their mother, Elizabeth,

7

with her dark eyes and hair. Wessley was already big; people mistook him for sixteen or seventeen. He was a good athlete, a fine tennis player, muscular for his age and lithe. Alexander was eight, a smaller, stockier version of his brother but just as attractive.

'Are you coming to watch me play on Friday?' Wessley asked through a crumby mouthful of sponge cake.

James nodded, sitting back in his chair and sipping iced lime juice.

'It's my sports day, too,' Alexander added.

'When?' James asked, laughing.

'Soon.'

'It's not for ages yet,' Wessley told his brother crossly.

'Next month,' James said. 'We'll be there, won't we, Wes?'

'I suppose so.'

'Will Mum come as well?' Alexander wanted to know.

James shrugged. 'Your mum's very busy; we'll have to see.'

'She'll be away on business.' Wessley sounded resigned and world-weary.

'Will she, Dad?' Alexander asked.

'I'm not sure.' James smiled. 'I'll ask her and see.'

'Better get her to check in her Filofax first,' Wessley told him.

'I'll do that, too,' James said, getting up at last. 'Now, go and get changed and decide what you're going to do until dinner time.'

Alexander put the large glass to his lips and drained the remains of his drink in several noisy gulps. 'I'm playing in the garden with my Action Men,' he announced, banging the tumbler on to the old refectory table.

'I'm going round to Simon's house,' Wessley told James.

'Right.' James nodded, gathering up his sheaf of papers. 'I'm going to read through this lot.' He heard the boys clattering and slamming around upstairs as he settled into a comfortable armchair by the open French windows overlooking the garden. James turned over the first page of his new novel and began to read through the typescript.

James wrote books. His heroes and heroines were attractive and usually intelligent with a degree of wit and ambition. He wrote about London and New York and of torrid sexual antics although there was, he hoped, more often than not humour in their coupling rather than just lurid fucking. His books were for 'adults': they concerned power and lust and avarice, but mostly James wrote about relationships; marriages in turmoil, wayward children, reluctant spouses, affairs of the heart. His protagonists were strong and astute, people who knew what they wanted and where they were going. They were usually women. James smiled at the thought.

James's work sold well both at home and abroad, especially in America where business had been good in the past and James had been described as a sort of masculine Marilyn French – something that had never been properly explained. If James had lived alone, and in somewhat reduced circumstances, he'd have had no trouble supporting himself from such earnings. He'd been writing for years – he'd taught classes on writing, creative literature and poetry classes at his Polytechnic. He had taken Open University Summer Schools and had even signed creased paperback editions of his own work. Now all of that was over: no more undergraduates, no more lectures, no more tutor seminars with panic-stricken final year students, no more examinations to set, no more marking, no more internal politics in higher education.

The boys came downstairs again, breaking James's

9

reverie. Alexander marched out through the French windows into the garden, with his box of toys ready for guerrilla warfare amongst the tatty flower-beds. Wessley, dressed in garish Bermuda shorts complete with a T-shirt with 'Bermuda Windsails' printed across his chest, sat opposite his father for a moment.

James looked up. 'All right, Wes?'

Wessley nodded. 'How's the book going?'

James scratched his head. 'I'm not sure.' He laughed. 'I'm never sure until it's finished and then it's normally too late.'

'Is Mum eating with us tonight?'

James shook his head. 'Too busy. She's having a meeting with Nick and Ruby until around eight-thirty.'

'Don't they have any homes to go back to either?' Wessley asked.

'Well,' James sighed, 'once this office is opened in New York things won't be so frantic.'

Wessley didn't look convinced. 'What time's dinner?'

'Be back by half-six, we'll eat at seven.'

'Right.' The boy nodded. 'It's the school tennis tournament in a few weeks' time. Is anyone coming to see me play?'

James grinned. 'I expect so.'

'Is Mum?'

'I don't know, why not ask her?'

'Because she's never here,' Wessley grumbled.

'A slight exaggeration, Wes.'

'She's never here,' Wessley muttered to himself, walking away.

James ignored him – he'd soon get used to this new way of living. He heard the front door slam before starting on his work once more.

* * *

After their evening meal the family sat together in the lounge watching television. The French windows were still wide open and the evening air was warm and close. Elizabeth arrived home a little later just as James was kneeling at the side of the bath, washing Alexander's hair.

'Hello, Mum,' Alexander called out, his eyes tightly shut against the soap suds.

'Hello, you.' She looked down at the scene for a moment. 'Your hair needs a trim.'

'It's okay,' Alexander told her, taking a face flannel to wipe at his eyes as James finished rinsing his hair with the shower attachment.

Elizabeth smiled at James. 'All right?'

James grinned back up at her. 'Fine. Wes is downstairs watching TV.'

She nodded. 'I know, I just spoke to him – he's in the grumps as usual.'

James didn't respond. He stood up and lifted Alexander out of the soapy water, wrapping a bath sheet around him before drying his hair.

'That hurts,' Alexander complained.

Elizabeth laughed. 'Don't be such a baby' she said, turning to leave the room. 'See you in a minute,' she told James, touching him on the shoulder.

James watched her, comparing Elizabeth's immaculate dark suit with his own rather dishevelled and water-spotted jeans and T-shirt. He looked at Alexander, staring into his son's pretty face and beautiful dark eyes.

'Come on then, you, let's find some clean pyjamas.'

He picked the little boy up and carried him into his bedroom.

Elizabeth came into Alexander's bedroom just as James was finishing a story. She'd showered and changed into a

11

loose-fitting white cotton dress, short and childlike and rather fetching. She bent over to kiss Alexander and spent a few minutes talking to him while James returned the damp towel to the bathroom.

'Are you going to have dinner with us tomorrow?' Alexander asked her.

'We'll see, darling. I'll try.'

James followed Elizabeth down to the kitchen where she made coffee and rootled around in the refrigerator for the remains of their salad. James was busy pushing soiled clothes into the washing machine. Wessley came through as he heard the sounds of food preparation.

'What's for supper?' he enquired.

Elizabeth looked across the kitchen at James and they both laughed.

'When did you last eat?' she asked.

'A while ago.'

'Two hours ago, plus snacks since then, no doubt.'

'I'm growing,' Wessley protested.

'You've hollow legs,' James added, standing up.

'What do you want?' Elizabeth asked him.

Wessley pulled out a chair and sat down at the kitchen table, 'What are you having?'

'Whatever I can find . . . sandwiches, salad and cold potato by the looks of it.'

'Is that all?'

'I had a business lunch,' Elizabeth explained, starting to place things onto the table.

They sat down together, James drinking a mug of coffee, Elizabeth nibbling a sandwich and Wessley tucking into a plate piled high with food.

'Are you coming to my tennis tournament, Mum?' Wessley asked. 'It's in two weeks' time.'

Elizabeth hesitated. 'In the daytime?'

'Afternoons.'

'I'll try,' she said.

'Can't you do better than that?' Wessley was annoyed.

'No,' Elizabeth insisted, 'I'm going to New York in two weeks' time and there's lots to be done before, lots to plan and scheme.' Elizabeth turned to James and grinned.

'Just one afternoon then,' Wessley insisted, 'the Friday, the final.'

'How do you know you'll make the final? Don't start counting your chickens already,' Elizabeth warned.

'I'll make the final, no sweat.'

'Like mother like son,' James said.

'What if I win and you're not there?' Wessley continued.

'Your dad can video it for me, I'll watch it later.'

Wessley groaned. 'Dad can't handle that kind of technology. He still uses a manual typewriter, he won't even adapt to the word processor you got for him.'

'I like my typewriter,' James explained. 'I'm very attached to it in fact, we've been together for many a long year.'

Wessley gave his father a scathing look. 'You must be the only writer in the country who has a word processor and doesn't use it.'

James shrugged. 'I'm still learning,' he replied, smiling at his son. 'I keep it nice and clean, you have to admit that – I dust it and keep the VDU sparkling.'

'It's easy for you,' Elizabeth added. 'We didn't grow up with all this technology; we had to use our brains, we couldn't just plug in and switch on.'

'No, you were both part of the sixties generation – we've been studying that in history, hippy, dippy, dopey,' Wessley remarked disparagingly.

'You make us sound like war criminals,' James said and

both he and Elizabeth laughed. 'Anyway, sunshine, have you got any homework to do?'

'A bit.'

'Then you'd better say good-night and get yourself sorted out.' James continued to smile but there was steel in his grey-green eyes.

Wessley kissed his parents good-night. 'Come to my matches,' he told his mother as she hugged him.

He went round the large table to kiss James, 'Sports kit,' he said into his father's ear in a rasping stage whisper.

'Airing cupboard,' James whispered back, breathing his son's strange sweaty adolescent aroma; half boy now and half man.

"Night then.' Wessley turned to them at the kitchen door. 'Wake me early, Dad, I want to wash my hair in the morning.'

'Yes, oh-great-master, anything else?'

Wessley spent a moment deliberating. 'No, not right now, thanks all the same.'

'God,' Elizabeth said as he left, resting her head on the back of the chair and staring up at the ceiling, 'do you think we made a mistake in not sending them both away to school?'

'No, but sometimes I wonder,' James replied. 'Not to worry, it can only get worse.'

Elizabeth sat up and stared across the table top at him and burst out laughing.

'How was your day?' Elizabeth asked later as they prepared for bed.

'Busy,' James replied as he turned on the shower. 'What about you?'

'The same,' she said as James stepped under the powerful jet of hot water. Elizabeth sat on the closed

14

toilet seat with her moisturizer and a hand mirror, working the expensive cream into her neck and face. 'I shall really be very pleased when this New York office is set up and working.'

'Come off it, Liz, you love all of that jet-setting, it's glamorous, exciting . . .'

'To one of your characters, perhaps; to me it's only knackering.'

James laughed. 'ERN Limited takes over the world.'

'Hardly, it's just a very small office in New York.'

'I rang Jenny Grove today,' James said.

'Who is Jenny Grove?' Elizabeth asked, curious.

'The counsellor.' James pulled the shower curtain back quickly, popping his soapy head out, suds dripping down over his face. 'You gave me her name and number, remember?'

Elizabeth yawned and nodded. 'She's really Ruby's contact, I just passed on the message, I don't know anything about her.'

James resumed his shower. 'Are Ruby and Nick working as hard as you?'

'Of course they are.'

'Are they as excited over the American connection?'

'Yes, I suppose so . . . What's she like?'

'Who?' James asked, stepping out of the tub.

'Jenny what's-her-name?'

He reached for his towelling robe and slipped it on. 'She sounded very nice.'

'Nice?'

'Yes.' He started to rub his wet hair with a towel.

'Not a very descriptive word.'

'Isn't it? Well, anyway, I thought I'd probably go along and see what's what.'

'What do you think it will achieve?' Elizabeth asked.

'Make me feel better?'

'About what?'

'Oh, things, you know . . . Myself probably.'

'But I don't understand, what things? What's the matter?' Elizabeth was genuinely confused.

James shrugged.

'Oh, come on,' Elizabeth persisted, her voice registering a mixture of disbelief and irritation. She moved from the toilet seat and began to brush her teeth. 'There has to be a reason.'

'I'm not sure,' James insisted, picking up a comb and pulling it back through his damp hair. 'To gain control over my life perhaps.'

Elizabeth dabbed at her lips with a fresh hand towel. 'When did you lose control of your life, James?' she asked. Their eyes met and they stood staring at one another for a long uncomfortable moment.

James laughed and tried to make a joke out of it. 'I'll go along and meet her and see what happens . . . It'll be good material if nothing else.'

'Fine, then go and find out.' She went into the bedroom.

James followed her through. 'You will try to make Wes's match, won't you,' he said, changing the subject as they got into bed.

'I'll try,' Elizabeth replied, 'I always try.'

James reached over and kissed her. 'Too much work, too many fingers in too many pies.'

'I wish Wes wouldn't keep making me feel so bloody guilty about everything,' Elizabeth admitted. 'I thought we'd explained everything to them and I was stupid enough to think they understood.'

'They do. It's what the family is for, though.'

'What?'

'Making one feel guilty.'

'Well, we all benefit. I'm not working my socks off for myself and, besides, I won't always be so busy.'

'Stop worrying, Liz, they know the score, they're intelligent kids. It isn't a big deal for them anymore, there haven't been any disasters since I took over the running of this place. It was a smooth transition of power!' James smiled.

'That's what worries me sometimes.'

'Stop it, Liz.' He laughed at her.

'No, really, I mean it, you do a much better job than I ever could.'

'So what?'

'So, it's yet another failure I have to face.'

'Don't be ridiculous, you're running a company, multi-million dollar PR contracts, flights to New York every other weekend, the works.'

'It isn't quite like that yet, and my mother always talks to me as though she knew I'd always make a bad mother.'

'You're not a bad mother, Liz, for God's sake . . .'

'You didn't see the way Wes looked at me when I arrived home this evening.'

'Wes is going through pubescent angst, one day he's high the next low . . . this is just the start,' James explained.

'God forbid, he already looks twenty-one.'

James chuckled.

'Come here,' he said, putting his arms around Elizabeth and drawing her close to kiss her. 'We were already married at twenty-one.'

Elizabeth reached up to him, tracing a line with her finger across his collar bone and then, placing a hand on James's shoulder, pulled him down onto her. She loved it when he kissed her breasts, the warm wetness of his

17

mouth and tongue against her hard nipples, arching her back and tensing her muscles as he went down on her, everything giving way inside to the wonderful sensation as he kissed and lapped at her genitals, wrapping herself around him as he entered her. James came quickly. Elizabeth rarely climaxed during intercourse but this never particularly bothered her although for years it had caused James considerable consternation and worry.

They talked for a while afterwards in sleepy, disjointed phrases. Elizabeth suggested something about a holiday and then lost her thread and fell asleep. James rolled over onto his stomach, moving away from her, rousing momentarily as his skin touched the cool sheets before he too drifted off into deep, dreamless, sleep.

The heat wave continued for some days. James went to watch Wessley play tennis on Friday afternoon, sitting with Alexander on a grassy bank at the side of the court. James's old friend Geoff wandered over to join them halfway through the second set when Wessley was busy grinding his opponent into the burning, red concrete.

'What's the score?' Geoff asked, flopping down at James's side on the dusty, dry grass.

'It'll go to a third set,' James replied, not taking his eyes off the ball as it was passed between the players in a trance-invoking, metronomic rally. 'Wessley just lost the first,' he added.

'He'll win the match though, easy,' Alexander told them proudly.

'He's looking good,' Geoff admitted, leaning forward and resting his arms on his knees.

'Good boy!' James cried as Wessley suddenly broke the spell with a ferocious backhand pass down the line.

'Second set!' Alexander clapped his hands together as the players walked over to the court side.

Wessley looked across at them, allowing himself a fleeting grin and a little wave before sitting on the bench and taking a drink from his coach.

'What are you doing here?' James asked, turning his attention to Geoff.

'I've half an hour before evening surgery, I remembered you saying that Wessley was playing today.'

James nodded, pleased. 'So, how are things?'

'Good.' Geoff smiled, lying back and closing his eyes against the sun.

'Dad, can I have an ice-cream?' Alexander pestered.

'It'll ruin your appetite for dinner.'

'Please,' Alexander pleaded, putting his arms around his father's neck and hugging him tightly.

James laughed. 'Are you trying to strangle me or show me some love?'

Geoff squinted at them. 'Let him have an ice-cream, James. I'll have one, too.'

Alexander pushed his father over as James fiddled in his trouser pocket for some change. They rolled over and over together on the grassy bank, laughing as money spilt out everywhere. Alexander gathered up the silver and ran off towards the ice-cream vendor.

'You're a great help,' James told Geoff, dusting himself down and returning to his place.

'It won't do him any harm.'

'A great help,' James repeated, watching as Wessley walked back on court, making ready to serve.

In the end it was an easy victory. Alexander went to congratulate his brother while the two men remained on the bank talking. They had been friends for thirty years, from their first days at school when they were seven and on through university until now. They were physical opposites; Geoff was dark and swarthy with mischievous eyes. He'd pulled James through some scrapes and always, always, made him laugh, made him see the funny side. Geoff was of average height, brawny and strong with powerful shoulders and arms. His raven black hair and cunning little smile made him very appealing. He was twice married and twice divorced. James was taller and slimmer with fair hair and grey-green eyes. Always slightly unkempt, Geoff looked a little the worse for wear, a hirsute man with a perpetual five o'clock shadow. He had a lived-in, rumpled quality. In truth he couldn't give a damn, people either accepted him or they didn't. James was more careful. Geoff struck up an immediate rapport with strangers, James was cautious, preferring to wait and see. Geoff's patients adored him and James adored Geoff. They were close, like brothers, only children who'd come together all those years ago.

They went down to congratulate Wessley as he came off court soaked in sweat, his sports bag slung across one shoulder.

'It was a massacre,' Geoff said, slapping Wessley on the back.

'Great win, Wes.' James put an arm around his son's shoulders. 'You wiped him off court.'

'He's a good player, too,' Wessley said with obvious pleasure.

'Well, I have to love and leave you,' Geoff announced as they reached the cars under the shady trees at the road side. 'Duty calls.'

'Thanks for coming,' Wessley said, smiling.

James opened up the back door of the car and felt a wave of heat brush against his bare legs. 'What are you doing tonight?' he asked Geoff.

'I have a date.' Geoff winked at him.

'You're always seeing women,' Alexander said with distaste.

Geoff picked him up, holding the boy so that their eyes were level.

'Listen, son,' he laughed, 'in a year or two it's all you'll be interested in, too.'

Alexander pulled a face. 'Yuk, I don't think so.'

Geoff put him down again, patting his head. 'We shall see about that.' He grinned at James and then turned to Wessley who was stowing his kit into the back of the estate car. 'Great match, Wes.'

'Come and watch me next time?'

'Of course, if I can.' Geoff passed on, placing a hand on James's shoulder. 'I'll call you tomorrow – are you in for lunch?'

James nodded.

'Good. How's work?'

James slammed the back door shut as the boys got in and shrugged. 'It's hard.'

'Did I tell you that the dates for my exhibition are virtually fixed now?'

'No, you never tell me anything.'

Geoff laughed. 'Two more pictures and I'll have enough to hang.'

'Don't you wish you could give up work and paint full-time?' James asked, only half joking.

'No way, I don't have your discipline, if that were the case I'd never do anything.'

James waved him away and, getting into the hot car drove back to Camden.

Elizabeth was home that evening by six and they sat down to eat as a family for the first time in a fortnight. James had roasted a chicken which they had with new potatoes and a green salad. She helped him clear away afterwards and later, having put Alexander to bed, they sat together on the comfortable sofa in the lounge, a warm breeze coming through the open French windows.

'God, I miss all of that sometimes,' Elizabeth admitted taking James's hand in her own and turning it over, examining it carefully as she spoke. 'I suppose that sounds awfully false.'

'Not at all, why should it?'

'Well, I can say it because I know it's not something I do with any regularity. It has novelty value these days.'

'You can't do everything, Liz,' James said. 'Don't start feeling guilty, it's ridiculous.'

'I can't help it.' She turned to him, looking into his eyes. 'Do you think I've changed?'

'In what way?'

'Oh, I don't know, harder I suppose.'

James sighed. 'Don't be silly, of course not.'

'You would tell me, wouldn't you?'

'Yes and you're not.'

'I do miss it sometimes, James, I miss the safety of it all, that retreat into chores and domesticity.'

James laughed. 'You were never into chores and domesticity, there were always home-helps and those bloody awful nannies.'

Elizabeth laughed too. 'I know, but you can understand what I mean . . . I love my job, I adore it but, sometimes, I wonder just what the fuck I'm doing when I've all of this . . .'

'I thought it was because of all of this, I thought that was the purpose. Materially you can provide the lot,' he said with calculated humour.

'But are you happy?' she asked.

22

'You keep on asking that. Why shouldn't I be? It's not hard, Liz, Jesus there's not much involved anymore. The place is cleaned, the boys aren't any bother, we have every labour-saving device known to science, even the ironing is taken away and returned in pristine, knife-edged, condition . . .'

Elizabeth kissed him on the lips. 'I think we're symbiotic or something.'

'What?'

'We couldn't survive without the other.'

'That's one way of describing us, I suppose.'

'How would you describe us?'

James put his arms around her. 'We're both doing what we want. I don't think we should discuss it.'

'Why not?'

'Because it's a fragile thing – it works and we get on with our lives, it doesn't matter how or why.'

'What about your work?'

'Work's okay.' James nodded. 'No better and no worse than before. It's great being able to concentrate on a book without other distractions.'

'The children are distractions.'

'Not in the day, though. No more sulky teenagers to deal with, no more crap from the powers that be.'

Elizabeth yawned. 'I've got to work tomorrow,' she groaned, 'do you mind?'

'Yes, but I understand.'

She kissed him again. 'Once the New York office is functioning things won't be so frantic.'

'Can I have that in writing?'

Elizabeth laughed. 'I promise.' She reached up to him then, kissing him on the lips. 'I promise.'

Wessley returned from a friend's house just as Elizabeth was in the kitchen making a chocolate drink.

23

'Okay?' James asked, looking up from watching television.

Wessley nodded. 'I'm tired, think I'll go to bed.'

'Right.' James smiled at him. 'All that tennis got to you?'

Wessley grinned. 'Probably. Where's Mum?'

'Kitchen.' James pointed, turning back to his programme.

'See you then.' Wessley went into the kitchen where Elizabeth was pawing over the *Guardian* as she waited for the milk to boil. 'Hi.'

'Hello, Wes. Want some chocolate?'

'No thanks,' he said, opening the fridge door and taking out a can of Coke.

Elizabeth turned over a page of the newspaper. 'So, what are you doing over the weekend?'

Wessley shrugged. 'Nothing much. I've got tennis coaching in the morning, I might go out with Tom afterwards. What are you doing?'

'Guess?' She took the saucepan off the hob and poured the hot milk carefully into their cups, stirring up the chocolate as she did so.

'Work,' Wessley groaned. 'You're always working.'

Elizabeth placed the cups and saucers onto a small tray along with a packet of biscuits. 'I know, darling, it's what grown-ups do.'

'We never have normal family weekends.'

Elizabeth laughed. 'The last weekend I spent here you were never in and when you were you argued with Alexander the whole time.'

Wessley looked at her. 'Do you know if you'll be able to come to my tennis tournament yet?'

Elizabeth shook her head, picking up the tray. 'Not yet.'

'Oh, Mum,' Wessley complained.

'I'll try,' Elizabeth insisted.

He stood up and followed her out. 'Try,' he told her, turning away and running up the long staircase.

'Children,' Elizabeth breathed, placing the tray onto the old gun chest and flopping down next to James.

'What's up? Wes giving you a hard time?'

'Wes always gives me a hard time; makes me feel like "The Wicked Witch of the West".'

James chuckled, reaching forward and picking up their drinks, handing one to Elizabeth.

'Wes just wants you to see him play in a tennis match, that's all. He's very good, you should have seen him this afternoon.'

'Now you're trying to make me feel guilty.'

'I'm not,' James insisted, 'but it's natural for him to want his mum at court side.'

'It's the weekend of my New York trip,' Elizabeth sighed.

'The final's on Friday afternoon, he may not even make it.'

'He's brilliant, he's bound to make it.' Elizabeth sounded defeated.

'Look, it's next Friday. Leave a window in your diary, a clear space, take an afternoon off.'

Elizabeth put her cup down and reached over for her briefcase on the floor by the side of their sofa. She opened it and retrieved her Filofax, turning to the relevant section. 'Okay, but I'm flying out on a Sunday, it'll mean me working up to the last minute.'

'You'd do that anyway.' James laughed.

'I'll probably have to hold a meeting here next Saturday morning. Ruby, Nick and possibly George,' Elizabeth said, sipping her drink.

'George.' James smiled at her. 'He must be the only secretary in the world to look like a heavy-weight boxer.'

'He isn't anything of the sort, George is a sweet boy.'

'He has definite pugilistic tendencies.'

'Nonsense – and he's a personal assistant, don't call him a secretary.'

'Why not? Will he flatten me?'

'Of course not, he's very gentle, he only looks like that, he can't help his build.'

'God knows what your clients must think when he apes his way into a room . . . I bet they think he's a bodyguard, you know the sort of gorillas that surround the likes of Frank Sinatra.'

'Do you mind if we meet here next Saturday?'

'No.' James took her hand. 'Come on, let's get to bed, we can watch the late film.'

'Very romantic, the characters in your novels make much more exciting advances.'

'That's fiction, Liz,' he grinned.

'In your books it's all inwardly, outwardly, downwardly, thrustingly . . .' She began to giggle as James started a play fight with her all over the sofa.

'It's not like that at all,' he insisted, staring into her eyes as they lay half on and half off the crumpled cushions. 'It's more like this.' He began to kiss her, holding her tightly in his arms.

'Let's go to bed,' Elizabeth murmured. 'I'll get a crick in my neck this way.'

James laughed. 'Well, that's not very romantic.'

'Who cares,' she replied, pulling herself up and her skirt down. 'God, you're a randy sod sometimes.'

'Sometimes!' James said with mock outrage. 'I thought that was what I was here for, kept here locked away in your Camden love-nest.'

Elizabeth got up from the untidy sofa, pushing her hands through her messy hair. 'A love-nest would imply a toy-boy – you hardly come into that category.' She took his hand and pulled him up.

'I'm still in good condition,' James exclaimed, pretending to be shocked.

'For a man of your age.' Elizabeth smiled.

'I'm thirty-seven. What do you expect?'

'Come on, Grandpa, do you think you'll make it up the stairs?' Elizabeth put an arm through his, helping him on his way.

'Very funny,' James said, leaning against her, 'very funny.'

She reached behind and pinched his bottom before racing up the stairs ahead of him, James on her heels trying to grab her, both of them laughing hysterically as they reached the top and chased along the landing towards their room.

James was still fast asleep when Wessley came in the next morning, tugging at his father's arm for a ride to his tennis coaching session.

'What's the time?' James asked, sitting up abruptly and staring blankly into Wessley's face.

'Nine.'

'What time do you have to be there?'

'Nine-thirty.'

'Right.' James started to get out of bed. 'I'll be with you directly.'

'I can't be late, Dad,' Wessley insisted.

'You won't be, just give me five minutes, okay?'

Wessley gave him a disapproving look. 'I'll wait on the front step.'

Elizabeth stirred as James began pulling on clothes he'd dropped the night before. 'What's up?'

'Wessley's tennis class,' he said, jumping on one foot as he pulled a sock onto the other.

She reached out and brought the bedside alarm close to her face. 'Jesus, I said I'd be at the office for ten.'

'Okay.' He reached across the bed to kiss her, grabbing the car keys from the side table as he moved away again. 'See you later then.'

'Is Wes going to be a tennis player?' Alexander asked halfway through the session. Tired of playing with Action Man, he'd produced a crumpled comic and had been leafing his way through it.

'I don't know,' James replied, looking up into the clear blue sky and breathing in the fresh morning air.

'I bet he could be, if he wanted.'

'It's very tough, I'm not sure if Wes would really want that kind of life.'

'He would make millions of pounds and buy us everything.'

James grinned. 'Well, that's probably jumping the gun a little, we'll have to wait and see, won't we?'

'It would be good though, wouldn't it?'

'Yes,' James agreed. 'I suppose it would, if that was what Wessley wanted.'

'Then one of us would be famous.'

James laughed at that. 'I have a certain reputation, you know.'

'Yes, but you don't appear on television or in the magazines.'

'I've been interviewed on television.'

'That was ages ago.'

'And I sell lots of books.'

Alexander didn't look very convinced.

'And I've been in magazines with my picture and everything.'

Alexander looked over at the tennis court where his brother was practising his service action. 'I think he could be a tennis player, Dad. If he wanted to be he could.'

James sat back and roared with laughter.

They were back in Camden by eleven o'clock. It was hot and James went through the house opening windows and doors in an attempt to create a breeze. Wessley changed and went next door to find Tom. Alexander's friend, William, came round to play and James went onto the patio, lying out on the swing seat with a can of beer and the typescript of his latest novel. He watched the children playing on the climbing frame for a while before turning his attention to the work by his side. He read through the first few pages, striking out some words, writing others above them. He completed the first chapter by lunch-time when he made some sandwiches and opened another can of beer. Geoff rang and they chatted for a while, James balancing the kitchen phone under his chin as he buttered the bread. Geoff was telling him about his new woman.

'What does she do?' James asked.

'She's a solicitor.'

'Really?'

'Why so surprised?'

'Well, no reason. It's just that most of your women recently haven't seemed too well qualified.'

Geoff's laughter gurgled out of the receiver. 'She's called Veronica.'

'And how long have you known her?'

'Almost two weeks.'

'And she's still speaking to you, isn't that something of a record for you?'

'Oh thou green-eyed monster,' Geoff retorted, laughing. 'What are you doing today?' he asked.

'Working.' James watched as Alexander came in from the garden. He pointed to the sink and the soap dispenser. 'What about you?'

'I'm on call.'

'What about Veronica?'

'She's using up all my hot water taking a bath.'

James grinned to himself. 'Listen, I have to go.'

'I'll probably drop in on Monday,' Geoff told him.

'Fine, see you then.' James replaced the phone and went across to supervise Alexander.

After lunch James and Alexander lay together on the sofa in the lounge watching the cricket on television. Elizabeth discovered them asleep when she returned an hour or so later. She paused in the doorway, Alexander had his head on James's chest, his little arm thrown across his father's body. She smiled at the scene and, for a brief moment, felt apart and withdrawn from them, as though the children had turned away from her and towards James. It was irrational and silly, she knew, but it was a thought that concerned her.

Chapter 2

When Geoff called in at Monday lunch-time the house was once again tidy and clean. Mrs Reed had cleared away the debris of the weekend and departed. Geoff helped himself to a cheese sandwich and the two men sat out on the patio enjoying the warm sunshine.

'Are you still going to see that shrink?' Geoff asked through a mouthful of food.

James nodded. 'Tomorrow morning, and she's not a shrink.'

'A woman, eh?'

'Yes, very good, Doctor, well picked up – a woman,' James said sarcastically.

'You'll probably fall in love with her then.'

James laughed at the idea. 'I haven't even met her yet.'

'You will,' Geoff insisted. 'You like that sort.'

'What sort? What are you talking about?'

Geoff didn't bother to elaborate. 'God knows why you want to go and see a shrink.'

'Counsellor,' James snapped impatiently.

'Counsellor then.' Geoff smiled at him, looking mischievous and deadly. 'Why are you?'

'I think my relationship with Liz could be better and I think it's my problem, something that I have to work through.'

'You and Liz are fine, where's the problem?'

'All relationships have problems,' James sighed.

'Tell me then and I'll solve it.'

James laughed. 'Come off it, Geoff, wouldn't that be a bit like the blind leading the blind?'

Geoff grinned slyly. 'Is it a sexual problem?'

'Don't start,' James complained, looking up into the clear sky but smiling all the same. 'It isn't a sexual problem exactly,' he said softly.

Geoff flipped open the tab on another can of beer, pouring some of the contents into his mouth. 'You're really serious about this shrink, aren't you?' He wiped his lips with the back of his hand.

'Counsellor,' James insisted. 'Yes.'

'You're the only sane person I know. She'll ruin you.'

'She'll help me.'

'To what end?'

'I don't know. Sometimes I feel completely out of control . . .'

'Crap, man,' Geoff said immediately and with obvious disbelief. He put an arm around James's shoulder, pulling them together, jerky little movements which made their bodies bounce against one another. He laughed infectiously, making James smile. 'Has Liz put you up to this?'

James shook his head. 'No.'

'Then who?'

'Me,' James replied. 'It's for me, to try and discover what went wrong.'

'Nothing went wrong.'

'It all went wrong,' James said, suddenly serious.

'Like what? You have everything, kids, home, wife, successful wife,' he added. 'Time for your writing career . . .'

James laughed at that. 'My career, writing the same novel for the past ten years, capitalizing upon my initial success.'

32

He stood up, breaking apart from his friend and, walking across the patio, turned at the far end. 'The law of diminishing returns, don't you think?'

'So, you're not going to write the great British novel, so what?' Geoff sounded exasperated.

'That's not what I'm talking about.'

'Listen, James, everyone starts off with their dreams but most of us just have to settle for what we can grab in the end.'

James didn't look convinced. 'What was your dream, Geoff?'

'I wanted to be a top surgeon, I wanted to be really good.'

'You are really good.'

'I'm a good GP, I'm not a brilliant surgeon; I'm not top flight.'

'Yes, and what if you had been? You'd never have been able to devote any time to your painting. Perhaps that's what you should have done anyway.'

'Art doesn't pay the rent; in the end you take whatever compromise is the least bitter.'

'Do you think I've compromised?'

'Did you want to stay in teaching for the next twenty-five years?'

James shook his head.

'There you go then, you took the next opportunity.'

'The main chance.'

'You did what was sensible, the best of both worlds really – the kids needed someone around, didn't they?'

James shrugged, putting his hands into the pockets of his shorts. 'Liz gets depressed because she thinks I've taken over her role too.'

'Well, so you have. What use is Liz to those children

when she's six thousand miles away being the career executive in New York?'

'Don't say that.' James winced. 'She loves the boys, too.'

'Liz has never been interested in children, there's no reason why she should be. She shouldn't pretend, that's all.'

'Do you think she pretends?' James looked at him closely.

'Don't you?'

'She had them.'

'Liz is good at making money,' Geoff smiled, 'and she supports the arts.' He raised his can of beer and drained it. 'Here's to the acceptable face of capitalism.'

James laughed. 'I still love her after sixteen years, that's what you can't stand,' he accused.

'What do you know about love?' Geoff stood up and belched loudly. 'You're a bloody writer, it's all just grist to the mill, another experience to write down and experiment with.' He laughed as he picked his crumpled jacket up from the back of a patio chair.

'And you do, I suppose. Two divorces and a string of so-called girl-friends.' James followed Geoff through the house and out to his battered old Saab. He carried the doctor's bag, handing it to Geoff in the street.

'I'll call you tomorrow. When are you seeing her, this shrink in disguise?'

'In the morning.'

'God help us and preserve us,' Geoff said, looking up to the heavens.

'You're just an old bastard, Geoff. Why don't you get married again and have some kids – why don't you have some kids anyway?'

'I like yours, why would I want any of my own?'

34

James hit the top of the rusty car. 'Go and cure the sick,' he laughed.

Geoff pulled away, exhaust smoke pouring out of the back. He waved through the open window, ground his way through the gears and was gone.

James checked his watch. He had a meeting with his agent that afternoon and wanted to look reasonably presentable.

Zane Lillywhite was James's agent in London and had represented his interests for ten years. Zane was big and looked younger than his thirty-seven years. He was bright, if a little abstract at times, and had maintained his American accent even though he'd lived in London for the best part of fifteen years. Tall and attractive with an unruly mass of curly tow-coloured hair, he had large, sometimes plaintive, brown eyes. James wasn't Zane's biggest client but his books sold well and had appeared on the best-seller lists, though James had never really received the critical acclaim he'd hoped for.

Zane worked out of a large literary agency which had its offices just off Bond Street in Henrietta Place. James walked into the impressively modern reception area where large pictures of their most famous clients, past and present, were proudly displayed. The Sloaney girl behind the desk called Zane's office and a few moments later Rosamund, his assistant, came down.

'Hello, James, how are you?'

'Fine.' James grinned at her. She was tall and all in black – black dress, shoes, tights, long black hair. She chatted as they made their way up to Zane. James hardly knew her, she was just one more in a long line of attractive women who'd worked for him. Rosamund had a wonderful smile which she used often and to full effect. She showed James into the office where Zane was sitting behind his big desk, leaning back in the impressive executive chair, telephone receiver in his left hand, fountain pen in his right. He smiled and motioned for James to sit and then continued his conversation. One of his clients had just won a literary award and he was congratulating him. James felt a little hard done by, having never received an award of any kind.

'Well now,' Zane began, replacing the telephone receiver and smiling. 'Hello, James.' He scribbled a note onto an open telephone pad as he spoke.

'How are you?' He put the pen down.

Zane was wearing a dark Yves St Laurent suit jacket over a striped Jaeger shirt and blue Levi jeans. He smiled wide, exposing his perfect, white, American teeth. 'How are Liz and the boys?'

'Fine,' James smiled back.

'Well now,' Zane said once more, sitting back and resting his hands for a moment on the arms of his executive chair. 'I've read the new book and . . .' he was smiling again, '. . . I think I outlined my thoughts, didn't I?'

'You didn't like the title,' James replied.

Zane turned to an A4 block, flipping pages backwards and forwards, ignoring James's attempt at sardonic humour. 'I think it was the ending that was giving us the trouble.'

'Yes?' James looked at him expectantly.

'Would she really go away like that?'

'Yes,' James answered without hesitation.

'You don't think she'd return?'

'No.'

'No?' Zane looked perplexed, like a big, soft beagle.

'Is it too depressing for you, Zane?' James grinned.

Zane laughed. 'Not to me, but what about your readership, give them some hope.' He stood up and, removing his jacket, rolled up the sleeves of his striped shirt, exposing thick forearms. 'Give them something, James,' he said, sitting down again, letting James reflect for a moment. It was their usual game. 'This is fiction after all.'

'I just think she would have left.'

'And what does the reader want to happen?'

'They will want her to leave, too.'

'No, James,' he replied, looking more serious. 'That's not what they want.' Zane reached for the telephone and buzzed Rosamund, asking her to bring some tea.

Zane returned to the A4 pad. 'I was talking to Michael in New York the other evening,' Zane began. 'He thinks that *Couples* is absolutely terrific.'

'Good.'

'Everyone gets back together in that one, don't they?'

James smiled.

'And I saw Martin this lunch-time,' Zane continued. 'He was asking me what you were working on at the moment.'

'Oh yes,' James grinned; Martin was his editor. 'What did you tell him?'

'I said you were busy.'

'Martin will like this ending.' James pointed to his typescript.

Zane ignored the remark. 'The middle section drags on a bit if I remember correctly,' he said, just as Rosamund brought their tea, the white china cups chattering on their saucers.

James took his tea and sat back into his comfortable chair, waiting for Zane's next comment.

'So,' Zane continued, taking a sip of tea, 'just a couple of little changes and I think we can offer this to Martin.'

James nodded. 'A couple of changes.'

'Yes.' Zane nodded in agreement, sitting back in his chair and looking ever so contented.

'You always say that.' James laughed. 'It's always much more.'

Zane grinned, opening his hands. 'What can I say? I love the book. The title's awful, we'll have to think about that, but don't worry, it's going to be absolutely terrific.'

James smiled. Zane always said that as well. 'I'll make a happy ending then, just for you, Zane.'

'No, no, not for me,' he insisted. 'Not for me. I know that life isn't really like that, but literature isn't necessarily anything to do with the real world.' He looked hard at James. 'Remember this is fiction we're talking about, fiction.' The telephone rang and Zane picked it up. 'Two minutes, Rosamund,' he said, beaming across the desk as he replaced the receiver. 'Thanks so much for coming in to see me, James.' He stood up and guided James to the office door. 'How's the new book coming along?' he asked almost as an afterthought as he pulled the door open.

James made some encouraging noises.

'Call me in a few days. We must have lunch together soon.'

'Right, yes, thanks, I'll be in touch.' James took the offered hand and felt Zane's vice-like grip before walking out of the office.

Elizabeth was cooking supper that evening. 'Why have you set five places?' Alexander asked, coming in from the garden a little later.

'Ruby's eating with us,' Elizabeth explained.

'What are we having?'

'Lasagne,' Elizabeth replied, turning to look at the dirty child as she poured herself a glass of wine. 'What have you been up to?'

Alexander looked down at himself. 'Playing.' He smiled at her.

'Go and ask Daddy if he'll put you in the bath.'

'I can bath myself.'

'Yes, but I want you to wash that muck off.'

'I can do that too,' Alexander assured his mother.

Elizabeth took a big sip of the wine. 'Go and ask him anyway, tell him that we'll be eating in about an hour.'

Alexander nodded before setting off upstairs to find James. 'Shall I tell Daddy to have a bath as well?'

'Yes, why not,' Elizabeth smiled, stepping out into the warm evening air to find Wessley lying on the swing-seat reading a book. 'Dinner in an hour,' she said. 'Ruby's coming.'

Wessley looked up at her. 'How come you were home early today?'

'I got tired,' she said, thinking how gruff his voice was these days. 'All right?'

She sat down on a patio chair opposite him and crossed her legs.

'You seem to be a little off with me these days, Wes, a bit angry with me.'

'I'm not angry with you,' he said curtly.

'You have to understand that I'm working absolutely flat out on this American thing. It won't always be so frantic as the last few months.'

'I'm not angry,' Wessley repeated, sounding annoyed.

'Sometimes you seem to find it hard to have a civil

tongue in your head where I'm concerned,' Elizabeth snapped.

Wessley sat up and closed the book. 'Are you going to talk business all evening?'

'I doubt it. You like Ruby, she especially asked if you'd be here.'

'Oh, Mum.' Wessley looked embarrassed. 'She did not.'

'She did,' Elizabeth said, drinking the remains of her wine before standing up. 'Perhaps I'll change before we eat, what about you?'

Wessley shrugged.

She turned to leave, pausing for a moment to look at him. Sometimes it was almost a mirror image, a shiver ran down her back. Elizabeth smiled at him before returning to the house.

While Elizabeth had a shower, James went down to greet Ruby who was sitting on the patio with Wessley.

'Sorry,' James apologized, kissing Ruby on the cheek as she stood up to greet him. 'We're all a bit behind, would you like something to drink?'

'Wes has been keeping me company.' She beamed at Wessley, taking his arm as they walked into the house.

Alexander appeared in the kitchen, his T-shirt hanging out of his trousers. 'Hi, Ruby,' he greeted.

She bent to kiss him. 'God, this kid is *so* gorgeous.'

Wessley poured wine for them, handing the drinks around.

'God, you're so grown up,' Ruby took Wessley's arm again, 'and so cute.' She winked at James.

Wessley squirmed with embarrassment.

'Come on,' James said, 'let's go through to the lounge, Elizabeth won't be long and then we can eat.'

40

James liked Ruby, she was a vivacious woman with a ready smile and a good sense of humour. She had a mass of curly reddish-brown hair which she wore long. Her skin tanned easily and she was showing of her shoulders in a low-cut cotton dress that dipped at the neck and rode high above the knee.

'So, James, how's the book?'

James smiled. 'That's what everyone asks.'

'That's because we're all interested,' Ruby assured him.

'It's as well as can be expected,' he replied.

'I loved the last one. I even bought my own copy.'

'That's good,' James chuckled.

'Yes.' She laughed. 'Did you base your career woman on me or Elizabeth?'

'Neither.'

'It was me, wasn't it?' she teased. 'Not quite such a slut perhaps, but there were definite tendencies.'

'What's a slut?' Alexander asked.

'A hussy.' Ruby laughed.

'What's a hussy?' he persisted.

'Oh God, what have I got into?' She turned to James. 'Help me.'

'You started this . . .'

'Started what?' Elizabeth was standing at the doorway, looking fresh and cool in a blue denim skirt and loose-fitting white cotton top.

'They won't tell Alexander what a slut is.'

'Oh, it's someone who isn't very tidy, isn't it?'

'Yes,' Ruby grabbed this explanation with relief, 'that's right.'

'Come on then, let's eat,' Elizabeth said.

The boys were the first up on their feet, chasing through to the kitchen.

41

James laughed to himself. 'Of course, I haven't fed them anything today.'

Elizabeth kissed his cheek as he passed by. 'Poor you.'

Ruby looked at Elizabeth's damp hair. 'It suits you tied back, Liz, very sweet.'

Elizabeth grimaced. 'Too sweet, not quite the thing for the office methinks.'

'Food,' James insisted, grabbing their hands and pulling them on into the kitchen across the hallway.

'So,' James began later, when Alexander had gone to bed and Wessley had disappeared into his room to watch television, 'what's happening, Ruby?'

They were sitting out on the long patio with just the light from the lounge, darkness descending all around. It was still very warm. Elizabeth was relaxing in the swing-chair with Ruby, James sitting close by on a hard garden chair, resting his arm on the circular wooden table top.

'Nothing much.' She grinned. 'I've stopped seeing Tim, I suppose Liz told you that.'

James nodded. 'I was sorry about that.'

Ruby shrugged. 'Well, that's life I suppose.'

'You were together for a long time.'

'Don't remind me, five years.'

'No hope of a reconciliation, then?' he asked.

'No,' she said firmly.

'How do you feel about it?'

'Oh, I don't know, my emotions are a bit confused really, they seem to range from boredom to frustration.'

Elizabeth burst out laughing, spluttering on her coffee. 'God, Ruby, I'm sorry . . . but really, why can't you just be distraught like the rest of us?'

'When have you ever been distraught?' she asked

Elizabeth. 'You nabbed this lovely man and enjoyed ecstasy ever after.'

'Well, never mind, dear,' Elizabeth said, patting her friend's knee, 'there are plenty more fish in the sea.'

'I'm thirty-eight.' Ruby sounded shocked. 'It's all right for you men,' she said, turning to James. 'You improve with age, wrinkles and grey hair are a turn-on.'

'For whom?' Elizabeth wanted to know. 'Not for me.'

'For twenty-five-year-old floosies, I suppose,' Ruby said. 'After all, that's what Tim's caught. Mind you, Tim did have other added extras, his own company, houses all over the place, that rather smart Rolls Royce . . .'

'You'll find someone else,' James consoled.

'That's what my mother told me.' Ruby laughed. 'She said she'd never liked Tim anyway, said he was the sort of man who went home at night and changed into women's clothes.'

Elizabeth hooted with laughter. 'Oh, Ruby, really.'

'And, did he?' James asked.

'No.' Ruby sounded almost disappointed. 'It might have made things a bit more interesting if he had.'

They all giggled at the thought of heavy-weight Tim in women's clothes, all six-feet-four of him.

'Anyway, you can involve yourself in work,' James added. 'All these exciting new developments Stateside.'

Ruby nodded. 'Of course, Liz here gets to keep going on all the expense account junkets.'

'You could go as well,' Elizabeth replied, 'you don't like the flying.'

'That's true, of course,' Ruby agreed. 'I did offer to go over on the *QE2* but Nick and Liz declined to take me seriously.'

'What about Nick, didn't he want to go either?'

'Nick has Sally,' Ruby winked. 'They're inseparable,

like leeches.' She sounded incredulous. 'They've been married for eighteen months, eighteen bloody months, and they still act like they've just discovered sex. I tell you, James, it's absolutely vomit-making, isn't it, Liz?'

'Don't drag me into this, I think it's sweet.'

'It's bizarre, they'd make good subjects for one of your books,' she told James. 'He's classically good-looking, and knows it, and she's a sort of dumb blonde.'

'Sally's a highly paid model,' Liz added, just in case James had forgotten.

'Maybe we should have them round again. I could observe this ritual more closely.'

'And she talks "just like this",' Ruby said, mimicking Marilyn Monroe's voice. 'I can't bear her.'

'Oh, come on, Ruby. You know we're both as jealous as hell of her, she is absolutely gorgeous.'

'So gorgeous it's positively unreal,' Ruby grumbled.

James laughed.

'It's true,' Ruby insisted, peering at her gold watch. 'Jesus, is that the time?'

''fraid so,' James said, holding his wrist up to the light.

'Well, in that case, I'll have to love you and leave you,' Ruby announced, getting up from the comfortable swing-chair.

Elizabeth yawned and, standing up herself, hauled James onto his feet, too. 'Come on, lazy-bones, let's see our guest out.'

'Don't bother,' Ruby told her. 'Just point me in the right direction and I'll find the street somehow.'

Elizabeth put her hands on James's shoulder and rested her chin on them as they watched Ruby leave. James was standing on the next step down and they were both framed in the light from the doorway. ''Night, Ruby,' she called down to her friend.

'Thanks for a lovely evening,' Ruby said, then she blew them both a kiss and was gone, waving as she turned the corner into the square.

'That was nice,' James said as they undressed.

'Ruby was on good form tonight, she's been very down about Tim.'

'She'll soon find someone else,' James said, getting into bed.

Elizabeth went into the bathroom to clean her teeth, speaking through a mouthful of toothpaste. 'I hope so, someone younger perhaps.'

'Can't you find a suitable candidate in Manhattan? A nice young business associate or something?'

Elizabeth rinsed her mouth and came back into the bedroom. 'God, all that time she wasted with Tim, I always knew he'd dump her,' she admitted, climbing in beside him.

'How could you possibly know that?' James laughed, putting an arm around her as she snuggled up to him.

'Oh, I don't know, they just didn't seem right.'

'They lasted five years, that's longer than one in three marriages,' he said, reaching over to flick his lamp off.

'He was too old for her.'

'He was very rich, though,' James added.

'What does that have to do with anything?'

'Ruby likes all of that, doesn't she?'

'She's still been hurt, don't let that performance tonight fool you.'

'I know,' he said, drawing her closer, turning to face her in the darkness and kissing her, 'I know.'

'James?' Elizabeth asked after a long silence.

'What?'

'If there was anything wrong with us . . . you'd tell me, wouldn't you?'

'There's nothing wrong with us,' he said, hugging her tightly.

'No, of course there isn't, but even so you would tell me?'

'Cross my heart.' He yawned. 'Cross my heart.'

Elizabeth lay still next to him. Gradually he released his grip on her as sleep caught up with him. In a while he moved gently away and Elizabeth followed him, facing his back and putting her arms around him before falling asleep, too.

Chapter 3

James paused for a second or two before stepping inside Jenny Grove's office. His throat felt dry and there was a feeling in his stomach that he'd last experienced on his first day of school, a nervous anticipation, the fear of the unknown. Her secretary ticked off his name in a large desk diary and after a few minutes more he was ushered into the inner sanctum.

Jenny Grove was slim and tall with striking features and waist-long blonde hair which she tied back in a loose pony-tail. She had very green, very bright, piercing eyes. Moving from behind her desk, where she'd been writing something on a notepad, she greeted him, motioning to two easy chairs by the window where they sat. The office was large and airy, full of pictures and pot plants. Jenny Grove smiled easily but she seemed business-like too. She was wearing a comfortable beige skirt and a white top. The suit jacket hung over the back of her desk chair. James noticed her hands, rather beautiful hands with neatly manicured nails, long fingers with no rings.

'You managed to find us without too much difficulty,' she began, smiling. 'We are rather tucked away here.'

James nodded. She had an attractive voice, well modulated and steady without any discernible accent. 'I know Islington quite well.'

'You're a writer,' she stated.

James nodded.

'Of course, I've read some of your work.'

James felt immediately vulnerable; he wondered if she'd said it deliberately, if it was part of the treatment.

'And you're married?'

'Yes.'

'Children?'

'Two boys, Wessley and Alexander, fourteen and eight.'

'Yes,' she grinned. 'Your wife works and you work at home.'

'We came to an arrangement some months ago, Liz's job was taking up more and more of her time and energy . . . we decided that I'd give up my teaching post.'

'How has that worked out?'

James shrugged. 'It seems to be working out okay, at least this way we can guarantee that the boys' lives aren't too disrupted.'

'How did you feel about giving up teaching?'

'Relieved.' He laughed. 'Very relieved.'

Jenny laughed too. 'What sort of education were you in, a school-teacher?'

'An English teacher in higher education, a Polytechnic.'

'So, giving up the daily routine didn't worry you?'

'No, I swopped that routine for another . . . it also means I can concentrate upon my writing. My wife is in public relations, she has an expanding company, an office about to open in New York . . . Liz's career is very successful.'

'She's obviously able to earn more than you?'

'Oh, God, yes.' James laughed at the idea. 'When I gave up teaching at Easter her salary easily quadrupled mine.'

'What about the boys, how have they reacted to this new arrangement at home?'

'They seem all right. I think they miss Liz sometimes but, generally, its's turned out pretty well.'

'And what kind of a house-husband are you?'

'Pardon?'

Jenny laughed. 'What do you do in your capacity as a house-person?'

James thought for a moment. 'Not a lot really. I ferry the boys back and forth from school, I get their breakfast, usually cook their dinner and put their dirty clothes into the washing machine . . . that's about it really.'

'You have help?'

He nodded. 'A cleaner comes in three times a week, plus someone does the ironing.'

'How did you manage when the boys were younger? Presumably Liz worked then?'

'Oh, God, yes. Liz has always worked, we had nannies and home-helps, she returned to work as soon as possible after they were born.'

'What about your work, how does that fit in?'

'My routine is pretty fixed. Generally I'm free to work after I've returned from taking the boys to school, afternoons are generally free until three-thirtyish, I usually work in the evenings, too . . .'

Jenny smiled. 'Could you survive on your writing?'

'I could, my family couldn't.'

'You've had success, though.'

'I probably earn more than most but obviously not as much as some.'

'Does it bother you?'

'That Liz earns more than me?'

Jenny nodded.

'Not particularly. I don't really think about it,' he continued, feeling that further explanation was required.

'Elizabeth earns more than most people I know . . . she probably earns more than most people.'

'Tell me about your family.'

'My family,' he repeated.

'Yes, tell me about your parents.'

'My parents died when I was young.'

'How young?'

'Eight, when I was Alexander's age. They were killed in a plane crash in the United States.'

'What do you remember about them?'

'Not too much really. My father seemed a lot like Liz, a high-powered business executive.' He paused for a moment and then laughed. 'What does that mean, I've married my father?'

Jenny smiled as well. 'Not necessarily.'

'He was a cheery sort of fellow, but he was always away somewhere else, wheeler-dealing . . . my mother was accompanying him on a business trip when they died.'

'What about your mother?'

'She was gentle and kind, all those things . . . it seems like centuries ago now.'

'Do you have siblings?'

'No.' James shook his head. 'I was a spoilt brat only child. I was brought up by my father's mother, which was fine.'

'How did you get on with her?'

'My grandmother was old and slightly confounded by having a child in the house who set about wrecking tranquillity, but apart from that I suppose we rubbed along okay. She died several years ago, in her mid-eighties.'

'So you lived with your grandmother from the age of eight until when?'

'Until I went on to university, I suppose, although I

went off to boarding school when I was eleven, so it was mainly the long holidays when we were actually together.'

'How did you like boarding school?'

'Fine, I loved it actually. It was where I met my closest friend, Geoff.'

'You're still friends?'

'Yes, he's a GP in London.' James didn't say Islington, for some reason he felt it would be a bit too close for comfort. 'I enjoyed the order of school,' he continued. 'I suppose I'm a conformist, at least, Liz always says that, I like everything to jog along nice and easily.'

'Is Liz a conformist?'

'Yes, I suppose we both are, we haven't actually done anything out of the ordinary, we haven't rejected society and set up some kind of alternative life elsewhere.'

Jenny smiled. 'And yet you write, that's hardly nice and easy, that's not being a conformist, being an accountant is conforming.'

'Being a Polytechnic lecturer is conforming,' he added.

She laughed. 'A lot of people would say what you and Liz have done is rather unusual to say the least.'

'A lot of men would probably say that.'

'And some women, too.'

'The women are generally intrigued.'

'Staying at home doesn't bother you, then?'

'No, I have the routine, everything follows a logical sequence of events.'

'Some people might find such responsibilities hard.'

James laughed. 'Some men, you mean. They'd feel emasculated.'

Jenny smiled.

He looked at her. 'Well, it may be true but I don't think that's the reason I'm here today.'

'Why are you here?' she asked gently.

51

'I seem to spend most of my time listening to other people's lives unfolding in front of me, from Geoff's divorces to the boys' chatter, to my cleaning woman's family problems to Elizabeth's business complications . . . sometimes I feel that I'm not even there, it could be anyone – they all just want a kindly sounding-board.'

'Do you think that you are a good listener?' she asked.

'Yes, I'm a sucker probably.'

'They wouldn't confide in you if they didn't sense a deeper sympathy, people don't really talk to walls in the rational world.'

James shrugged. 'People ask me "how's the book?" and then go on talking about themselves . . .'

'So, you get angry with them?'

'I get annoyed, anger has always been a problem.'

'How do you express your annoyance?'

'I don't usually. I mean, I shout at the kids from time to time but that's just family life, I'm not really angry with them.'

Jenny smiled. 'Perhaps you're never satisfied with the quality of your anger, it may not provide the effect that you want.'

'I listen to myself and feel absurd. If I raise my voice I always cringe afterwards for how ridiculous it is.' James looked at Jenny and felt absurd. He wondered if any of the things he'd said made any sense at all. She, for her part, remained impassive, bringing the conversation back to his childhood so that when the session drew to a close they were talking about his parents, people he'd locked away and barely considered for years. After it was over James stepped onto the hot streets feeling very high, a positive sensation that lasted through lunch and into mid-afternoon when he was, once again, immersed in his work.

* * *

Elizabeth had lunch with Ruby. They were supposed to be discussing a new client but their business talk soon degenerated into a general chat about their respective lives.

'James looked well,' Ruby said. 'Giving up his teaching post seems to have done the trick.'

'Things couldn't have been worse,' Elizabeth replied. 'That job was driving him to distraction, I think it was the only sensible solution.'

'Anyway, it was a super evening, good food, and your kids are so great. Wessley,' she breathed, 'is going to be an absolute heart-breaker.'

Elizabeth tackled her pasta dish. 'Wes is giving me a hard time at the moment,' she admitted. 'I think he's punishing me for finally leaving home.'

'You haven't left home.' Ruby laughed at the idea.

'No, but you'd think it from the fuss he makes and the blackmail he employs.'

'Blackmail?' Ruby sipped her wine.

'Emotional blackmail, when I can't make a tennis match because I have to be here. That's why I've had to cancel Friday afternoon.'

'It'll do you good,' Ruby encouraged.

'It's bloody unprofessional, though.'

'At least you've got kids. Look at me, thirtyish and childless.'

'You could have kids if you wanted them. You just don't want them.'

'I might want them,' Ruby insisted.

'So have a child.'

'You have to have a man.'

'Get someone to donate sperm,' Elizabeth said nonchalantly.

'Who?'

'I don't know, a friend, someone you know well but don't want to get involved with.'

'I don't know anybody that well.'

Elizabeth shrugged. 'You don't want kids, you've always detested the idea of shitty nappies all over the place. They completely disrupt your existence, Ruby.'

'They didn't disrupt your existence,' Ruby replied, sounding like a petulant twelve-year-old.

'They did, you don't remember, that's all.'

'I could have nannies like you.'

'They only remove the work load, they don't make the guilt any less.' She looked at Ruby across the small table top. 'Perhaps I was just never maternal enough.'

'Crap, why shouldn't you have your career, too?'

Elizabeth laughed. 'For a minute I thought you were going to say " . . . my cake and eat it"!'

'You'd spend more time with them if you could, you *will* spend more time with them once the New York office is up and running.'

'I'm not sure if that's entirely true, but thanks anyway.'

'And Wessley will be fine, he's really grown up, he's a mature young man.' Ruby smiled encouragingly at her friend.

'He's fourteen years old, Ruby, a child. Wes only looks twenty-one, don't let him fool you.'

'Well, you're going to the damn tennis match now, that'll please him, won't it?'

Elizabeth nodded. 'I suppose so. It's this job. As long as I do it there will always be this distance, it's inevitable. I'm off to New York again on Sunday, just imagine how Wessley's going to react to that.'

'What does James say?'

'Oh, he gently encourages me to meet Wes halfway,' she sighed, 'and so I shuffle my diary around and make my new arrangements and make my apologies to new clients and, the thing is, I *really* want to meet them. I've worked hard to get the account.'

'It's a few drinks over lunch, Liz, that's all.'

'It's the icing on the cake, the conclusion to hard graft. I bet Wes will lose the match just to spite me.'

'Oh, Liz,' Ruby laughed, 'don't be so paranoid.'

'I can't help it, he doesn't remember how I used to zoom home from the office and carry on another few hours' domestic labour when the nanny departed and he went to a child-minder.'

'James helped.'

'Yes, of course he helped but James was also finishing a hard day's work and preparing to begin another on one of his books.'

'So, things are better now, so enjoy.'

Elizabeth laughed. 'There's just no solution. If I'd stayed at home I'd have felt resentful; I work and I feel guilty. You can't win.'

They walked back to the office in the hot afternoon and, once in the air-conditioned, high-tech efficiency, Elizabeth sat down behind her big desk and called George to take down some dictation. He wandered in, his biceps bulging through the white cotton of his expensive shirt, the sleeves rolled up high over them like a navvy's. James was right, George did resemble a heavy-weight boxer, a contender down on his luck.

'Hello, George,' she grinned, watching as he sat down in front of her. 'What's been happening?'

George took up the notepad in his enormous hands and, turning back the pages, reeled off a list of messages taken and people to call back.

Elizabeth leant back in her expensive executive chair and listened to George's rather lugubrious drone.

Sometime later she received a call from their business associate in New York, Howard Sands. He wanted to discuss some problems they were facing with the office there. Elizabeth had met Howard Sands on several occasions. She found him very bright and extremely forthright. He was a couple of years younger than her, expensively dressed, perhaps a bit too flashy but definitely a handsome man. She imagined him lolling in his office, feet up on the desk, leaning back in his chair as he spoke to her. After the initial detail of their business they discussed the time of her flight on Sunday, where she was staying and the work that lay ahead. He said that he'd meet her at Kennedy Airport and Elizabeth found herself flirting with him across the safe distance of their telephone connection. She was looking forward to seeing him in New York.

It was almost eight o'clock when Elizabeth walked into the house. Wessley was sitting in the lounge watching the television.

'Hello,' he said without looking away from the screen.

'Hello, Wes, where's Dad?'

'Upstairs. Alexander's been sick all evening.'

'Oh, no, really?' She put her briefcase down and rushed upstairs where she found James swabbing around the toilet with a disinfectant. 'Hi, James.'

'Hello. Alexander's just been sick again,' he said, flushing the toilet.

Elizabeth walked along the landing and into the little room where Alexander was lying, his face deathly white against the deep blue of his pillow case. The room smelt of pine disinfectant, and James had placed a bowl on the floor by his bedside.

'Hello, darling,' she said, sitting on the edge of the bed

56

and taking Alexander's cold hand in her own. She felt his forehead. 'Poor you, how do you feel now?'

'All right,' Alexander replied bravely.

James came in.

Elizabeth turned to him. 'Was he sick at school?'

'No, it came on around six, but there's a bug going the rounds at school – I was talking to some of the other mothers this afternoon.' He winked at the supine child.

'Should we get the doctor to come over and take a look at him?' Elizabeth asked.

James shook his head. 'I think it's just a tummy bug. Geoff happened to ring soon after Alexander was sick for the first time, he offered to come over but I really don't think it's necessary.'

Elizabeth turned back to Alexander. 'Is there anything you want?'

He shook his head pathetically.

She stood up at last, patted his hand and followed James out of the room.

'I hate it when they're ill,' Elizabeth admitted, pouring them both a mug of coffee from the percolator in the kitchen.

'Kids recover quickly.'

'You don't think it's appendicitis or anything, do you?'

James shook his head, carrying his mug to the table and sitting down.

'He isn't in any pain, I'm sure it's just a twenty-four-hour thing. Geoff said to keep him off milk and solids for a while.'

Elizabeth joined him at the table. 'Poor you,' she said sympathetically.

He smiled. 'It's to be expected, Liz. They can't be one hundred per cent all the time, they do pretty well; one can hardly describe our kids as being of the sickly variety.'

'No, thank God,' she agreed. 'I always feel so guilty, though.'

James laughed. 'What have you to feel guilty about, for God's sake, Liz? These things happen, it isn't anyone's fault.'

'No, I know, I can't help it all the same.'

'What's for dinner?' Wessley asked, coming in to the bright kitchen. 'I'm starving.'

'Have you been up to see your brother?' Elizabeth asked.

'Yes.'

'Would you take him up a glass of water, Wes?' James asked.

Wessley nodded. 'Does he want anything in it?'

'I suppose a drop of orange wouldn't hurt. I've done a Lancashire Hot-Pot for dinner,' he told Elizabeth. 'Hope that's okay.'

'I'm starving.' She smiled at Wessley as he left the kitchen with his brother's drink. 'Do you mind if I go up and change, James?'

'No, dinner will be ready in about twenty minutes barring any further sudden emergency upstairs.'

'Oh,' she said, pausing at the door, 'I forgot to ask, how was your meeting with Ms Grove? Are you allowed to tell me?'

James shrugged. 'I think so. Later though, when the house is less frantic.' He winked at Elizabeth.

'He says he feels sick again,' Wessley announced, coming downstairs.

'I'll see to him,' Elizabeth said, running up the staircase to Alexander's room.

James told Elizabeth all about his first session with Jenny Grove as they lay in bed together that night.

58

'What's she like?'

'Nice,' James replied, 'she seems astute and clever.'

'What does she look like?'

'She's attractive in a kind of academic way.'

'Is she married?'

'I don't know.'

'What colour is her hair?'

'Blonde.'

'How old is she?'

'Hard to say really, early forties I'd guess.'

'And she's really beautiful?'

James chuckled in the darkness. 'I didn't say that, she's a very handsome woman. Why the interrogation?'

'I'm just curious,' Elizabeth said. 'How did you feel afterwards?'

'Good,' he admitted. 'Extremely good.'

'So you're going to continue seeing her?'

'Absolutely, for a while at least.'

'And you talked about your family? Isn't that Freudian or something?'

'I'm not sure.'

'Nothing else, only your parents?'

'My childhood really,' James said, 'and my grandmother, of course.'

'And that made you feel good?'

'Yes.' James laughed, he hadn't divulged everything because he wasn't sure how Elizabeth would react and he wasn't entirely certain that he had worked it all out yet. It was, after all, just the beginning.

Elizabeth moved closer, kissing him and then resting her head on his smooth chest. 'I'm glad you got something out of it, James.'

He placed his arms around her. 'I think it'll be good.'

'Ruby was talking about having a child today.'

'She's not pregnant, is she?'

'God, no, she's just getting broody – thinks that time is slipping by too fast.'

'Well, she is thirty-eight,' James said.

'Yes, but it's not impossible, she could still conceive,' Elizabeth insisted.

'Would you like another kid?' James asked. 'We could start one now if you liked.'

'You've got to be joking! Why, you don't want anymore do you?' She sounded unsure for just a moment.

'Well . . .' James began hesitantly. 'It's not impossible, Liz.' He turned them over until Elizabeth was on her back and he was on top of her. 'Nothing is impossible.'

Elizabeth gasped as he moved a warm hand between her legs. There was a sudden, discernible tension between them, and Elizabeth became wet just at the touch and taste and sound of him. His hands moved across her body, gentle caresses at first and then harder. His mouth found hers and Elizabeth wrapped her limbs around his waist, taking him inside her almost immediately. They lay together rocking in this gentle, teasing, cradle, James finally coming with a rasping ejaculation. She felt the fluidity of his movement cease as the ecstatic spasms racked his body, as his muscles grew hard and tense around her and then everything was softness as they lay together.

Elizabeth stroked back his damp hair and felt secure in the knowledge of this moment. There was no work to worry over, no kids, nothing – only the two of them.

Chapter 4

Elizabeth worked for most of Saturday. Her partners Nick and Ruby came to the house with George. They were going over the final details concerning the New York office before Elizabeth's departure the next day. James had a few words with them before taking the boys out; Wessley to his regular tennis coaching and Alexander to Geoff's flat in Islington.

'Mum's always working,' Wessley complained as they all got into the Volvo.

'She saw you winning your tournament, what more do you want?' James asked, slamming his door and pulling the seat belt across and into position.

'And we went out for a pizza,' Alexander chipped in.

'And Mum paid,' James grinned, starting the engine and pulling away from the kerb.

Wessley smiled too. 'It was a good match, wasn't it.'

'Yes, excellent. Very good.'

'Can we watch Wes practise this morning?' Alexander asked.

'No, I told you,' James explained patiently. 'Tom's father is picking him up afterwards and taking them swimming.'

Alexander stared out at the traffic on the Camden Road. 'I never go swimming,' he moaned.

James laughed. 'You go every week with the school.'

'Not to the big pool, though, not to the leisure centre pool.'

'You're such a baby, Alexander,' Wessley told his brother. 'You always want to do exactly what I'm doing.'

'I do not.'

'You do.'

'I don't, do I, Dad?' Alexander insisted.

'Turdy-bum,' Wessley snapped.

'Shut up the pair of you,' James told them, pulling the car up to a halt at a red traffic light. 'Stop arguing.'

He opened his window, resting his arm on the warm paintwork, tapping his fingers on the steering wheel, looking at the sulky pair in the back.

Geoff's flat comprised the bottom half of a large Victorian town house. It had a garden, quite large and overgrown with a dilapidated greenhouse where the kids loved to play. The flat had two giant-sized rooms, partitioned by original sliding doors which disappeared into a groove in the wall when open, a smaller room and a kitchen with a bathroom extension tacked on the end. He used the front room as his studio, the back room to sleep in and the small room as a tiny lounge. He'd lived in the flat since he'd first practised medicine, buying it almost fifteen years before at what now seemed a ridiculously bargain-basement price. James loved the place, he always felt comfortable in it.

Geoff was sunbathing when they arrived, sprawled out on the long grass wearing an awful pair of paint-splattered shorts which had a broken zip held together with safety-pins.

'Your front door is wide open,' James informed him, casting a shadow over Geoff's prone form.

'I need the through draught in order to dry the new painting,' he replied, shading his eyes with a big hand.

Alexander sat down beside him and examined Geoff's

thick body. 'You've got a big tummy,' he concluded after a few moments.

Geoff laughed. 'It's all the pop, son, all the pop.' He sat up. 'Don't worry, James, no one's going to steal anything, they'd have to put it there before they could take it.'

James shook his head. 'You're totally hopeless.'

Geoff nodded. 'You're right, you're right, come on,' he said standing up, lifting Alexander with him, throwing the child over a shoulder and marching into the house, 'I'll show you the picture . . . see what you think.'

Alexander laughed as he was jiggled up and down across the lawn and into the cool interior.

James watched their antics and couldn't resist smiling. 'He'll be sick, Geoff, he's only just got over one bout.'

'Daddy's an old moaner,' Geoff said, lifting Alexander off his shoulder and putting him gently down. 'An old worrywart, isn't he, Alexander?'

Alexander looked up at his father and grinned, taking James's hand as they walked through into the large front studio-room to admire Geoff's work.

'Well, now, what do you think? You can be brutally honest.' He moved to James's side placing a heavy arm around his shoulder as they stood in front of the large canvas. It was a vast brooding Norfolk landscape, a distant windmill against a smoke-grey sky with knifing shafts of streaming white sunshine. He'd captured the openness of the area, the wide arc of countryside against the endless horizon.

'North Norfolk,' James said, nodding, 'you took a reel of photographs . . . I remember. Of course, I'm not an art critic,' James teased.

'For God's sake, man, give me an opinion, I'm not asking you to write an article for the bloody *Guardian*.'

'I like it,' Alexander piped, taking hold of Geoff's free hand, 'it reminds me of last year in that cottage by the sea.'

'Thank you, son. Now the father,' he insisted, turning his face so that his nose was almost touching James's cheek.

James laughed at last. 'I like it, marvellous, marvellous.'

'You're not just saying that now?' Geoff grumbled.

'I love it, how much do you want for it?'

Geoff kissed his friend's cheek, a sloppy wet kiss, laughing before turning them away and back out of the room which smelt of fresh oils. 'Seventeen hundred.'

'Really?' James sat down at the kitchen table as Geoff prepared their lunch. 'And you've got about twenty others in the exhibition.'

'They're not all as big as that one.' Geoff handed knives and forks to Alexander who started to set the table. It was a routine he knew well.

'How do they price them?'

'God knows, by the yard probably.'

'Do you think you'll sell them all?'

Geoff shrugged. 'A few.'

'I wonder how much that one of the boys is worth now,' James mused, goading Geoff into a response.

'You wouldn't sell it, I know you wouldn't. He couldn't be such a Philistine now, could he, Alexander?'

Alexander paused from his table-setting to look at his father. He turned to Geoff after a moment's consideration and shrugged before trotting off to fetch the glasses.

'Thanks a lot.' James laughed.

'There, you see, kids sense these things, they don't express them verbally, but it's obvious to them.'

'What's a Philistine?' Alexander asked, sliding the glasses onto the table top.

'An uncultured person,' Geoff explained, grinning at James across the kitchen. 'Someone who sees great art only in terms of what it's worth to their bank balance.'

Alexander looked at his father and then at Geoff, 'What's for lunch?' he asked, 'I'm starving.'

The two men looked at one another and burst into laughter.

'So,' Geoff began after lunch when they were sitting outside drinking beer under the scrubby little apple tree. 'What's new?'

'Nothing,' James replied, resting his head against the tree trunk. He looked out from under the shade at Alexander who was crawling across the long grass involved in an imaginary jungle war. 'Liz has found us a holiday home on Majorca, a luxury villa away from the tourist traps with a swimming pool and a secluded cove.'

'Sounds fabulous.'

'The only snag is that she can't come.'

'You're joking.'

James shook his head, rolling it back and forth against the knobbly wood. 'It's just me and the boys and you, if you want.'

'Me?'

'It's free, apart from the airfare, but that's next to nothing these days.'

'Why can't Liz go?'

'Guess.' James turned to his friend.

'She's a busy woman.'

'A busy woman,' James agreed. 'Well, anyway, are you in or what?'

'When?'

65

'Whenever.'

'Don't be so bloody vague, man.'

'Really.' James felt hot and drunk now. 'It belongs to one of her business associates, some fabulously rich bloke who hardly ever goes there.'

'Yes, and we'll arrive only to find him in residence with his lovely wife and six children.'

'No, no, no, this is bona fide. Liz's no fool, she recognizes a deal when she sees one.'

'She's paying then I take it?'

'Bring your paint box, Geoff, she'll be a patroness of the arts then.'

'Are you going to work?'

'I expect so – think about it. Tell me when you're free and we can try to get a flight.'

'Right, you're on. How long for?'

'A couple of weeks, that should be enough of sea, sun and Spain. I take it that your holiday plans are pretty open this year.'

Geoff nodded. 'I said I'd take Veronica on a dirty weekend somewhere.'

'What's a dirty weekend?' Alexander asked, creeping towards them through the long grass, ready to pounce and shoot.

'Geoff's coming to Majorca with us,' James announced. 'That's good, isn't it.'

Alexander nodded. 'What's a dirty weekend, though?'

'It's a euphemism, son,' Geoff replied.

James raised his eyes, looking up at the sunlight splintering through the canopy of scruffy leaves above them. He waited for Geoff's further explanation but when he looked again, Alexander was having a rolling play fight with the big man, shouting and laughing as they tangled together across the untidy lawn. James closed his eyes

–

and fell fast asleep in the hot afternoon, the voices of Alexander and Geoff becoming more and more distant.

When James woke up again it was still warm but he could see dark clouds in the sky for the first time in over two weeks. He was lying under the apple tree on the dusty earth, a thick root sticking into his side. He stood and stretched his arms, yawning as he started walking towards the house, the atmosphere stormy and threatening.

'How long have I been asleep?' James asked, entering the kitchen.

'A couple of hours, no more than three,' Geoff said.

James yawned. 'We were supposed to be going along to the National Gallery. I'd promised Alexander he could feed those revolting pigeons.'

Geoff smiled. 'Not to worry, you needed the sleep and we've been doing artistic things. Your son's got quite a talent.'

James sat down next to the child, examining his picture of a beach and blue sea. Everything was painted in garish, primary hues, acid-yellow sand, cobalt-blue sea and sky.

'That's you, Daddy,' Alexander said proudly, pointing to an impossibly brown man with beach-coloured hair, horribly out of proportion with huge feet and arms that swung like an orang-utan's.

'Good, isn't it,' Geoff beamed, pouring tea. 'I think he's caught you very well indeed.'

James grimaced. 'And where is this beach?'

'Majorca,' Alexander replied, still concentrating upon his work, pointing out the people in his picture, Geoff and Wessley on the beach and Elizabeth miles out to sea in a precarious-looking sailing boat.

'Very good, sunshine,' James told his budding artist.

'We'll take it back to show Mummy, unless Geoff wants to exhibit it, of course.'

Geoff laughed, sitting opposite them and handing out the mugs of tea. 'Alexander rang Liz a while ago. She said not to hurry back, she's cooking the evening meal and . . . oh yes, I've been invited to dine with you.'

'Have you?' James pretended to be surprised.

'Yes, Mummy said you both have to be on your best behaviour, though.' Alexander looked at them in turn, giving each a warning glance.

'Are you free, then?' James asked.

He nodded.

'What about Veronica?'

'She's out of town.'

'Who's Veronica?' Alexander asked.

'A new friend,' Geoff told him.

'It's a pity she's not around, we'd love to meet her wouldn't we, Alexander,' James said teasingly.

Alexander nodded. 'I've liked all your girl-friends, Geoff,' he said, looking quite serious.

'Have you now?' Geoff smiled. 'I'll have to watch out for you in a few years' time then, won't I.'

Alexander, who had no idea what Geoff was talking about, smiled back before taking a sip of his tea and resuming work on his painting.

Late that night James lay with Elizabeth as a thunder storm raged overhead, the window frames rattling every time it rolled across the heavens. The warmth of the last few days began to dissipate from the house and the smell of rain filled their nostrils as it lashed down. Forked lightning illuminated the dark room from time to time, casting fleeting and exaggerated shadows across the walls.

James got out of bed to look at his sons but found them fast asleep and impervious to the racket outside.

'They're shattered,' Elizabeth remarked as he climbed back into the bed. 'I sometimes wonder if that coach is working Wessley too hard.'

'Wessley needs someone to work off all that energy of his,' James concluded. 'Hitting tennis balls for all he's worth is bloody good therapy.'

'Do you think he could be a tennis player?'

'A professional, on the circuit?'

'Yes.'

'Do you?'

'I don't know, his coach seems to think there's something there.'

'When were you talking to him?'

'He brought Wessley back from the pool. I didn't understand the details.'

'We'll have to see, I suppose, it depends on what Wes wants to do. I can't say I really imagined him being a professional sportsman, though.'

'What do you imagine him being, then?'

'I don't know, are we supposed to be guiding him towards a career choice at fourteen?'

'I don't know either . . .', but Elizabeth's words were drowned in a huge clap of thunder right above them. She grabbed James's hand in shock and gasped for breath feeling stupid and feeble-minded. 'Do you think Geoff disapproves of me, James?' she asked after a while.

'No, of course not.' James curled a strand of Elizabeth's hair round his fingers, he laughed at her suggestion. 'Why should he?'

'Oh, I don't know, I believe he thinks our situation is all wrong.'

'Who cares what Geoff thinks?'

'You do, he's your best friend.'

'He's your friend, too.'

'It isn't the same, besides, you've known him for all of your life.'

'So?' James laughed again. 'What does that have to do with anything?'

'You know him better than anyone else.'

'Don't be ridiculous. You're jealous of him that's all. You always have been.'

'You love Geoff.'

'Yes, I agree, I do love him but I married you, Liz, and that's the major distinction.'

Elizabeth bit into his shoulder. 'He got you stinko at our wedding. He got you so pissed the night before we got married that you barely made it to the registry office.'

James chuckled at the memory. 'He was a medical student, for God's sake.'

'What does that have to do with anything? You weren't a medical student, he was trying to sabotage the wedding.'

'No,' James assured her, kissing her lips. 'He wasn't, I know he wasn't.'

'How can you be so sure?'

'Because he wouldn't do anything like that. He's scared of you.'

It was Elizabeth's turn to laugh. 'Don't be absurd.'

'It's true, he's in awe of your success.'

Elizabeth hooted with laughter, putting a hand over her mouth to stifle the sound, turning to James in the darkness.

The hot spell had finally broken and Sunday dawned grey, chilly and rainswept. Elizabeth was up early putting the finishing touches to her packing. James made breakfast and coaxed the boys into getting ready for the drive to Heathrow.

70

—

'Can we watch the planes taking off?' Alexander asked as they drove away from the house.

'If you like,' James replied, watching the greasy road as the windscreen wipers moved back and forth in hypnotic rhythm.

'It's raining, dummy,' Wessley told his brother. 'You can't go on to the observation area if it's raining.'

'It might have stopped by then,' Elizabeth remarked. 'Besides, a bit of rain won't hurt, you won't melt.'

Wessley sighed and stared out of his window.

'Have you got everything?' James asked.

'Yes,' Elizabeth nodded, turning a page of the *Observer* colour magazine.

'Is someone meeting you at the other end?'

'Howard Sands,' she said.

'That's good of him.'

'Not really, he wants to pick my brains, he thinks I'll be jet-lagged and therefore not quite *compos mentis*. He thinks I might let a few things slip.'

'I thought he was supposed to be your associate.'

Elizabeth flipped another page and examined an advert for a new kitchen. 'He is, but you know what these American business types are like.'

'So you don't trust him?'

'It's not a case of not trusting. So far everything has been fine but we obviously have our ideas about things and Howard has his.'

'Sounds wonderful,' James said.

'It is,' she assured him, 'it really is.'

Alexander cried when it was time for Elizabeth to leave them. Wessley remained impassive with an angry look in his eyes. Elizabeth kissed Alexander and then turned to her eldest son.

71

'Don't look like that, Wes, the wind might change and then you'll have a permanent scowl on your face.'

Wessley did not alter his expression.

'Give me a kiss goodbye,' she told him.

Wessley pecked her on the cheek.

Elizabeth let it pass and reached forward to kiss James. 'How do I look?' she asked as they broke apart.

'Like a woman who is going places.'

She grinned. She was wearing black trousers and a long black jacket over a cream round-necked cotton top. 'What do you think, Wes?'

'You look all right,' he sulked.

Elizabeth picked up her briefcase. 'Right then, be good kids and I'll see you all next weekend.'

'Bring us something back,' Wessley called after her as she walked away.

Elizabeth turned and nodded, waved, and then was gone.

James took Alexander's hand and put an arm around Wessley's shoulder as they walked out of the departures building towards the parked car.

James had hoped to get some work completed after lunch but the change in the weather, the fact that the boys were forced inside because of the rain, resulted in them being argumentative and fractious. He'd just settled one row between them and was sitting down with his typescript in the lounge again when he heard them shouting. Wearily James put his work down once more and went into the kitchen to find out what the trouble was this time. Alexander was screaming. He was holding his hands against a gash on his forehead, blood running down between his clasped fingers. Wessley stood, white-faced

72

and frozen to the spot. James grabbed a length of kitchen paper.

'What happened?' James demanded, forcing the frightened child's hands apart and blotting the wound with the thick wad of crumpled paper.

'I pushed him away from me,' Wessley began, his voice breaking with fear and emotion. 'I didn't mean it, Dad.'

James examined the sharp corner of the work-surface where a deposit of Alexander's scraped skin remained, a piece of scalp containing tiny strands of hair.

'For God's sake, Wes, he's only a baby.' James moved the sobbing boy to the table and into the light, attempting to get a better look at the injury. Blood dripped from the sodden paper forming a spotty trail across the floor tiles. The front door bell rang.

'Go and answer that, Wes,' James commanded.

Wessley remained rooted to the spot. The bell rang once more.

'Wessley,' James shouted. 'Answer the bloody door.' In a moment he heard Geoff's voice.

'What happened here?' he asked, bending down to look at the injury and tut-tutting as he saw the damage.

'Sibling rivalry,' James answered, standing away, relieved that medical expertise was suddenly on hand.

'It was an accident,' Wessley said, standing at the door as though afraid to advance any further.

James scowled at him. 'You pushed him.'

'It's going to need a stitch,' Geoff said. 'Come on, let's get him to the surgery.'

James picked up Alexander and they rushed out of the house and down the front steps to the car.

'God,' James sighed, 'what a day.'

* * *

When they returned Wessley went straight up to his room and Alexander lay on the sofa in the lounge. Geoff had shaved a small section of hair away from the child's hairline and had put in six neat stitches which looked angry and incongruous against Alexander's perfect skin. In a short time his colour had returned and he was asking for something to eat. James made him a peanut butter sandwich and put his favourite video on. Rain poured down, battering, wind-blown, against the French windows.

'Jesus,' James sighed as he returned to the kitchen with further instructions for milk-shake and cake.

'Sit down,' Geoff commanded. 'You look worse than the kids.' He was making tea and munching Mrs Reed's supply of digestives.

'I'm supposed to be responsible for them,' James complained, leaning forward, resting his elbows on the smooth table top and pushing strong fingers through his hair.

'These things happen,' Geoff soothed. 'Children fight.'

'They don't try to kill one another.'

'You'd be surprised.'

'What do you know about kids?' James asked, feeling angry, wanting to hurt someone, anyone. He looked at his friend. 'I'm sorry, Geoff.'

Geoff nodded. 'Hot sweet tea, that's what I prescribe for you, old son.'

James broke into a smile at last. 'I'd better go and see Wes.'

'Leave him, he'll be all right, just leave him to calm down.'

James watched as Geoff poured boiling water into the pot. 'He needs a good talking to.'

'Wes was really upset, James, don't be too hard.'

'That's easy for you to say, you don't have a delinquent on your hands.'

Geoff grinned, shaking his head. 'Neither do you.'

'God knows what Liz will say when she phones.'

'Don't tell her.'

'How do I explain the stitches?'

'It isn't as serious as it looks, there won't even be much of a scar.'

'Yes, Doctor.'

'Come on,' Geoff instructed, handing over a mug of tea. 'We'd better go and sit with the laddie, make sure he doesn't drop off to sleep yet.'

'Why not?' James asked, sounding anxious again.

Geoff laughed. 'Just a precaution, it was a nasty bang on the head. I'd prefer him to stay awake for a while, just to make sure he isn't concussed. Then I must be off.'

'Jesus,' James breathed.

'It's nothing,' Geoff said firmly, leading the way through, 'nothing at all.'

'Thanks for everything,' James said a little later as he saw Geoff out of the house.

'Call me if you're worried. And don't give Wes too much stick.'

'No, Doctor.'

Geoff started to get into the rusty old Saab when he stood up again, smiling across the top of the car. 'Don't you want to know why I came round in the first place?'

James looked vacant for a moment, he'd forgotten that Geoff had just called in on the off chance. 'Yes, why?'

'Majorca.'

'What about it?'

'Last two weeks in July any good?'

James nodded.

'Right then, do we organize the flight ourselves like big boys or will Liz's secretary do that as well?'

'I hadn't thought. We can do it, I suppose.'

'You'd better check, old son. Maybe she's laying on a private jet, too.'

James laughed. 'I doubt it.' He waved Geoff away, watching as plumes of dirty exhaust smoke belched from the car's rear end.

'Alexander's okay now,' James told Wes, sitting on the end of his bed. 'How are you?'

Wessley shrugged. He was sitting in a small armchair by his bedroom window reading a tennis magazine. 'I didn't mean to do it, you know. It was an accident.'

James looked at him. 'You have to be careful with us, Wes. We're delicate, we tend to bruise and cut easily.'

'I'm sorry.'

'It's your brother you should be apologizing to,' James reminded him.

Wessley nodded. 'I know that.'

'You also have to remember that you're strong for your age. Alexander isn't going to stand much of a chance against you.'

Wessley looked at his father. His eyes brimmed with unshed tears. 'I don't know what happened.' His voice sounded unsteady then.

'Is everything all right?' James asked gently.

Wessley nodded.

'Nothing you want to tell me?'

'No.' He cleared his throat. 'Nothing really.'

'Right then.' James stood up. 'Let's forget it, come down and help me get tea ready, pay your penance.'

'Will you tell Mum?' Wessley asked as they walked downstairs to the kitchen.

'I'll have to, Wes.'

'God, she'll go crazy.'

'Nonsense,' James insisted.

'She will, she always goes crazy at me.'

'Haven't you got that the wrong way round?'

'What?'

'You heard.' James handed him some plates.

'Why does she have to work all of the time?'

'You know why,' James said, rinsing out the tea pot and switching on the noisy waste-disposal unit.

'It never used to be like this. Mum used to be here sometimes.'

'Once the New York office is opened things will be different. How many more times do we have to have this conversation, Wes?'

Wessley shrugged. 'My friends think I'm odd.'

'In what way odd?' he asked, already knowing the answer.

'None of them has a mother who works and a father who stays at home.'

'I work at home,' James reminded him.

'Is it always going to be like this?'

'Like what? A nice house, good food, everything you could possibly want? Luxury holidays abroad?'

Wessley dug his hands deep into the pockets of his jeans. 'I mean is Mum ever going to be here?'

'She'll be here next weekend. Perhaps if you were to try behaving a little more reasonably . . .'

'I knew it,' Wessley interrupted. 'It's all my fault.'

'You're a bit of a grouch, Wes, come on now, admit it.'

'It's adolescence,' he replied.

Alexander appeared at the kitchen door, wearing his stitches with pride.

'How do you feel?' Wessley asked him.

77

'All right.'

'I'm sorry.'

Alexander looked up at his brother. 'It doesn't hurt much now anyway.'

Wessley grinned. 'You can play on my computer tonight if you like.'

Alexander beamed. 'Great, can I really?'

Wessley nodded. 'As long as you're careful.'

'I will be,' Alexander assured him.

The two boys sat down and began an animated conversation concerning a Dungeons and Dragons computer game a boy at school had. James looked on. It was as though nothing had happened. It was as if the afternoon's fracas had never taken place. He smiled to himself, sitting down at the table with them. His mind wandered on. It was spats, outbursts, like that afternoon's which made James wonder if their domestic arrangement did put unfair pressure on the boys. Wessley appeared to be punishing Elizabeth for being such a great success and being away from him. Elizabeth had missed great chunks of their lives, she'd always concentrated upon her work and he'd always encouraged her. They'd managed to muddle through the baby years with paid help. He examined the children's faces. Handsome boys – there was no doubt about that, and intelligent, too. James had never really worried about them before but he thought about Wessley pushing his brother against the sharp corner of the work-surface and a cloud of doubt embraced him. There was something appealing and beautiful about Wessley but also something dark and unknown.

James tried to remember his own childhood. He attempted to sift through the years and remember what he'd been like at fourteen. He knew that he hadn't been as accomplished as his eldest son, not so good academically and certainly not such a brilliant athlete. Perhaps Wessley and Elizabeth were at odds because they held up a mirror to the other. Alexander was more like himself, James considered, physically like Elizabeth but with his temperament. There was a certain easy-going side to his nature that James hadn't wanted either of his sons to inherit. It was the side that irritated Elizabeth. It was the side that allowed him to settle for an almost unavoidable literary career; a journeyman writer who wasn't about to soar into the stratosphere. A husband who would encourage his wife's career. A man who had never really wanted to define success in the way Elizabeth saw it. A person who was quite happy to plod on at his own pace, churning out a long list of books which groaned on his shelves and were popular to an extent. James finished his tea. Everything in his life was set within constricting little boxes. He stretched out his arms and tried to prevent the walls from pushing in even further. He attempted to break out, to be something different but it was useless. He was easy-going, good-natured James. Even Jenny Grove had suggested that his anger wasn't angry enough!

'Dad,' Alexander called him for the third time.

'What?' James asked, smiling at his son.

'Can I have some more toast?'

'We're going to have some supper later,' James reminded him. 'You don't want to spoil your appetite.'

James looked at his children, from one to the other, before getting up to satisfy Alexander's hunger pangs. 'I think you must have worms,' James told him.

The boys looked at one another and laughed.

Chapter 5

Howard Sands was waiting for Elizabeth looking immaculate and casual at the same time, an Armani jacket and slacks, a neat white shirt with a button-down collar and a dark, silk tie. They shook hands. It was just after two o'clock in the afternoon, New York time and she felt a little speedy with fatigue. No matter how she tried to ignore it, jet-lag always caught her out.

'The flight was delayed,' she explained. 'I hope you haven't been waiting around.'

Howard took her bag as they walked out into the bright sunshine amidst the chaos outside the TWA building at Kennedy Airport. 'No, I waited in the clubroom,' he explained. 'I even managed to get some work done.' He laughed, holding his slim, black briefcase up in the air.

They drove to Manhattan in Howard's sleek, midnight-blue BMW. They crossed the Triborough Bridge into the city and jerked their way through heavy downtown traffic. Heat shimmered off the car's bonnet but, inside, the efficient air-conditioning system kept them both cool. Elizabeth gazed up at the miraculous skyscrapers. She always forgot her cynicism about jet travel and big cities as soon as she saw New York again. Every cliché ever written about it was absolutely spot on as far as she was concerned. Howard eventually pulled into the New York Hilton on the Avenue of the Americas where a liveried door man helped Elizabeth out. Howard opened the boot and waited for the bellhop to remove her baggage.

'I thought we'd have a working dinner this evening,'

Howard said, closing the boot lid and returning to the driving side of the BMW, smiling across the top of the car at Elizabeth.

'Fine,' Elizabeth replied, suddenly feeling the oppressive heat bearing down on her.

'Good, I'll meet you for drinks around seven-thirty then. Is there anywhere special that you'd like to dine?'

'No.' Elizabeth shook her head.

'Great, it'll be a surprise then,' and, ducking down, he climbed back into the powerful car and was gone.

'Nice wheels,' the bellhop breezed as they walked into the cool hotel.

Elizabeth agreed, walking across to the reception desk to register her arrival.

Later, Howard took her to Abuzzi, an Italian restaurant a few paces from Tiffany's, which had a festive quality with bright oil paintings covering the walls. It was a hot evening and Elizabeth had worn a simple black dress, the only adornment being her wedding ring and a fragile, gold chain necklace. Once inside the restaurant Elizabeth realized that she was hungry and ordered breast of chicken with prosciutto and mozzarella in marsala sauce. Howard ordered mignonettes of beef with shallots. They drank a lot of wine and Elizabeth felt flushed and sated and extremely comfortable.

'We haven't talked much business,' Elizabeth said as she picked up her cup to finish the coffee.

'We've talked enough,' Howard assured her. 'We can get down to work tomorrow.'

'If I ever wake up tomorrow.' She groaned. 'All this marvellous food *and* jet-lag, God, I'll be like a zombie.'

Howard laughed. It made him look even more attractive. Elizabeth had never really seen him in a totally

81

relaxed mood before. Their brief meetings had been strictly business, their dinners with clients or partners.

'It's not late,' he said, 'I'll take you back to the hotel in a little while.'

Elizabeth nodded. There was something so unmistakably American about Howard, his size she supposed, and the healthy sheen he exuded. He was dark, swarthy and muscular and Elizabeth suddenly wondered what he looked like without clothes.

They had a seven-thirty breakfast meeting the following morning, Howard and three button-down Wall Street executives, in the Hilton's 'Hurlingham's' restaurant. Elizabeth had been the last to arrive, sitting down as the introductions were made, realizing that they were all wearing grey suits apart from Howard who wore black. After the initial pleasant chat it was down to work with a vengeance with Elizabeth having to explain why her company could represent the PR requirements of a large American corporation better than their existing people. Elizabeth had done her homework well, she'd come prepared and was, as Howard said later, able to cover all her bases.

The three grey men had departed by nine-fifteen. Howard sat back and shot her an admiring glance. 'That was pretty nifty,' he admitted.

'God,' Elizabeth groaned, 'I still feel hung-over, they must have wondered what had stumbled in.'

'You look great,' Howard told her, smiling, his dark eyes meeting her own. 'Really, you look smashing.'

Elizabeth laughed at his very English expression.

By Thursday Elizabeth had seen so many people and attended so many meetings that she could no longer remember the names or the faces of anyone they'd met. They tended to work out of Howard's large suite of offices high in the Seagram Building from where Elizabeth could look down at the traffic and the people below. The Sands Corporation was very impressive with muted colours and thick carpeting, the hum of computers and air-conditioning and full of Ivy Leaguers, intelligent, quick and sharp. It amused and fascinated Elizabeth to watch Howard in his own environment, jacket off, shirt sleeves rolled up, collar button undone, the physique of a navvy amongst the swish of his Park Avenue suite.

It was that afternoon when, coming out of a meeting with some of his associates, Howard suggested the Russian Tea Room.

'What?' Elizabeth had turned to him in surprise.

'The Russian Tea Room, you need a break.'

Elizabeth followed him along the corridor and into his office. 'What about work?'

'Forget about work, we've done enough this week, we deserve a treat.'

'We're meeting someone there, aren't we?' she asked. 'Another client.'

'Come on,' Howard instructed, pulling on his jacket and taking her arm, leading her towards the elevator, 'hot coffee and cakes, cream cakes, that's what we want now.'

As they emerged into the steaming heat of that New York afternoon, Elizabeth felt a sense of freedom, a sense of being herself without having to balance work and motherhood and marriage, without having to continually divide herself up into little pieces. It was a wonderful feeling but also terrifying, and it frightened Elizabeth to death.

'This is so lovely,' she told Howard, looking around the restaurant with its red and gold Edwardian decor.

Howard grinned, pleased at having pleased her. 'And you're free for the rest of the day too.'

'Really? No more people to meet?'

Howard shook his head. 'Nope, not until eight o'clock tomorrow morning.'

'I can do some shopping then. I promised the boys a treat and something for myself, of course, and I can go back to the hotel and have a long soak, and . . .'

'. . . and you can have dinner with me this evening,' Howard interrupted, 'if you like.' Their eyes met.

Elizabeth agreed without any hesitation, it was exactly what she would like.

'Have you ever been to the Tavern On The Green?' he asked. 'In Central Park?'

'No.'

'It's great, they have tiny lights strung in the trees and we can eat outside on the terrace and,' he laughed at himself, 'it's beautiful and,' he paused.

'What?' she looked into his eyes.

'Romantic?' he suggested.

Elizabeth put a forefinger up to her mouth, moving it slowly over her bottom lip. There seemed no need to reply.

Across the restaurant from them sat an old woman, an actress perhaps, very old but immaculately dressed and made-up. Her face had been painted, the eyebrows shaved and pencilled in, frosty blue eyelids and wonderfully long lashes, comical in their audacity. She wore a black fur pill-box hat, her blonde hair curling beneath it. Big silver earrings in the shape of African dance masks sparkled in the light, and her real lips, now thin and drawn, had been supplemented by the brightest red lipstick. Elizabeth imagined the lips being painted on, a scarlet gash which bled slightly into the tiny lines and creases around the mouth. The woman's skin glowed with make-up, a theatrical base onto which had been daubed roses for cheeks. Her outfit was incredible, beautifully executed in red and black: black top, red skirt, red cuffs with large black buttons, black polka-dot gloves. She was a wonderful sight and yet somehow tragic; gorgeous under hot white lights on some distant stage but scary in close-up.

'Look at that,' Elizabeth whispered, tapping Howard's arm.

Howard turned to sneak a look. 'Jesus, isn't that what's-her-name?'

'Who?'

'That film star from all those Warner Brothers films in the thirties . . . you know, Joan Crawford.'

'Joan Crawford died years ago.'

'Well, *she* looks as though she died years ago.'

'Stop it,' Elizabeth replied, breaking into a fit of giggles.

Just then the old woman lifted her hooded eyelids and revealed the brightest blue eyes which seemed to flash at Elizabeth before turning their attention towards the waiter. The look made Elizabeth stop laughing. She imagined that the old woman had heard their whispered conversation, and she felt suddenly guilty.

Afterwards, after their dinner, after the twinkling lights high up in the dark trees, after the bubbling champagne, they'd returned to the Hilton. Elizabeth invited Howard to stay and he, looking suddenly much more serious, accepted. Later, as Howard slept in her hotel bed, Elizabeth prowled the room. Eventually she sat looking out at the bustling city which, even at this hour of the morning, never stopped moving. Down Sixth Avenue and across to Fifth Elizabeth gazed at the illuminated Empire State

Building which glowed through the murky darkness. Behind the thick glass, hermetically sealed away from the walking dead who inhabited the streets and slept over subway gratings, the scavenging hordes, the drug gangs – everything that was vile – here she was, sleeping with a man other than her husband, an infidelity twenty storeys high and, yet, none of it mattered, at least, not then.

Howard had been consistent with Elizabeth's fantasy, though it had all been over and done with quicker than she would have liked. She was used to one man, it was extraordinary to be with, to feel and to touch another. She'd never seen anyone with so much body hair. Naked, Howard's legs looked almost satyr-like and his chest and tummy were covered in a coiling forest of curling black hair. Their love-making had been violent with a sense of urgency, each responding to the other's desire, each wanting the other without reserve. Elizabeth felt his big hands roam her body, sometimes gentle, sometimes hard. She held him tight, biting him, feeling his penis inside her, encompassed by him, caught on the edge of eroticism as the dream became a reality. Her head swam and everything inside dissolved, she was wetter than she'd ever been as Howard finally pushed himself into her, catching the rhythm as Elizabeth reached a sudden climax and called out in a voice she hardly recognized as her own. On and on until her strength began to wane, until there was precious little left, and then Howard came, the rhythm slowed, became disjointed until they parted. They turned to each other then and Elizabeth took him into her arms. Howard whispered that he loved her and she, afraid to believe anything else, wished it were true with all her being.

Elizabeth returned to their bed at last. Howard turned over as she climbed in beside him but he didn't wake. She lay in the darkness for a long time considering just what she'd done and what she would do now, for the truth was that Elizabeth had fallen in love with him. This realization frightened her. She was out of control, she had no idea of what the future held. In two days she would be back in London and she knew that it would be unbearable.

They took their eight o'clock meeting at the Hilton the following morning and then Howard, insisting that they eat a proper breakfast, walked Elizabeth along Sixth Avenue to the Rockefeller Center where they sat on the Plaza, the golden sculpture of Prometheus in front of them, the spray from the waterfall and fountains cooling the steamy atmosphere. Under green canopies of leaves and thick, verdant foliage, they ate, not speaking very much, but anyone could see, by the expressions on their faces, that this was an affair of the heart.

'This is ridiculous,' Elizabeth said, smiling as she reached for her cup of coffee.

'What is?' Howard asked.

'This. I hardly know anything about you.'

'You know everything that's worth knowing.'

'I don't know anything about your family, or where you come from or if you have brothers and sisters, if you're married or divorced, if this is a common sort of event for you.'

'Boston,' Howard began. 'I come from central Boston, where my parents still have a house, and I have two brothers, one older, one younger.' He smiled to himself at this list. 'I graduated from Harvard Business School and I've worked here ever since. Oh, and I'm thirty-two and I'm divorced, no children, and, no, this isn't a common sort of event for me.'

'So,' she breathed, 'what's to happen?'

'What do you want to happen?'

Elizabeth shrugged, the laughter suddenly absent from her voice, her face serious now. 'God knows,' she said, reaching into her bag for her sunglasses. 'I don't know what's happening, at least, I *know* what's happening I just don't know where it's taking us.' She stared at him. 'Or how to deal with it.'

'I want to be with you, Liz.' He was serious now.

Elizabeth slipped her glasses on and looked up at the flags of the United Nations which fluttered around the Plaza on the esplanade. 'I'm married with two children,' she sighed, turning her gaze onto him again, 'what am I thinking of?'

'What is it they say in movies? "This thing is bigger than both of us"?'

Elizabeth smiled. 'Is it, though?'

'Sure is,' Howard replied without hesitation. 'It is for me.'

She took his hand across the table. Her life had just fallen out of control. She was in love with him.

On Saturday afternoon Howard insisted on taking Elizabeth to view the Frick Collection housed in a Beaux Arts mansion on Fifth Avenue. After touring the rooms of the house and admiring old Henry Clay Frick's paintings they sat in the Garden Court at the centre of the building, a glassed-in cloister with a fountain and flowers and stone benches between the Ionic columns. Elizabeth faced Jean Barbet's bronze angel and listened to the sound of the splashing water.

'So,' Howard began, reading her thoughts, 'home again tomorrow.'

'And then what?' she asked bleakly.

'Whatever you want, I guess.'

88

'That's not very helpful, Howard.' She turned to look at him, wretched that they were about to part.

'Then stay.'

'That's impossible, don't even think it.'

'Why is it?'

'Why?' she laughed in exasperation. 'What do I do, call James and say: "Oh, hello, James, I'm staying in America because I've fallen in love with my business associate"?'

'Sure, if you like, why not?'

'Because it's not as simple as that, life isn't as simple as that.'

Howard sat forward, clasping his hands together in front of him, elbows resting on his knees, staring at the floor. 'Then we'll just have to wait and see,' he said at last. 'I'll be over in a few weeks anyway.' He lifted his head to gauge Elizabeth's reaction.

'I want you,' she replied, 'that's all I know.'

'Come on,' Howard instructed after a moment, 'I'll show you the Guggenheim now.'

Elizabeth took his hand and kissed him on the lips. 'Can we forget about the Guggenheim?' she asked as they stood on the steps of the Frick Collection.

'I thought you wanted some culture.'

'Let's go back to the hotel,' she suggested.

'Now you're talking.' Howard laughed, pulling her onto Fifth Avenue and stepping out into the road to hail a yellow-cab.

There was no satisfying Elizabeth as far as Howard was concerned, she always wanted more of him. 'You'll be the death of me,' he gasped, coming up for air, their limbs and the crisp bed linen tangled together.

'But what a way to go,' she sighed, moving onto him, pressing herself against his hard body, wanting him inside her again. There was little grace in their passion, she knew that, there was heat and sweat and the smell of sex in the air and a desire for him that was unnerving.

In the morning it rained for a short while. The hot streets were fresher as the sun was partially hidden behind fast-moving clouds. Howard drove Elizabeth to the airport and waited with her in the Ambassadors Clubroom. They didn't say very much. The last few days had been like a whirlwind, and now it was time to leave Elizabeth felt sick and full of desperation. When the flight was called, and the first-class passengers invited to board, they kissed and Howard told her, once more, that he loved her. Elizabeth cried, it was wonderful and yet so terrible, her emotions were razor sharp. Finally, kissing him again, she broke away and almost ran towards the boarding gate.

James's week had started with his session at Jenny's office which had left him with a feeling of unease. They had talked about his childhood again and James had begun to remember things concerning his parents that he'd long forgotten . He returned to Camden in the early afternoon and had tried to work. Rain battered on the window of his study obliterating his view across the garden. He stared at the words on the page. Conversations rattled through his head but they were mixed up with the things Jenny had said. In the end he went down to prepare the evening meal, pausing every now and then to scribble something in his notebook.

The following day James had lunch with Ruby in town. He'd been to see his editor that morning and arranged to meet her in a little Italian restaurant close to Covent Garden; tucked away along a side street, dark and outwardly unprepossessing, it had been a favourite hideaway for years.

'You look very business-like, James,' Ruby smiled, 'a briefcase and everything.'

'Don't be sarcastic,' he told her, leaning across the table to kiss an offered cheek.

'How are things?' he asked, picking up a menu.

'Things are busy . . . heard from Liz?'

James nodded. 'She's busy as well.'

'This bloody New York office,' Ruby sighed, 'they want us all over there for the official opening.'

'Sounds like fun.'

Ruby pushed a hand through her curly mass of hair. 'It's going to be hell, James, absolute bloody hell.'

James laughed, she always reminded him of characters he wanted to write about but could never capture with enough precision or, perhaps, he valued their friendship too much to even try. 'You know that you love it all, Ruby.'

She laughed too, nodding her head in agreement. 'I know, that's right, I do.'

Ruby shrugged off her light, beige jacket, hanging it on the back of her chair. It felt warm in the little restaurant. A lazy ceiling fan turned slowly in the centre of the room to little effect.

'How are you, James?' Ruby suddenly asked during their meal.

'Me?' James grinned. 'The same as ever, I suppose.'

'I've been worried about you.'

'Have you?' he sounded surprised. 'There's no need.'

'Ever since I gave Liz the name of Jenny Grove I've been concerned.'

'Stop fishing, Ruby,' James laughed. 'How do you know Jenny Grove anyway?' He undid the top button of his blue shirt and slid the tie knot down.

Ruby pulled a face at him and forked some more

cannelloni into her mouth. 'A friend of a friend. I never actually consulted her if that's what you mean.'

'She seems good,' he said. James suddenly thought of Jenny in her bottle-green cardigan and expensive tweed skirt. He had no idea where she was taking him, but he trusted her. He was still so confused about the whole thing but relieved, if not amazed, that he was at last talking to someone. 'It's going well but I've only been a couple of times. I don't know what will happen.'

'Does anything have to happen?' Ruby asked.

He shrugged and then grinned. 'I have no idea.'

'I told Liz off, did she tell you?'

'No.' He pushed the remains of his Spaghetti Marinara away and reached for his glass of mineral water. 'I can't imagine anyone telling Liz off.'

'Don't you ever argue with one another?'

'Hardly ever.' He tried to remember their last argument.

'God,' Ruby breathed, 'how boring. I argued with Tim all of the time.'

'Yes, and look what happened.'

'Yes,' she replied defiantly, 'we had five great years. Don't try to side-track me. I told her that she should let up on the old work front a bit.'

'Liz's life is all about work, Ruby, you should know that by now.'

Ruby nodded, looking up at their handsome waiter and smiling wide as she chose her dessert.

James ordered coffee.

'God, you're so stuffy.' Ruby sounded exasperated. 'Here, try some,' she ordered, pushing a spoonful of pink ice-cream into his mouth.

James laughed and dabbed at his lips as a trickle of

pink ran down onto his chin. 'How did Liz react to your advice?' He couldn't resist asking.

'She said you were all right, that she didn't want you to see Jenny Grove and . . . oh, yes, that I should mind my own business, so to speak.'

'Serves you right.'

'Why are you seeing Jenny Grove?' Ruby asked after placing her gold American Express card on top of their bill and handing up the plate to their waiter.

'Peace of mind?'

'Who has peace of mind?'

'Don't you?'

Ruby shook her head. 'Maybe I should be seeing Jenny, too.'

'Maybe.' James smiled.

'You're not going to tell me, are you? God, I've known you for nearly twenty years and you still don't trust me.' Ruby laughed, she knew how ridiculous she sounded.

'I don't know,' James told the truth at last, 'I have no idea . . . really.'

They parted outside the restaurant. The sky was leaden but the day was uncomfortably close. He kissed Ruby good-bye and watched as she walked away. He'd known Ruby for as long as he'd known Liz and liked her well enough, but he sometimes felt that he hardly knew her. They didn't mix socially very much because Liz worked with her all day. There were sides to her that he didn't admire. She was capable of great ruthlessness and didn't suffer fools easily. Her business acumen had helped the company in a profound way. Liz and Ruby and Nick, they were equal partners but, sometimes, Ruby had proved to be the rock, the one who had no doubt, the one who dragged them all forward. He watched until Ruby had turned the corner at the top of the street and then he turned, picking up his briefcase, and headed for the tube.

Geoff made another 'house-call' that evening. Everything was fine and he assured James, once more, that scarring would be minimal. The boys disappeared upstairs after a while leaving the two men together in the kitchen.

'No date tonight?' James asked.

'No.' Geoff shook his head. 'I think we've knocked it on the head.'

'I see,' James sat down and looked at Geoff across the table top. 'This is all very sudden.'

'You win some, you lose some,' Geoff replied, opening a can of beer and drinking straight out of it.

'So, what now?'

'Majorca.' Geoff grinned. 'Two weeks of sun, cheapo Majorcan red wine and Sangria.'

'And some painting perhaps?'

'Oh, I'll take my paints. What about you? Are you proposing to work?'

James nodded. 'I expect so.'

'Well, I just want to relax and take lots of lovely siestas by the luxury pool.'

James laughed. 'Don't count your chickens, pal, none of us have ever seen this place. Elizabeth only has some pictures to go on.'

'Have you seen them?'

'Not yet.'

'Let me know when you do.'

Geoff drained the remains of his beer and crumpled the can in his hand. 'How did Liz react to the lad's injury?'

'She said we were lucky that you were here.'

'Praise indeed.' Geoff chuckled. 'When's she back?'

'Sunday.'

'Are you coming to my opening on Thursday evening?'

'Of course, I'm bringing the boys.'

'What about Liz?'

'It's in her diary, so I suppose it's possible.'

Geoff pulled a face.

'She's very busy,' James insisted.

'I want her to buy a big painting for her office.'

James grinned. 'Always an ulterior motive, eh, Geoff?'

'She likes art, it's me she doesn't like.'

'Don't be ridiculous.'

'It's true. Besides, she terrifies me.'

James roared with laughter. 'Yes, and pigs might fly.'

'Liz is very formidable.'

'Crap.'

'It's true.'

'Listen,' James began, changing the subject, 'are you staying? We're having some delicious home-made soup for supper, you're welcome to join us.'

Geoff shook his head. ''Fraid not, I've got to see a man about an exhibition, there's nothing hung yet.' He stood up, placing the twisted beer can into James's hand. 'Can you come over to the gallery on Sunday afternoon? You can see the space and made some suggestions about where to put the paintings.'

'I'll see,' James replied, following his friend out, 'it all depends on whether or not Liz's flight is in on time.'

Geoff looked down at his scuffed shoes. 'Try, James, I need all the support I can get.'

James placed a hand on his shoulder. 'It'll be fine, don't worry, I bet you'll sell everything.' He stepped out into the cool evening air.

'Oh,' Geoff said, pausing at the front gate, 'can you bring Alexander to the surgery sometime tomorrow, I think those stitches can come out.'

'That's quick.'

'We want to prevent scarring if possible, bring him over tomorrow afternoon, after school.'

James agreed and watched as the noisy Saab lurched away, a plume of noxious exhaust smoke trailing in its wake. He went back into the house and returned to his work.

Chapter 6

Elizabeth returned to work late on Monday morning. She met with Ruby and Nick, going over the main events of her New York trip. Everything was on schedule, the office would open on time and she'd spent an exhausting week meeting existing and prospective clients with Howard Sands. She felt shattered but knew it had all been worth while. The others were pleased with the general progress and Elizabeth had the satisfaction of knowing that she'd done a good job. Nick had to rush across town to a meeting with a client and Elizabeth arranged to meet Ruby for lunch. She spent the remainder of the morning with George going through a backlog of mail and telephone messages.

Ruby looked up from her desk as Elizabeth walked into the office. 'For someone suffering from the dreaded jet-lag you're looking pretty sensational.'

Elizabeth smiled and sat down. She'd purchased a new black suit which was short with a neat, fitted jacket. Everything was new, a white blouse with pretty lace collar trimming and some black, suede shoes. 'Do you fancy a walk before lunch?'

Ruby nodded. 'If you like, I just have to make one call then I'll be with you.'

They walked along Piccadilly and into Green Park where they sat for a while. The sun had finally broken through the clouds and felt warm against their faces.

'Something has happened,' Elizabeth began, looking

straight ahead of her across the park and towards Constitution Hill.

'What is it?' Her senses were suddenly alert. 'What's happened?'

Elizabeth took a breath and turned to face her friend. She looked into Ruby's brown eyes. 'I'm having an affair,' she said simply.

Ruby stared. 'An affair?' she said at last. 'I can't believe this, Liz. Are you joking?'

'No.'

'Who?'

'Howard Sands,' Elizabeth replied, her voice calm and controlled. 'Isn't it obvious?'

'Howard Sands?' Ruby repeated as though to thoroughly convince herself. 'Jesus,' she added under her breath.

'I know,' Elizabeth nodded, 'I know, Ruby, I know it all, you don't have to say anything.'

'Then, why are you doing this?'

'Because . . .' she turned away at last, 'because I can't help myself. It doesn't have to make any sense, does it?'

Ruby shook her head in disbelief. 'Does James know?'

'No.'

'What's going to happen, then?'

Elizabeth shrugged hopelessly.

'Are you going to see him again?'

'He's our business associate, of course I'll see him again.'

'Are you in love with him?'

Elizabeth smiled rather nervously, she felt ridiculous and self-conscious. 'I don't know,' she prevaricated.

'I can't understand you, Liz. You're married.'

'I know that,' Elizabeth replied quietly, 'don't you think that I know that.'

98

—

They had a quiet lunch in a small brasserie off Regent Street. Both women ordered a club sandwich and then hardly touched it.

'I'm not going to say anything to James,' Elizabeth told Ruby.

'It was a fling then,' Ruby concluded. 'A bit naff, Liz, and not very clever in the circumstances.'

'What circumstances?'

'The threat to your marriage for one, AIDS for another.'

'No one else knows apart from you and Howard, there's no threat to my marriage unless you tell James.'

'So, you're not going to sleep with Howard again?'

'It's not as easy as that. James and I have been married for sixteen years – people grow apart.'

'So, you don't love James anymore, is that it?'

'Of course I still love James, it isn't like that. God, Ruby, you're beginning to sound like my mother.'

'You need to get a grip of yourself, Liz, this isn't just about you and James, there are the boys to consider as well.'

'I know, I'm not quite that despicable, I do understand where my responsibilities rest.'

Ruby nodded. 'So, what are you going to do about Howard Sands?'

'God knows,' Elizabeth breathed.

'I don't believe you're even in love with him.'

Elizabeth didn't answer. Ruby was right; it was senseless even to contemplate another life, the complications would be endless and horrendous.

She took Ruby's arm as they walked towards the office. 'Are you really so shocked?'

'I think you're mad,' Ruby said, sounding irritated now, 'quite mad.'

99

'But I want him,' she replied, 'I can't think about anything else.'

'Don't tell me about it. I can't be stuck in the middle between you and James.'

'But I need your support,' Elizabeth insisted.

'Then you're out of luck, Liz. I can't support the break-up of your marriage and, what's more, you shouldn't expect me to.'

They walked on in silence, Elizabeth feeling that she'd been put very firmly in her place.

They all went to Geoff's opening the following Thursday evening. It was held in a gallery in Charlotte Street. Both boys looked terribly grown up and smart. Geoff came across to greet them, gliding carefully through the impressive gathering. He'd already imbibed a large quantity of the hospitality wine and was floating.

'You're late,' he said, shaking James's hand and kissing Elizabeth on the cheek.

'We are not,' Elizabeth replied, smiling at Geoff and then looking around at the people and the pictures.

'You missed my little speech,' Geoff said, leading them over to a table where drinks were being dispensed.

'Oh, no,' James said with mock distress.

'And the champagne.'

'The boys were looking forward to that.' Elizabeth laughed, taking a glass of Coke and handing it to Alexander.

'Are the press here?' James asked.

Geoff nodded, looking slightly the worse for wear. 'I've been interviewed and had my picture taken in front of some of the paintings.'

'Come on then, Geoff,' Elizabeth instructed, 'show us around.'

'Right.' He found them each a programme and led the way.

Wes and Alexander quickly became bored and wandered off to amuse themselves. Elizabeth fell into conversation with some Japanese businessmen, leaving James to shadow Geoff for the rest of the evening, delighting in the praise being heaped upon his friend.

'I bought us a picture,' Elizabeth announced later on the drive home.

'Did you?' James sounded pleased. 'Which one?'

'I want it to be a surprise.'

James smiled. 'Is it for the house or the office?'

'For us,' she said. 'God knows where we'll hang it, I think we'll have to redecorate to place it properly.'

'That was very sneaky of you,' James told her, stealing a glance as they drove along. 'Geoff didn't mention it.'

'Geoff was too high to understand anything. I hope he doesn't have a morning surgery.'

James laughed. 'He'll have sobered up by the time I take Alexander in after school.'

'Last day tomorrow,' Wessley reminded them.

'Poor Dad,' Elizabeth said. 'I hope you're both going to be kind over the next two months. Or is it three?'

'We always are kind to him, aren't we, Dad?' Wessley said.

James groaned. 'Never mind, we'll soon be on holiday.'

'Oh, yes,' Elizabeth said, suddenly remembering, 'George got your flights sorted out today, so you're all set.'

'What will you do when we're away?' Alexander asked.

'Work,' James and Wessley said in unison.

They began to make love that night but, in a while, Elizabeth pushed James back and went down on him, taking his erect penis into her mouth. James gasped, at

101

first with surprise then with pleasure. He felt a little cheated because he'd wanted to make love to her but this feeling soon became lost as his climax built. He watched Elizabeth's head moving, the pulse of his shaft against the soft wetness of her mouth, her tongue circling the head of the engorged penis, licking and teasing over its tautness. A greater urgency overtook James and he pushed himself against her, his muscles tensing as he came to a shattering climax, pumping copious streams of semen into Elizabeth's mouth.

'What was all that about?' he asked softly, as Elizabeth lay beside him.

She turned out the light and laughed in the darkness. 'Didn't you enjoy it?'

'What about you?'

'I don't always have to come with you, darling,' she assured him. 'Let me do it my own way sometimes.'

James sighed, feeling sleepy but somehow unsatisfied. 'Are you all right, Liz?' he asked.

'Fine,' she murmured.

He kissed her on the lips and, soon afterwards, fell asleep.

They all went to Cambridge at the weekend; a long-standing arrangement to visit some old friends. Marisa was the head of a Community College and Rupert a computer programmer. The visit wasn't wholly social as Rupert was to suggest some changes to the system of computers Elizabeth used in the office. They arrived after dark and were immediately welcomed into the cosy terrace house in Mawson Road.

'We've virtually been lying down in the road to save you a parking space,' Marisa said, kissing them all as they trooped into the narrow hallway. Over supper everyone

—

talked animatedly, catching up on the events and happenings since they'd last been together almost six months before.

'I told Sammy and Martha you were coming,' Marisa said, 'perhaps we can arrange to meet up with them tomorrow. I'm not sure when, though. Sammy was still in Birmingham when I called, setting up one of his photographic exhibitions. Martha wasn't even sure if he'd be back.'

Elizabeth was pleased. They'd all been at university together. Sammy had since made a reputation for himself as a freelance photographer, travelling widely both to work and to show his photographs. Martha had never worked full-time, devoting the last couple of decades to bringing up their four children. The first, John, had been born whilst she was still an undergraduate and, consequently, Martha hadn't completed her English degree. The last child had been born three years ago.

'The last time I spoke to Martha,' Elizabeth said, 'she was talking about going back to finish her degree.'

'She'll never go back,' Marisa replied. 'She was never really interested in academia after she met Sammy.'

'Martha's always been absolutely besotted with him,' Rupert remarked, smiling at Marisa.

'Well, that's all right,' James said. 'We don't all have to be high flyers.'

'Of course not,' Elizabeth agreed, 'but Martha could have made something of herself.'

'She married Sammy and had kids, perhaps that was always enough.'

Elizabeth looked blank and turned the conversation away to Marisa's work and the latest developments in education.

James listened to the after-dinner talk, watching them

carefully but not really listening. They were clever and bright, all accomplished in one way or another, the products of comfortable middle-class backgrounds. His gaze wandered around the long, expensively furnished room. There were bookshelves crammed to bursting point, African carvings and exotic gourds decorated in ethnic style. Two large antique, gilded mirrors above the two open fire-places. Everywhere was clutter: academic texts, Rupert's word processor with its expensive colour printer, objets d'art, some rare, some trivial, Chinese prints and dark, rich oil paintings. Two sofas formed an L-shape where Wessley and Alexander sat watching television, laughing like drains.

'I've just bought your new book,' Marisa was saying, 'will you write something in it later?'

James smiled, he should be grateful he supposed but he knew that his work wasn't to Marisa's taste at all. She was an intellectual preferring philosophy to his kind of froth.

'I liked the cover,' Rupert commented, 'very attractive.' He reached over and grabbed the heavy book from the top of his VDU. 'Here,' he said, handing it across the table complete with a pen.

James looked at the gaudy illustration, glitzy palm trees, the Hollywood sign, the gorgeous blonde. He scribbled something inside before passing it back. James was fond of them. There was something comforting in having known people for so long, a tacit but deep appreciation each for the other. They were growing older but they could still be their selves of twenty years before, without the accrued baggage of the years. They had all done well, and took pleasure in this. They'd stayed together and had children just like they were supposed to. Scions of the middle classes who hadn't been blown off course and gone to hell. They had worked hard to increase the pot of gold.

The others slept in the next morning but James and Marisa were up by nine o'clock. They ate breakfast in front of the open sliding glass patio doors that took up the entire end wall of the kitchen. James looked out into the tiny garden with its neat patch of lawn and the pretty flower borders on either side. They chatted about Geoff's exhibition the previous week. Marisa had wanted to get up to town for his show but had been too busy.

'I think it's almost our duty to support artists,' she said, 'especially those we know.'

James nodded, thinking how bloody patronizing Marisa could sound at times. He changed the subject and said he wanted to go into town. Within half an hour, whilst the others were just beginning to stir, James and Marisa were striding purposely across Parker's Piece towards the town centre.

Once on King's Parade they called into Corpus Christi College, standing in the courtyard for a while, trying to avoid a group of Japanese tourists, as James took a few pictures, posing Marisa against an archway.

'What's this for?' Marisa asked. 'Research or just plain blackmail?'

'Research, of course.' James grinned, handing the camera to her. 'Here, it's fully automatic, you can take one of me if you like.'

'Well, darling, if it ends up on the back of a dustjacket just remember that I want a picture credit.' She peered through the viewfinder and snapped a shot of him grinning madly. 'There,' Marisa said, handing the camera to James, 'another classic for the family album.'

'I'm writing something about Cambridge,' James replied. 'I just need a bit of background, that's all.'

They stepped onto the street again, walking past the rows of bicycles propped up along the wall outside. 'What are you writing about Cambridge?' Marisa asked pointedly.

'It's just an idea,' James replied, 'just a germ of an idea.'

'God, we're always scouring your books to make sure we haven't appeared in them yet, is this going to be the one, I ask myself? I mean, do we have to leave the country?'

'Don't worry, I won't write anything bad.'

'You don't understand what a strain it is.' Marisa laughed. 'I always get Rupert to rush straight down to Heffers to get each new book of yours and we read them like the clappers, I can tell you.'

James took her arm and they wandered into town where they bought a few things; James a map of the city, Marisa a new jacket and some salad things from her favourite stall in the market.

'God, that jacket was expensive,' Marisa complained as they doubled back on themselves, calling into Fitzbillies to buy cakes for everyone. 'Let me pay,' Marisa insisted as James took out his wallet, 'it will expunge my guilt for being so selfish.'

James laughed. 'You can afford it,' he insisted, taking a box of cakes from the assistant.

'I wouldn't bet on that.'

'When are we seeing Sammy and Martha?' he asked as they stepped onto the street again.

'I'll call them later,' she said. 'They're always dead to the world until lunch-time at weekends.'

When they arrived everyone was up and the long table

in the main room was full of spent breakfast things. Elizabeth was still sitting there with the last of the coffee reading the *Guardian*. She'd tied her hair back and was wearing blue jeans and one of James's baggy sweat shirts. In the bright sunlight, streaming through the window behind her, she looked all of twenty again.

'Cakes,' Marisa announced, putting her packages down on the table.

Elizabeth folded her paper back and smiled at them. 'Good trip?' she asked, eyeing Marisa's carrier bag.

Marisa shook the jacket out and held it up, it was black and fitted. When she slipped it on over her cotton top, it looked positively couture even against her old denim skirt, bare legs and sandals. 'It's to go with my black skirt,' she remarked to Rupert.

'Have I said anything?' he protested.

Rupert made some fresh coffee and they all sat outside eating the scrumptious cakes. Afterwards Rupert and James went inside to clear away the breakfast things and prepare lunch. Marisa and Elizabeth remained in the bright sunshine watching the boys bat the tennis ball between them.

'They play well together,' Marisa remarked, 'despite the age difference.'

Elizabeth shaded her eyes. 'You wouldn't have said that last week when Wessley cut Alexander's head open.'

'Well, all children fight from time to time.'

'Thank God Geoff called in.'

'Fate,' Marisa said. She looked hard at Elizabeth. 'What about you? You look as though you've got a lot on at the moment.'

'We're all terribly busy,' Elizabeth admitted, 'but that's good, isn't it?'

'I suppose it's good,' Marisa readily agreed, 'as long as

107

you enjoy it. But something's up, I can tell. What are you plotting?'

'I'm not plotting, don't be silly, Marisa.' Elizabeth laughed a little too shrilly. She hated it when Marisa seemed able to see into her mind.

'God, don't be so infuriating, Liz. You never tell me a thing, I always have to drag it out of you or hear it second-hand from Ruby.'

'There's nothing to tell. Stop being so dramatic, Marisa, I'm just tired, that's all, and a wee bit distracted because of work.' She looked into her friend's doubtful face. 'Really, that's it.'

Marisa sighed and looked across at the boys again. 'I wonder if Wes would give me a game of tennis this afternoon.'

'I expect so. Aren't you coming punting along the Backs with us?'

Marisa stretched up her arms to the clear blue sky, 'I'm not sure, Rupert always gets so bad-tempered, he insists upon propelling us and then almost invariably loses the punt-pole.'

Elizabeth smiled, 'I expect Wes will play, any excuse to show off.'

Alexander dropped his bat at that moment and ran to his mother. 'Wessley's cheating,' he grizzled, getting up onto Elizabeth's lap.

She stroked his hair back examining the pink line where the stitches had been. 'You're too hot, go and sit in the shade.'

Alexander cried harder. 'I want to play.'

'Then don't complain,' Elizabeth laughed.

'But he's cheating,' the child repeated, outraged that Elizabeth could be so calm.

Marisa sighed and got up from the hard-backed kitchen

chair, carrying it into the house with her. 'I'd better go and check on the men,' she announced. 'Then go and phone Sammy and Martha, find out when they're coming.'

Elizabeth closed her eyes, feeling the heat of the sun against her face, her thoughts drifting away to New York and Howard Sands.

The afternoon proved to be sweltering. Marisa and Wessley went off to play tennis whilst the others hired a punt out on the Cam and took their trip past the Backs. Marisa and Wessley got onto one of the public tennis courts on Christ's Pieces and had a ferocious game through the hottest hours of the day. Wessley was in the shower when the others returned and Marisa was lying out on the grass, a large glass of orange at her side.

'Who won?' James asked, casting a shadow over her face.

Marisa sat up, putting her dark glasses on. 'Wes, of course. I think he should be a professional, you'd never have to work again.'

The others came out and sat down with them.

'I lost,' Marisa announced, 'before you ask.' She turned to Elizabeth. 'Do you play tennis?'

'Badly,' she smiled.

'Then where does Wessley get his talent from?' Marisa queried, as though attempting to uncover a great mystery.

'God knows,' James said, lying down and closing his eyes. 'I don't have any hand to eye co-ordination.'

'Maybe it was the milkman after all,' Ruper stage-whispered to Marisa.

'I'll make some tea,' Elizabeth announced, standing up and leaving them to their speculation. She could hear them laughing as she stepped into the kitchen, the stone tiles cool beneath her bare feet.

Marisa came in after a while. Elizabeth was sitting at the round kitchen table waiting for the kettle to boil.

'I spoke to Sammy earlier. He sounded very subdued. Said Martha was out, but they're coming for dinner tonight.'

'Sammy subdued?' Elizabeth remarked. 'That's not like him.'

'No. Still, I expect we'll hear all about it.'

They all dressed casually for dinner. It was hot and all the windows in the house were open. A light breeze fluttered the flames of the candles on the long table in the living-room onto which eight place-settings had been crammed. They'd almost given up hope of Sammy and Martha arriving when their car pulled up on the opposite side of the road.

'Why were you so funny over the phone?' Marisa asked Sammy, when they were all settled with celebratory glasses of champagne.

'Oh, nothing, really.' He seemed embarrassed. 'Just a little local difficulty.' Sammy was a big man, he'd put on a lot of weight over the years and had gone from being cuddly to rather porky. He had a shock of red hair and he wore glasses with bright red frames. His white shirt had a stain down the front, the material was still damp where he'd attempted to sponge it off.

'Well,' Rupert began, proposing a toast, 'to old friends and happy memories.'

Alexander sneezed and coughed. He'd never had champagne before and the bubbles went up his nose. Wessley sat next to him, nonchalantly sipping his drink and glancing contemptuously at his brother. After some initial banter, the conversation became strained and eventually everyone fell awkwardly silent.

110

'It's no use,' Martha whispered, 'we can't spend the remainder of the evening like this.' She turned to Sammy. 'We'll have to tell them.'

Marisa looked first at Rupert and then at Elizabeth. 'What is it?' she asked. 'I knew there was something wrong when we spoke earlier.'

Sammy laughed nervously. 'Really, it's nothing.'

Martha looked as though she would cry at any moment.

'You're not pregnant again, are you, Martha?' Elizabeth asked worriedly.

'No,' Martha replied. She took a deep breath.

'I just found out today that Sammy's having an affair.' She looked from one friend to the other, her dark eyes swimming with tears. She turned to Sammy finally. 'After twenty years it's quite a shock.' She sounded wounded, like a frightened animal.

'It'll be all right,' Sammy said to the shocked room. He suddenly seemed very assured. 'Let's not spoil the evening.'

Elizabeth stared at James, trying desperately to think of something to say. She felt sick.

'Shall we eat then,' Marisa announced gaily, her voice full of false joie de vivre, conscious of Wes and Alexander sitting wide-eyed on the window-seat. 'Come on, everybody.'

After Martha and Sammy had gone, after the boys were in bed, the four friends sat down on the sofas listening in silence as the antique clock on the mantelpiece twelve o'clock.

'God,' Rupert said, 'that has to be one of the worst evenings of my life.'

'Poor Martha,' was all Marisa could summon up.

'I don't think we were very much help.' James picked up the remains of his wine and swallowed the lot. 'She

111

told us the news, there was a minute's silence and then we all carried on as if nothing had happened.'

'Well, nothing has happened, they're obviously still together,' Elizabeth interjected.

'She'll never get over it,' Marisa insisted. 'Never.'

'I wonder who it is?' Rupert sounded intrigued.

'A photographic assistant, I bet,' James replied.

'Poor Martha,' Marisa said, 'I'd better call her during the week, take her out for lunch, have a chat.'

'I'd leave it, darling, she'll call if she wants to talk.'

'I think they wanted to talk tonight but we were all so totally useless.'

'God knows what the boys thought,' James said. 'I hope they don't think this is how we all conduct our lives, squalid affairs in the back seats of cars.'

'How do you know it's squalid?' Elizabeth challenged and then regretted it.

Everyone turned to her. 'Come on, Liz,' Marisa began, 'Sammy and Martha have been together for ages and he's not exactly catch of the week, it must be someone pretty peculiar.'

'Well, these things happen,' Elizabeth concluded, lamely.

James stared at her over the rim of his wine glass. She had a funny look about her he thought, strained and emotional, a definite edge, something brittle. He rested his head onto the soft cushions of the sofa and closed his eyes. It was late and they were all incredibly tired.

'What's an affair?' Alexander asked on the drive to London late the next morning.

Elizabeth stared out at the passing countryside. After Martha's revelation, the weekend had taken a distinct nose-dive. Even the weather clouded over on Sunday. It rained all morning and a chill wind blew down Mawson Road as they packed up the Volvo. Elizabeth remembered Martha's awful, frightened face, her short black hair scraped back making her cheeks look hollow. Her attractive features seemed distorted into a mask of bile, anger and hate but, most of all, confusion. Sammy, as usual, seemed intent upon maintaining a jovial front. Happy Sammy, the life and soul of the party, ever-ready boy with a quip on the tip of his tongue. Elizabeth wondered if this was to be her own ultimate fate, a squalid scene in front of friends who squirmed with embarrassment and then went on to change the subject.

'Mum? What's an affair?' Alexander asked again.

'It's when a man dumps his wife for someone else, stupid.' Wessley was exasperated by his little brother's ignorance.

'Is it, Mum?'

'It might be expressed a bit more politely,' Elizabeth remarked. She watched the slapping windscreen wipers for a while, wishing that they were home. Wishing that she was three thousand miles away . . . wishing, wishing, wishing.

Wessley looked thoughtful for a moment. 'Well, I think it's cruel . . . having an affair is cruel.'

James smiled. 'You're right. I think it's cruel, too.'

'Would you have an affair, Daddy?' Alexander asked, looking incredibly innocent.

James laughed and shook his head, peering through the steamy window, conscious of Elizabeth sitting stiff and silent beside him.

Chapter 7

As soon as they were settled back at Camden, Elizabeth rang Ruby. She got her answering-machine, which featured Ruby's tra-la voice informing all callers that she was at Tim's flat in Hampstead. Elizabeth dialled the number and finally got her friend.

'What are you doing at Tim's?' she asked straight away. 'I thought it was over.'

'It is,' Ruby insisted, 'but my place is being decorated and lots of my stuff's still here. Besides, Tim's away in Germany somewhere.'

'Can I come over?'

'Of course . . . by yourself?'

'Yes, why do you ask?'

'No reason.'

'Right, see you in a few minutes, then.'

Elizabeth drove through the rain to Hampstead and after telling Ruby about the weekend, lay back on one of Tim's luxurious matching white sofas and looked up at the ceiling. 'I have to see Howard,' she announced.

'Just because Martha and Sammy are going through a difficult patch doesn't mean you have to follow suit.'

'I'm not,' Elizabeth insisted. 'I just have to see him, that's all, simple as that.'

'It's hardly simple.'

Elizabeth turned her head to one side, looking hard at her friend. 'What am I going to do, Ruby?'

'Well, I know you've just had this fling with Howard but . . .'

'It's more than that.'

'How did it start?'

'How do these things start?' Elizabeth replied, sounding mysterious.

'Usually when two people get the hots for one another. Of course, it's helpful if they are unattached.'

'Don't be so censorious,' Elizabeth complained.

'You're a married woman with two children.'

'I know that, for God's sake, don't you think I understand the implications? Don't give me another lecture.'

Elizabeth decided to tell her friend the truth at last. 'Ruby, I'm in love with Howard Sands,' she said simply.

'Don't be ridiculous.'

'Why is it ridiculous?'

'I should have thought your weekend in Cambridge would have taught you a lesson.'

'Sammy and Martha have always been wrong for one another.'

'Says you.' Ruby was irritated now.

'Don't you think so then?' Elizabeth seemed surprised.

'What do I know?' Ruby replied. 'You're the expert. Don't be so judgemental, Liz, these are our friends you're talking about.'

'What has Sammy got to look forward to now? What do they talk about, for God's sake?' Elizabeth was getting hysterical.

'Listen, Liz, you're going a bit over the top.'

'I damn well feel like going over the top!'

'Calm down,' Ruby soothed, pouring them both another cup of tea. 'You're just over-reacting to the situation, it must have been dreadful.'

'It was,' Elizabeth agreed, sipping the hot tea, tears welling in her eyes and spilling onto her cheeks, 'it was ghastly.'

Ruby moved swiftly to Elizabeth and, removing the expensive china from her shaking hand, put an arm around her shoulders, holding her close as great sobs shook her body.

James was working when Elizabeth returned in the early evening.

'Gran called,' Wessley informed her as she dropped the car keys onto the hall-stand.

Elizabeth groaned inwardly. She looked at her reflection in the hall-stand mirror, moving a coat aside to get a better look. Her eyes seemed huge against pure white skin. She turned to Wessley. 'What did Gran have to say?'

'They're coming to stay next week.'

Elizabeth attempted to gather her senses. 'Did Daddy speak to her?'

'Yes.'

'I see, and when, exactly, are they arriving?'

'Tuesday until Thursday.'

It was all Elizabeth needed. 'Good, well, it will be a good time to see them, just before your holiday. They couldn't have chosen a better time.'

Wessley grinned. 'Oh, Mum, don't be like that.'

'Like what?' Elizabeth feigned innocence.

'Like you don't want them to come.'

'As if I wouldn't want to see my own mother,' she replied with mock horror.

'You know how you and Gran argue all the time.'

'Not all of the time, Wes, don't exaggerate.'

Wessley followed her into the kitchen where he helped Elizabeth get supper ready. 'Will Sammy and Martha divorce now, Mum?' he asked, setting the places at the old table.

'I don't suppose so . . . These things happen.' She started to scrub the new potatoes. 'People get over it, I guess.'

'Sammy kept laughing,' Wessley commented.

'Sammy was overwrought.' Elizabeth said, dropping each finished potato into the saucepan of water at the side of the sink. 'It was hardly the sort of thing I wanted you two to witness. I just hope it hasn't warped you for life.'

'Oh, Mum,' Wessley complained, laughing, 'I know what the score is.'

'Nonsense, you're fourteen years old, you barely know what day of the week it is.'

'You looked sad,' he commented.

'Yes, well, it was a bit of a surprise for me, too.'

Wessley placed the last knife and fork on the table. 'It's a pity,' he said before leaving to do his homework, 'we were all having a good time until then.'

Elizabeth nodded, running fresh water into the sink. 'Until then,' she agreed.

That night in bed James and Elizabeth started to make love but broke apart after a while and lay silently in the heavy darkness.

'What's wrong, Liz?' James asked. 'Is it Sammy and Martha?'

Elizabeth considered; it would be so easy to agree and discuss their friends' problems. 'I'm just tired, James,' she said instead, 'exhausted with this New York business and now I have to contend with Mother and Dad next week.' It was partly true, her mother was reason enough to cast a gloomy spell.

'Is that all?' James's laughter was soft and comforting. 'We can manage that situation, besides you'll be out most of the time.'

'I'll have to play truant for one day at least.'

117

'They're old, Liz, it's only for three days. It'll be all right.'

'I feel guilty about them and guilty about not coming to Spain with you all . . .'

'You've got no reason to feel guilty,' James insisted, his voice soft and deep. 'Why not change your plans and come to Majorca, two weeks won't make much difference to your empire building.'

'I can't,' she said, 'I really can't. Don't tempt me.' Elizabeth coveted those two weeks when Howard would be in London, time in which to reaffirm the truth of her situation.

James leant over and kissed her good-night. 'We'll deal with your parents, Liz,' he assured her, 'really we will.'

Elizabeth reached up and held him tightly. She felt so confused. At last she let him go, and James turned away to sleep while Elizabeth lay restless beside him. Why did she continue sleeping with James? Was it a misplaced sense of loyalty or did she feel sorry for him? Perhaps deep down she still loved him, had only lost touch with her true feelings over the years. But her need for Howard was compulsive. She *had* to have him, and this desire both overwhelmed and frightened her.

Elizabeth arrived home late on Tuesday evening and her parents had already been in the house for several hours. She faced them in the lounge thinking how elderly and shrunken they had become. Her father was over eighty now although he looked tanned and handsome still, his strong hands gripping her shoulders as he kissed her cheeks.

'Hello, Daddy,' she said, smiling demurely, noticing the high polish on his black shoes as he stepped back to allow her mother in.

'Mummy.' Elizabeth took the little woman into her arms and kissed her cheek, smelling the old-fashioned face powder and the strong eau-de-Cologne. Her mother was wearing an expensive, brown travelling suit over a white, silk blouse which had a fussy bow at the neck, her blue-grey hair frozen into a sleek coiffure with two little curls turned under at either side of her forehead. They were, Elizabeth conceded, still a handsome couple, her mother, at seventy-nine, alert and sprightly, her father tall and immaculate. Oliver and Alice had once been a fabulous couple. He'd made his money out of rubber and they'd spent their early married life on the family plantations in Singapore. Consequently both retained a colonial attitude to the world, anachronisms alive and kicking at the latter end of the twentieth century.

After dinner her mother sat in the kitchen, watching as Elizabeth made coffee.

'You look tired, Elizabeth,' the old woman remarked.

'I know, Mummy, that's because I *am* tired. We're rushed off our feet at work.'

'James looks well, though.' She lowered her voice a little as though fearing the men might hear their conversation from the lounge.

'He's better for having given up that tedious job,' Elizabeth explained.

'Well,' her mother sighed, 'I suppose he must make a decent enough living from his books, you certainly see them rywhere these days. I just wish they weren't quite so adult.'

'Mother,' Elizabeth laughed, 'what's that supposed to mean?'

'All those *words*.' Her mother wrinkled her nose.

'Actually he doesn't make all that much, it's difficult to earn a decent living from writing.'

'So, you keep him, then?'

Elizabeth lifted down the good coffee cups and saucers from a cupboard. It amused her to tease the old woman, it gave her satisfaction. 'We don't really see it in those terms. With James at home all the time I can get on with my work without having to worry about the boys.'

'Oh, Elizabeth, when did you ever have to worry about them?' Elizabeth felt her hackles beginning to rise but took a good, deep breath and let the moment pass. 'What do you want to do tomorrow, Mummy?' she asked instead.

'I hadn't really thought, darling. Won't you be at your office all day?

'I could meet you for lunch, we thought that might be rather pleasant.'

'Can you do that?'

'Of course,' Elizabeth laughed, 'I can do what I want, I'm the boss.'

Her mother nodded. 'You certainly are, darling. We're both terribly proud of you, of course we are.'

Elizabeth looked across at her, the compliment had sounded a bit backhanded to her. 'So shall we have lunch?'

'I'm sure we'd enjoy it. You know, we don't get to London nearly enough these days and your father likes Gloucestershire so much it's hard to get him to shift.'

Elizabeth breathed a silent sigh of relief. They would all meet for lunch the following day. James would bring them into the city. Elizabeth's guilt would be expunged – at least for a while.

James was up early the next morning. He had a nine-thirty appointment with Jenny Grove. Alice and Oliver were under the impression that he had an urgent meeting with his agent and he didn't disabuse them. They waved him away at the front door, delighted to have their grandsons to themselves for a while.

James began by telling Jenny about the events in Cambridge at the weekend.

'How did Liz react?' Jenny asked.

'I think she was pretty disturbed by the whole thing, the fact that none of us seemed able to make any direct comment to either of them.'

'It's a shocking bit of news to hear. How did you feel about it?'

'I was upset. I've known Sammy and Martha for years, and always rather admired Sammy. He's the kind of man you'd never expect to have affairs, if you can actually expect that of any man,' he finished.

'So, you don't admire Sammy anymore?'

'Yes, I do, I suppose. I just feel differently about him. I always saw him as being set apart . . . as being good.'

'For not having affairs?'

'For being so reliable. He's a lovely man.'

'What about you, James? Have you had affairs of the heart?'

'Not since I was married, a few flirtations, a few heart flutters. I'm too much of a coward to have affairs,' he laughed at himself, 'I always think of the consequences!'

'So, you take a moral stance,' Jenny said, smiling.

'No, not really, I take a coward's stance.'

'And yet you disapprove of Sammy's affair.'

'Not really disapprove, it just seems ridiculous, that's all. Sammy's hardly the sort you'd imagine having affairs.'

'And what sort are they?'

'Oh, I don't know, people who aren't Sammy.' He smiled. 'Sammy looks married, you can spot it a mile away, just very, very married.'

121

'You said Elizabeth took their news badly.'

'Yes,' James agreed, 'she went off to see her best friend as soon as we got back to London.'

'To talk about it?'

'I suppose so, they're close.'

Jenny nodded. 'So, you haven't discussed it with Liz?'

'It's difficult.'

'In what way?'

'It's almost as though it's an infection or something . . . we seem to have lost a lot of friends to marriage break-ups and separations.' He looked into Jenny's eyes. 'Perhaps we both feel that it's tempting fate too much to discuss it.'

'You've said previously that your relationship with Elizabeth is changing, what did you mean?'

'I'm not sure,' James admitted. 'It's subtle, something almost elusive, but, I know it's there, has been for some time.'

'You mean an attitude?'

'I don't know.' He shrugged. 'Maybe we've just become too casual with each other. When you're married for a long time most things become automatic and that doesn't help.'

Jenny made no comment, just nodded encouragement.

'Maybe it's just a result of the changes we've experienced since Easter.'

'Do you regret those changes?'

'No.' James was positive.

'You could be seeing things more clearly, now that your life is more balanced, now that your work is more focused.'

'Possibly. But I think it's probably more to do with how I relate to women.'

'And how is that?' Jenny asked him.

'I'm generally confused.' James laughed. 'And a bit scared.'

Jenny brought the session to an end, suggesting that they start with this the next time they met, and asking James to attempt an understanding of what was troubling him.

James left the session feeling disturbed and dissatisfied. For the first time he was disappointed with Jenny, as though she hadn't let him speak the thoughts which had suddenly come tumbling into his mind. The last thing he wanted now was lunch at the Savoy with Alice and Oliver but it could hardly be avoided.

In the event it turned out rather better than he'd hoped. Elizabeth was late and talked nineteen to the dozen to make up for her lapse, thus nobody noticed his pre-occupation.

Elizabeth parted company with them outside the Savoy, returning to work whilst the others went on to Harrods to shop.

Ruby stuck her head around Elizabeth's door in the middle of the afternoon.

'How are things?' Ruby asked. 'I've only got a few minutes so make it interesting, I only want to hear the awful bits.'

Elizabeth laughed and buzzed George to ask for coffee.

'Lunch was fine. We're all being so terribly polite. Elizabeth pulled a face. 'I laughed at Daddy's excruciating jokes and even managed to smile when Mummy was telling stories of my youth to the boys.'

Ruby chuckled. 'Well done.'

'It won't last, of course. I know that she's just itching to say something bitchy about me working here and James working from home.'

'You can't really expect them to completely understand, Liz.'

'Why not? It seems quite logical to everyone else.'

George brought their coffee, placed the mugs on the desk and left quickly to answer an insistently ringing telephone.

'They keep advising me to go with James and the boys to Majorca,' she resumed when George had shut the door.

'They're right,' Ruby agreed.

'Geoff's going now.' Elizabeth made this sound a major stumbling-block.

'It's a huge villa, Liz. Geoff's not the problem.'

'No.' She looked directly into Ruby's eyes. 'Howard is arriving in London the day they all leave for the sun.'

'You haven't said anything about this before.' Ruby picked up a steaming mug, looking very stern.

Elizabeth grinned behind her own mug. 'I can't help it, Ruby, I have to see him.'

'You're being absolutely stupid, Liz. How are you going to keep this a secret?'

Elizabeth didn't reply to that. 'I'm cheating, I know, but what can I do?' she said instead.

'You can stop being so bloody ridiculous for a start.'

'Don't lecture me,' Elizabeth pleaded, sounding weary.

'You shouldn't have told me if you didn't want my advice. Don't you feel guilty about what you're doing?'

'Of course I do.'

The intercom buzzed and George announced her next appointment. Elizabeth sounded exasperated.

'Tell them to wait a minute,' she said, turning back to Ruby. 'What are you doing after work?'

'I have a date,' Ruby said, getting up to leave.

'Do you?' Elizabeth was surprised and smiled at last. 'You kept that quiet.'

'I wasn't sure if you'd be interested, your own life being so full of intrigue at the moment.'

'Oh, Ruby, don't be like that.'

'Well, anyway, I have a date *and* he's not married.'

Elizabeth didn't reply, watching her friend leave before asking George to bring in her four o'clock appointment.

'James is such a marvellous cook,' Elizabeth's mother said after dinner that evening. 'Doesn't he mind being head cook and bottle-washer?' They were sitting out in the mild evening, the scent of rose and honeysuckle in the warm air.

'He isn't exactly that, Mummy. We still have Mrs Reed.'

'I don't think I'd like it all the same,' Alice continued. 'I mean, it isn't very manly, is it?'

Elizabeth turned to her mother and laughed. 'Don't be absurd, James hasn't been emasculated by cooking the evening meal now and again.'

'You do cook sometimes then?'

'Of course, if I'm in on time.'

'What do the boys think about this arrangement?'

'They seem perfectly happy,' Elizabeth said airily.

'Of course, I'm old-fashioned, but I always think that children need their mother.'

'I *am* here, Mummy,' Elizabeth insisted. 'They're at school most of the time.'

'Won't you change your mind about going on holiday with them? Little Alexander is terribly unhappy about leaving you here all alone.'

'No, Mummy, I can't change my mind, there's just too

much for me to do here. We've explained it all to them and they understand.'

The older woman didn't look convinced. 'You and James need to spend some time alone, you both need a break.'

'Later in the year,' Elizabeth said. 'After September everything will be back to normal.'

'I wish you could have come shopping with me this afternoon, Elizabeth, you have such marvellous taste.'

'I'm sorry about that.' Her mother was making her feel guilty. 'Next time you're in town we'll have a day shopping together.'

Alice reached across and patted her daughter's hand. 'That will be nice, dear, I shall look forward to it.'

It began to get a little chilly and the two women went back inside. Elizabeth went upstairs to say good-night to Wessley and Alexander, then joined the others in the lounge.

'James,' her mother began, 'I was telling Elizabeth that she ought to reconsider her decision not to go on holiday with you.'

James looked from mother to daughter and back again. 'Liz just can't make it this time, Alice, we'll try to arrange something a bit later in the year.'

'I'll make some tea,' Elizabeth announced, stalking to the kitchen, angry as hell at her mother's intervention.

'You've done it now,' Oliver informed his wife, 'really upset the old apple cart.'

'Nonsense, Elizabeth should be going on holiday with her husband and children. You've let her get away with much too much, James,' she said, fixing him with a stern eye.

James excused himself and joined Elizabeth in the sanctuary of the kitchen.

126

'Do you want some help?' he asked, watching her angrily crashing cups and saucers about.

Elizabeth eyed him. Her period was due to start that day and, as usual, she felt edgy and tense. 'God, I'm sick of this house,' she seethed.

'Don't let Alice get under your skin, it's only hot air.'

'I know,' Elizabeth nodded, 'I know.'

'What's the matter, Liz?' he asked gently.

Elizabeth shrugged, sitting down at the table and staring blankly at the evening paper. 'Sometimes I just think it might be pleasant to live away from London completely.'

James laughed. 'You don't mean that. You love London, and besides what would happen to your work?'

'I'd give it up.' Elizabeth looked at him defiantly.

'And do what?'

'Have another baby, grow some vegetables, have a horse in the paddock.'

'Another baby?' James joined her at the table. 'You're joking.'

'I'm perfectly serious. Do you want to stay in London for ever?'

James shrugged. 'It doesn't really matter where I am, my typewriter can go anywhere with me.'

'Wouldn't you like to live in the country, it would be good for the boys too.'

'Since when have you had this desire to return to nature?' James asked. 'You'd go mad within six months, I can guarantee it. More than a weekend at your parents' place and you're climbing the walls.'

'That's because of Mummy.'

'Face it, Liz, you couldn't exist anywhere other than London.'

'We both like Norfolk, we could look for somewhere there.'

'Liz,' James began patiently as he poured boiling water into the large tea pot, 'you're over-tired. Alice is right, you do need a break.'

'Oh, not you as well.' Elizabeth was exasperated. 'I can't and that's it.'

'What about Nick and Ruby, aren't they taking a break, either?'

'None of us are, not yet.'

James sighed. 'If you really want to move out of London we can start to look. Were you serious about Norfolk?'

Elizabeth looked into his grey eyes. At that moment she was no longer sure what she was serious about or what she wanted.

Geoff's painting arrived on the morning of Alice and Oliver's departure. Elizabeth had bid them an early farewell in their bedroom before leaving for the office, her mother having extracted a promise that they would all come to Gloucestershire for a long weekend in September.

James and the boys waved the couple away soon after eight o'clock, Alexander crying as they left and, when their pristine Bentley was out of sight, they all trooped back inside to have their breakfast. This was when the front door bell rang and the picture was delivered. They took it out of its packaging and propped it up on the sofa in the front room.

It was a Norfolk seascape, bleak and grey, breakers foaming coldly onto the shore. Geoff had caught the atmosphere perfectly: brooding, wild, with a louring sky over the dramatic storm at sea. Wessley pointed out a little fishing vessel tipping in between the choppy waves.

'It's just like we were there,' Alexander said.

'Geoff's clever, isn't he, Dad,' Wessley declared. 'A doctor and a famous artist.'

James agreed.

'Don't you wish you could paint?' Alexander asked his father.

'No.' James shook his head. 'Writing is quite enough for this lifetime, thank you.'

'Where are we going to put it?' Wessley asked.

'I don't know. We'll have to see what your mother has to say on the subject.'

The boys lost interest and drifted off to play. James lifted the painting off the sofa and placed it carefully against a wall before going up to his study to begin work.

'I hate to say it,' Elizabeth told James that night in bed, 'but I'm relieved Mother and Dad have gone.' They were both sitting up in bed reading. For once Elizabeth had a book open and not a file of work.

'You've always found your mother too much,' James reminded her, as if Elizabeth needed reminding.

'I suppose it means we're too much alike. They say that, don't they, children who recognize themselves in a parent find them difficult to deal with.'

James laughed. 'They also say that you should always check out your mother-in-law because you're looking at your wife in years to come.'

'That's just sexist crap.' Elizabeth paused. 'You don't really think I'm like her, do you?'

'You just said you were.'

'I don't go on like her though, do I?'

'Not yet.' James grinned.

'I promised that we'd visit them in September.' She sounded thoroughly demoralized at the prospect.

'I know, it was the last thing Alice said as we waved them away.'

'What do you think?'

'It depends what you're up to.'

'I'll make some time free,' Elizabeth assured him.

She returned to her book but none of the words made any sense. Finally she switched her bedside light off, closing her eyes to the world and attempting to forget about it all. Everything she did had a sense of unreality about it now. She was making plans with James for September when she wasn't even sure that she'd be with him then. Yesterday she'd spoken of leaving London and giving up her job. Yesterday, too, she had almost decided not to see Howard again. Now, once more, he was all she could think of. Instead of a carefully managed divertissement, her affair with Howard Sands had progressed into something completely uncontrollable.

Chapter 8

James had his last session with Jenny Grove before going
to Spain. Tuesday morning was close and hot, weird
purplish-grey-black clouds rolled in from the west like
vast dirigibles scudding across the sky. The air was heavy
and still. Jenny's office windows were open and an electric
fan whirred on her desk in an attempt to circulate a little
breeze. James had dropped Wessley off for a tennis lesson
and had left Alexander with Geoff who, apart from a
couple of house-calls, was supposed to be packing his
suitcase.

Jenny met him at the door. She was wearing a short
skirt of muted grey checks with shades of lilac and a crisp
short-sleeved white blouse. She'd tied her long hair up
and looked very cool and business-like as she sat opposite
him, crossing her long legs and referring briefly to a
notebook on a side table. She smiled at him and they
began.

'Liz has seemed listless,' James admitted after fencing
around the subject. 'She's been down since her parents
visited, it's the after-shock I think.'

'You said she didn't get on with them,' Jenny
prompted.

'Her mother,' he said, 'it's really her mother. She's very
old, I just don't think they connect.'

'Do you connect with Liz's parents?'

'Yes, they've always liked me. I've got on with them
although I'm not sure if they really understand why Liz
works and I stay at home.'

131

'You *work* at home.'

'Yes, but they don't quite see it that way. I suppose it would be all right if I did Liz's job and she wrote books.' He looked out of the window as the dark clouds began to merge. 'Anyway, there's not much money in writing.'

'Are you really scared of women?' Jenny asked suddenly, referring back to their last session.

James looked a little embarrassed. 'Did I say that?' he said, knowing that he had.

She nodded.

He stalled. 'I think that most men are scared of women to some extent. I was always awkward about that initial contact.'

'Well, that's not quite the same as being scared,' Jenny commented.

There was a long silence in which James considered what it was he meant. He cleared his throat before he spoke again. 'Perhaps scared was the wrong choice of word. I think what I should have said was that I'm scared of my own reaction. The idea of being dependent upon a woman.' He looked at Jenny. 'I guess it goes back to one's childhood, and then falling into roles . . .'

'Is that what you think you've done?'

'Not really, not exactly . . . I'm not sure. There appears to be a certain blurring at the edges where our marriage is concerned. Elizabeth has the aggressive work role whilst I was never really interested in clawing my way to the top.'

'I see.'

'She's very successful,' James repeated for the millionth time. 'Well, anyway, all I'm saying is that Liz is the dominant one, and I've never felt very comfortable in that particular role.'

'What about the children, who disciplines them?'

'We both do.'

'And do you find that uncomfortable?'

'I think I attempt to rationalize everything. I never really lose my temper with them, if that's what you mean, I always try to make them understand what's happening, what's going wrong.'

'They don't see you as an authority figure, then.'

'I hope not.' James smiled.

'What about their mother?'

'She's hard on Wes . . . at least *I* think she's sometimes a bit hard.' James felt immediately disloyal.

'In what way hard?'

'Liz never lets him get away with very much.'

Jenny nodded, encouraging James to continue.

'Well, that's it really. I'm not criticizing her or anything. Maybe Wes needs a bit more direction . . .' His voice trailed away. 'Liz and me . . . we've been together sixteen years,' the sound of thunder rumbled overhead as he spoke, 'and she's been a wonderful wife and a good mother, don't misunderstand me. It's just that,' he paused once more, collecting his thoughts, 'it's just that – wouldn't it be awful if you woke up one day and discovered that it had all been a sham, a terrible pretence.'

'Is that what you think?' she asked quietly.

A huge thunder clap seemed to explode right over their heads. James jumped in surprise and then laughed out loud. 'Odin speaks!'

Jenny turned as a sudden torrent of rain began to slash from the leaden sky. She got up and pulled the windows closed. A flash of lightning lit up the heavens and crackled over the rooftops. 'You were saying,' she said, returning to her seat.

'I don't know what I was saying,' James lied.

'I think you're angry, James.'

133

'Perhaps it's mid-life crisis,' he suggested and then, more seriously, 'I always considered that Liz was really too good for me.'

'In that way?' Jenny got things back on track despite the crashing storm outside.

'She's a very clever woman, bright and intelligent.'

'Aren't you those things, too?'

'In different ways, perhaps I am.'

Jenny paused for a moment. 'Do you discuss this with her?'

'No.'

'What about your marriage?'

'My marriage is the same as it's always been. Liz has all the ideas and gets on with things whilst I've written a couple of decent books and spend the rest of my life regurgitating the same old stories under new covers.'

'That sounds more like feeling sorry for yourself.'

'Or the awful truth.'

'I'm not certain that you are being truthful. I don't believe that you can really see your writing career as being quite such a hopeless endeavour, the evidence doesn't support that at all.'

James thought of his agent, Zane Lillywhite. What would be Zane's honest assessment of his career to date?

'It seems to me,' Jenny continued, 'that you're using your writing as a shield to hide behind.'

'You mean escaping the realities of the world?'

'I was thinking rather in terms of Liz.'

James thought about that. 'Do you think I'm jealous of her success?'

'What do you think, James?'

'I've never thought of it in those terms.'

'Just don't see it as a way out.'

'A way out of what?' James was confused.

134

Jenny looked at her watch. 'Next time,' she told him softly but firmly.

Elizabeth arrived home late that evening and helped the boys to pack their bags. They were very excited although James seemed a little subdued.

'I bet you wish you were coming with us,' Alexander said later as he rubbed shampoo into his hair.

'I'd love to have come,' Elizabeth told him, 'but you'll be all right without me for a couple of weeks.'

'I'll miss you though, Mummy,' the little boy said seriously.

Elizabeth rinsed his hair and gently combed it away from his face, looking at the neat scar line which now looked less angry and dramatic. 'I hope you'll remember to send me a card.'

'I will,' he insisted, 'I'll write every day.'

Elizabeth laughed. 'Well, darling, perhaps not every day, you can call me on the telephone every few days if you like.'

Alexander nodded, turning his attention to his big plastic tug boat, holding it under the hand shower to see how long it would take to sink under the blue, soapy water.

Elizabeth left him and went into her bedroom where James was putting the finishing touches to his own packing. Wessley had met her along the landing wearing his schnorkel and yellow mask, holding up a pair of flippers.

'I see that Wes is getting into the holiday mood,' she said, sitting on the bed and handing James some socks to put into his bag. 'Are you ready?'

'Just about.' James stuffed the rolls of towelling socks deep into the corners of the sports bag.

'Sun-tan lotion?'

He held up a large bottle of factor 15. 'Everything – I made a list.'

Elizabeth laughed. 'And is Geoff taking the medical supplies?'

'Knowing Geoff I doubt if he'll even remember to pack an aspirin.'

'I wonder if I should have come after all,' she said.

'Don't say that, Liz, it's bad enough that you can't. Don't hint that you might have, it's too tantalizing.'

'Perhaps a break will do us both good,' she suggested. She hadn't thought of that until now.

James shrugged. 'You could always come out for a few days if you changed your mind.'

Elizabeth stood up. 'I suppose that's true,' she said, returning to Alexander and hauling him out of the tepid bath water where he was sitting surrounded by sunken ships.

When the boys were in bed, Elizabeth changed into tracksuit bottoms and a baggy T-shirt, and went down to watch television with James. She found him with all their travel documents spread out across the top of the gun chest.

'All set?' Elizabeth asked, sitting down beside him on the comfortable sofa. 'All systems go?' She'd always joked at his meticulous planning.

'Are you going to be all right when we're away?' James asked.

'Yes, of course.' She laughed with surprise at his question.

'You'll miss us you know, you'll miss those two monsters charging all over the place.'

'I shall revel in the peace and tranquillity.'

'It'll drive you crazy.'

136

Elizabeth smiled. 'I have so much to do I'll probably just work late at the office . . . I'll hardly be here.'

'Come out for the second week.'

Their eyes met and Elizabeth hesitated for a moment. 'I can't,' she insisted.

'A few days then, call it a business trip.'

'I'm up to my neck in work.'

'Well, at least think about it.'

'I will,' she assured him.

'But you won't come,' he added, folding away the air tickets and a map he'd been examining.

Elizabeth looked at the television screen. 'How did you get on with Jenny today?' she asked.

'I'm not sure.'

'What does that mean?' She kept her eyes on the news programme.

'I mean it's difficult to say how things go, it's not quite as tangible as that.'

'Well, does it make you feel better?'

James watched the programme too. 'I'm not even sure if it's supposed to do that, either.'

'What is it for then?' Elizabeth turned to him, feeling exasperated.

James shrugged.

'Are you seeing her because of me?' she asked.

'I'm seeing her because of me.'

'But there's nothing wrong with you.'

James smiled. 'There doesn't have to be anything wrong.'

'No, well, I suppose you know what you're doing. Does it help at all with your writing?'

'Not especially.'

'Are you going to continue seeing her after you get back from Spain?'

'What is this, Liz, twenty questions?'

'I'm sorry,' she said, feeling she'd exposed a raw nerve. 'It's just that you never talk about it . . . we don't seem to talk at all just recently.'

'Perhaps you're right,' James began, 'a few days apart will be good for both of us.'

Perversely Elizabeth suddenly wanted to tell James everything, confess her infidelity and let them deal with it there and then. She was desperate for some kind of response, something over and above his monumental reasonableness and understanding. She wanted to goad him into anger.

'James,' Elizabeth began. There was a tangible tension in the air, everything on the verge of spilling out. She watched his eyes as they met hers, saw fear and disappointment in them. 'I'm going to make a cup of something,' she mumbled, getting up. 'Coffee or tea?'

'You look awful,' Ruby told her the next morning.

'I feel wrecked,' Elizabeth admitted, dropping her briefcase onto her desk. 'I didn't sleep.' She explained what she had nearly done last night.

Ruby looked appalled. 'Wait a minute,' she said, stopping Elizabeth in mid sentence, 'you were actually going to tell James about Howard?'

Elizabeth nodded. 'Yes, at least, I wanted to tell him . . . I just couldn't.'

'God, you must be cracking up, Liz. What possible good would it have done?'

'At least I wouldn't have been lying to him,' Elizabeth said.

'That would have made his holiday, wouldn't it!'

'I wasn't thinking about holidays, I was thinking about James.'

'Well, that makes a change – you should have done that weeks ago, before you embarked upon this disaster.'

'I can't help it, I can't stop myself.'

'Pull yourself together, Liz,' Ruby snapped, lifting the telephone receiver and thrusting it into Elizabeth's hand. 'Here, call bloody Howard Sands and tell him the trip's off, tell him not to come.'

'I can't. It's four A.M. in New York.' Elizabeth sounded feeble-minded.

'This is your bloody life! Who cares what time it is. What about James and the boys?'

Elizabeth put a hand to her forehead and started to cry.

'Call him, Liz.' Ruby was adamant.

'I *can't.*' Tears poured from her eyes as she quietly replaced the telephone onto its cradle.

The day passed in a numb fog. Elizabeth got through her various meetings feeling detached and disconnected. Functioning on auto-pilot, she was often barely aware of what was being said or what she was saying. In the end she left early and walked into an empty house which made everything seem much worse. She took a long shower, afterwards staring at her reflection in the steamy bathroom mirror where she'd wiped a porthole of looking-glass. Devoid of make-up, hair pulled starkly away from her face, there, she decided, was the real truth: a woman nearing forty, successful, rich and even powerful; married for almost half her life, two children and all the rest. Elizabeth catalogued all the things she had achieved with James, all the things she could be on the verge of giving up. Ruby had been right, it was ridiculous, it was too much to lose but reason didn't enter into it. Howard Sands was above reason. The lascivious urgency of their affair made everything else meaningless. Elizabeth stared at herself, watching the rivulets of condensation slowly obliterating her face, twisting the image, distorting the line, corrupting the vision.

She lay naked on the bed in the late afternoon. The curtains moved slowly in the warm breeze allowing strong sunlight to mottle the room. She could hear the voices of children playing in the street outside. After a while she fell into a deep sleep, and was woken only by the sound of the front door bell. It was almost dark and Elizabeth's first thought was to ignore it but, when the bell was pushed again, she got up and peeped through the chink of curtain where she saw Ruby's car. On the third ring she pulled on her robe and went down to answer it.

Ruby smiled as she stepped across the threshold. They hadn't seen one another since that morning; Ruby had been in Birmingham for most of the day on business.

'Okay?' Elizabeth asked, following Ruby through into the kitchen where the bright lights hurt her eyes for a moment.

Ruby nodded. 'I've just driven down the M1 having negotiated that rabbit warren of a city centre.' She put her briefcase onto the floor and sat down, easing off her high heels. 'I'm exhausted,' she breathed, 'what about you?'

'I left early.' Elizabeth yawned as she filled a kettle for tea. 'I've been asleep for hours.'

'Good. You must listen to what your body tells you.'

'If I did that I'd be even more manic than I already am.' She looked at Ruby's suit, pinky-beige linen with a short skirt and long jacket, a Capellino silk shirt underneath. 'You look smart.'

'Thanks.' Ruby grinned, tugging at the other shoe. 'It's what I had on this morning, only you weren't taking very much notice then.'

'I'm sorry about this morning,' Elizabeth said quietly.

'Forget it.' Ruby kicked the uncomfortable shoe away and rubbed her sore heel. 'I'm sorry, too. It's none of my business . . .'

'Well, I know you think I'm making a huge mistake.'

'Yes, I do.' She stared at Elizabeth. 'Don't you?'

'I don't know what to think.'

Ruby laughed, pushing a hand through her curly hair. 'That's just like something Ingrid Bergman might have come out with in "Casablanca".'

'I suppose my life does rather resemble a melodrama at the moment.' Elizabeth smiled at the thought.

'What do you mean, "at the moment"? You've always loved melodrama. When we started this business in that grotty little office off Bond Street you used to pace about saying we were all doomed.'

'I did not.' Elizabeth was indignant. 'I was just a bit more cautious than you and Nick, there was a lot at stake.'

'Yes,' Ruby agreed, 'and just look at us now, an international concern.'

'One small office in New York,' Elizabeth reminded her.

'And one big affair. At least you'll have that if all else fails.'

'Don't be beastly.'

'Can I make a call?' Ruby asked, moving across to the wall phone.

Elizabeth busied herself making the tea and rummaging around in the fridge for something edible, half listening to Ruby's conversation.

'Who's your friend?' she asked when Ruby finally replaced the receiver. 'And why haven't we met him yet?'

'My new beau.' She sat down and picked up a slice of beef, folding it into half and putting it into her mouth.

141

'What's his name?' Elizabeth demanded.

'Benjamin.'

'Age?'

'Twenty-ish.'

'My God!' Elizabeth hooted with laughter. 'What's this, cradle-snatching?'

'Oh, ha, bloody, ha. He is a bit younger than *moi*, I admit.'

'So, what's going on?' Elizabeth poured them each a large cup of tea.

Ruby shrugged. 'I've taken your advice and found myself a sperm donor.'

'You're not pregnant?'

'Not yet, but I intend to be.'

'What does Benjamin think about this?'

Ruby tucked into the salad. 'I haven't told him yet.'

'You're really finished with Tim, then?'

Ruby nodded.

'But he was such a fabulous catch.'

'You haven't seen Ben.'

'What does he do?'

'He paints.'

'Not an artist,' Elizabeth groaned.

'A house painter. He's been doing out my flat for the last few weeks, that's why I was staying at Tim's place.'

Elizabeth laughed. 'You've picked up your decorator? Oh, Ruby, really!'

'He's absolutely bloody gorgeous, Liz.'

'How old is he really?'

'Twenty-three.'

'My God, a toy-boy! What do you know about him?'

'I know all the important bits and,' she paused to finish chewing her food, 'it's true what they say about younger men.'

142

'But what do you have to talk about?'

'Who's talking?' Ruby giggled, slopping tea onto her hand as she picked up the cup. 'No, really, Liz, he isn't stupid. He has a Masters degree and everything, he's doing a PhD at the LSE.'

'Of course,' Elizabeth laughed, 'how stupid of me. I knew there had to be a catch somewhere . . . only you could have your flat painted out by someone reading for a Doctorate.'

'Not at all,' Ruby insisted, 'London's full of them.'

'When are we going to meet this man?'

'Soon, I expect.'

The two women stared at each other for a long moment and then suddenly burst out laughing at the ridiculous nature of everything. Their sides heaved and they gasped for breath with each new gale of hilarity.

James stood on the terrace of the villa looking out over the Mediterranean as the sun began to set, casting a warm glow over the white building. They'd arrived in the late afternoon and driven the seventy or so kilometres to their holiday home close by Cala d'Or in a tiny bay. The villa was completely secluded, surrounded by hills and pine trees. A trail through the woods led down to a small cove that otherwise could only be reached by boat. The first thing they'd done was to dump their cases and go for a swim; only then were the boys convinced that the holiday had begun.

Now James stood with the sound of crickets in his ears, a glass of beer in hand.

'Alexander's dead to the world,' Geoff told him, emerging from the villa. His new shorts were too tight and cut into his stomach making it appear more of a beer-gut than usual.

143

'What about Wessley?'

'He's reading and listening to his Walkperson.'

James grinned. 'So, what do you think?'

'Bloody marvellous.' Geoff clinked his glass onto James's. 'Nice of Liz to fix this for us,' he remarked, toasting her.

James sat down at last, looking across at the still pool water. 'You know something, Geoff? I don't think I ever really wanted to be married.'

'What?' Geoff laughed, sitting down heavily in one of the flimsy terrace chairs. 'Come on, James, you're the most married person I know.'

'You're the most married,' James replied drily. 'It's true, anyway,' he continued. 'I mean it. I'm not sure if it's been really good for me or Liz, all these years together.'

'You're drunk,' Geoff concluded.

'I know what I'm saying.'

'Marriage was the making of you . . . Liz was the making of you.'

'You're so full of bullshit, Geoff. You never wanted me to get married.'

'I was jealous,' he admitted.

'Were you?' James asked, surprised.

'Of course.'

'But you married soon afterwards.'

'And divorced, and married again.'

'You liked being married.'

'I drove my wives crazy,' Geoff smiled, 'drove them absolutely spare.'

'With your philandering,' James agreed. 'They were perfectly fine women.'

'Perfectly fine,' Geoff nodded, reaching for another bottle of beer, 'but, then, that's me, James, a drunken old

144

bastard and likely to remain so, a career in the doldrums and a history of indecision.'

'Lots of people would see being a GP as the height of success,' James reminded his friend.

'Being a GP is second best.' Geoff took a swig from the fresh bottle as darkness slowly descended around them. 'I should have concentrated upon medicine or an art. Instead I've dallied with them both, and to what effect?'

'To good effect, I should say.'

'Ah, but, man, you're too forgiving.' He smirked drunkenly. 'You can't balance the two, something has to suffer. Instead of being a brilliant surgeon or a full-blooded artist, I compromised.' He wagged a finger in front of James's face. 'It's no good that, compromise is no good.' He shook his head slowly from side to side. Beer dribbled over his chin, dripping down onto the mat of black hair covering his chest.

James laughed. 'Okay, so, what if it's true? We all compromise. Look at me, I never wanted to fit myself into the role of husband, it's always seemed alien. I've never understood my own sex – men are such complete emotional cripples, looking for their mothers, most of 'em.' He laughed. 'Marrying their fucking mothers.'

Geoff placed a heavy arm around James's shoulders. 'You're drunk, my boy, and men don't marry their mothers, that's just another stupid lie . . . they seek for something of themselves and, when they discover how much better women are, they become disappointed.' His face was close to James's, his full lips wet and smoothly red, his breath warm against James's cheek. 'They always become disappointed.'

'Is that why you married twice?'

Geoff blinked and guffawed loudly. 'I married because I loved my wives and I divorced because I couldn't stand

145

being married to them, nor them to me.' He kept his face close, his dark eyes studying James's handsome features.

'I've been living on the edge of disaster for years,' James admitted.

'What do you mean, man?' Geoff asked, his voice reduced to a hoary, rumbling whisper.

'I sometimes think we've been together for too long, I sometimes think we're just clinging on . . . for the sake of the children as much as anything.'

'You love one another,' Geoff insisted, squeezing his hand into the muscles of James's shoulder. 'What's all this talk? It's that bloody silly shrink, isn't it?'

'Liz has her job,' James continued, 'and that's all she's ever really been interested in, everything else is reduced to her time after work. We're all just *there*, waiting.'

'You *are* drunk,' Geoff growled, 'and talking rubbish.'

'Drunk but making perfect sense. Sometimes I can really understand why Sammy went off and had an affair.'

'He was a bloody fool to tell Martha,' Geoff said. 'And what has it proved? Face it, James, we're creatures of impulse, driven by desires, we'll fuck anything if it's available to us, any woman.'

'There speaks a true expert,' James replied, ruefully.

'Don't tell me you've never strayed from the marital bed, a horny little preppy like you?'

'I haven't, not once.'

'Haven't you ever been tempted?' Geoff asked, his voice dark and carnal, thick with lechery.

James thought for a moment, looking up into the starry heaven. 'I never have, though.'

Geoff laughed throatily, placing both arms around James and hugging him tightly. 'You're a fucking virgin, then, my friend, a fucking virgin.' He stood up, a little unsteadily at first, stripped off the new shorts and ambled

146

towards the illuminated pool. The two white half-moons of his behind bobbled away from James in the darkness and then, with a blood-curdling scream, he jumped into the still water.

James sat back and laughed too. He watched as Geoff swam powerfully across the pool, lap after lap, hardly pausing for breath, as though taking on the world and proving that everything he said was true. The God's own truth.

In the morning the cook came in and made breakfast on the terrace for the boys. James arrived late on the scene, unshaven and unkempt.

'Daddy's hung-over,' Alexander laughed, sipping at a giant glass of freshly-squeezed orange juice.

'Don't,' James groaned, sitting down at the table. 'Don't start.' He looked around. A man was watering the plants and a maid in grey uniform hung out white sheets and towels. The morning sun splintered off the sea, forcing James to squint as he reached for the coffee.

The woman came out, clickety clack over the hard terrace. She was older, her salt and pepper hair scraped back into a tight bun, leathery brown skin, a handsome woman into middle age. She placed some warm milk on the pure white table cloth. 'For coffee,' she explained.

James attempted to pull himself together and smiled up at her. 'Thank you.'

'Is everything all right?' She flashed a smile.

'Fine, yes.' James cleared his throat. 'Do you come every day?'

'My name is Maria,' she said, nodding. 'My daughter.' She pointed to the bare-footed girl still hanging out the washing. 'My husband.' She gestured to the man watering the plants. 'He will take care of the pool and any other problems.'

'You're English is very good,' Alexander piped up.

Maria touched his head. 'How is your Spanish?' She laughed for the first time.

'I can say *Buenos dias*,' Alexander told her, 'and *gracias* and *por favor*.'

Maria clapped her hands. 'Bravo, little one.' She turned to Wessley, who was sitting back smiling at his brother's precocious reply. 'What about you?'

'*No hablo espanol*.'

Maria laughed again. 'Two beautiful boys.' She smiled and returned to the house, the tray at her hip.

After breakfast, when James and the boys emerged from the shady pine wood and onto the white sandy beach, Geoff was standing with his easel in the water, tiny waves lapping around his knees.

'Morning,' James called across to him.

'Morning, stay-abeds.' Geoff spoke with a brush clamped in between his teeth, sounding like an appallingly bad ventriloquist.

'*Buenos dias*,' Alexander cried, pulling off his T-shirt and running with Wessley into the water.

James followed the boys into the shallow water feeling the sand under his feet. He was wearing a baggy, white rayon shirt, his hat, blue cotton walking shorts and green mirrored sunglasses.

'Make way for the American gigolo,' Geoff remarked, grinning at James as he sat down close by on a small outcrop of rock. Geoff was wearing his awful new shorts and a vile orange vest, his hairy skin oiled and shining in the hot sun.

James laughed and took off his hat, dipping it into the Mediterranean. 'Have you met Maria?' he asked.

'Yes. Nice woman.' Geoff was working again, picking out the different hues of the water as the sunlight played on it.

James looked over to where the boys were swimming. 'I said we'd have lunch and dinner here today. Is that all right with you?'

'Sure.' Geoff turned to him. 'I can hit the nightclubs and discos.'

James grinned up at him.

'You've still got a good body, James,' Geoff commented, matter-of-factly. 'You should let me paint you.'

James laughed. 'You're joking, of course.'

'No,' Geoff sounded serious, 'it would be good for you.'

'Good for you, you mean, another prize exhibit for your next collection.'

Geoff chuckled. 'You're a handsome man, always have been, you haven't changed much over the years.'

'Luck.' James felt a bit embarrassed and played with his damp hat, watching the water droplets sparkling into the sea.

'Well, man, art is art, I'd like to do a nude of you before you go to seed.'

'To what purpose?' James asked coolly.

'Will you do it?' Geoff sensed victory.

'There's nothing special about me.'

'Man, you've a face, that's for sure. No wonder Liz grabbed you, hook, line and sinker all those years ago.'

James laughed. 'The boys have the looks, Elizabeth's looks. Why not draw them? Ruby says that Wessley will be absolutely sensational.'

'Be brave,' Geoff encouraged.

'I'd feel silly.' James grinned, looking down into the water at his feet, his hair flopping forward over his eyes.

149

'Why? Aren't you proud of what you have, what God has given you?'

'Not particularly . . . To be honest I've never thought that much about it.'

Geoff cocked his head to one side. 'Come on with you,' he said, 'it's time for a drink.' He shaded his eyes and looked towards the sun. 'Must be getting on for noon.' With that he gathered everything up and carted it back to shore with James trailing behind sloshing his legs through the warm sea.

They brought a picnic down from the house and ate it under the trees. The afternoon was hot and the boys darted in and out of the water while James and Geoff relaxed in the shade.

Eventually Geoff stood up and stretched. 'I'm going up to take a shower and look at my painting.'

'I'll hang around for the boys,' James said, lying on his back staring into the blue sky. He felt peaceful and safe for a moment, the Mediterranean lapping at his feet and falling away again. The voices of Wessley and Alexander came to him clearly, carried on the light breeze. He closed his eyes and took a deep breath, as though trying to suck everything that was good inside himself. James held it there until his lungs felt as though they would burst. He expelled the breath and knew that there could never really be any escape. The same reality was there wherever you were and a certain weariness overcame him, the sadness crept back inside, stealthily, like the cunning fox returning to his hiding place.

James watched the boys emerging from the sea. It was close to dusk now, the sun low on the horizon, and their bodies formed crisp, dark silhouettes against its crimson descent.

150

'Where's Geoff?' Wessley asked, picking up his towel and wrapping it around his shoulders.

'He went in for a nap,' James explained, starting to gather up their things.

'Geoff's lazy,' Alexander said.

'He's not, he's just old,' Wessley told him, 'isn't he, Dad.'

James laughed. 'Geoff's exactly the same age as me.'

'But you look young,' Alexander retorted.

'How old am I, Alexander?'

'Are you older than twenty-five?' the little boy asked after a moment's thought.

'Yes, unfortunately. I'm thirty-seven.' James hoisted the beach bag onto his brown shoulder.

'Wow!' Alexander said with amazement. 'That *is* old, isn't it?'

James laughed. 'No,' he insisted, 'it's the absolute prime of life.'

'What's the prime of life?' Alexander enquired.

'The state of highest perfection,' James told him, leading the way from the sandy beach and through the pine wood trail.

'Dad's just old,' Wessley confided to his brother. 'Old people always say they're in the prime of life.'

'But he's the highest prefection,' Alexander said dreamily.

'*Per*fection, dummy.'

'Come on you two,' James called back to them. 'We've got to shower and change before dinner. We're going to Porto Petro for a meal.'

The two children quickened their pace, Alexander stopping only once in the quickly fading light to pick up a pine cone to add to his already enormous collection.

Chapter 9

Elizabeth looked into Howard's face as she rode the length of him, his penis deep inside her now. His eyes were black and returned her stare.

'Liz,' he said, his voice tight and hoarse, 'don't let me come yet.'

Elizabeth grinned, biting hard into her bottom lip, grimacing madly. Howard drew his legs up, wrapping them around Elizabeth's body, using them as a lever to tug himself further up into her vagina. She climaxed without warning and then everything turned upside down as Howard rolled them over, coming inside her with a great rush and urgency.

'God,' he said as they lay together, staring into her eyes, 'that was good.'

She examined his face: there was something Slavonic there, something Russian or Polish. Howard was certainly different from anyone else she'd met. Everything he did was tackled with so much energy and determination. He made love without reservation, he ran his business without pausing for rest, like a hurtling express train. A big American man hurrying through life as if there were no tomorrow. Elizabeth touched his straight black hair, brushing it away from his forehead. For the moment she could feel safe with him, curled up together in her Camden bed, breathing him into her, marvelling at him, feeling the hardness under the silky smooth skin. There were no half-measures with him, no pauses for polite social convention, he went out and grabbed the things he wanted.

'What are you thinking?' she asked.

'That I never expected to be here with you like this.'

'Yes, you did,' she replied softly, tracing a line with her forefinger across his beautiful lips.

He took it gently into his mouth and caught it between his straight, white teeth before moving to kiss her. 'So, this is infidelity.' He grinned.

'Don't say that,' she warned him softly.

'Why not, if it's the truth?'

'Because I don't want to think about it, not now.'

'Coward,' he said, kissing her again.

Elizabeth kissed him back before rolling out from under his embrace and walking into the bathroom to take a shower.

'What are we going to do?' he called after her. 'We can't keep putting this decision off.'

Elizabeth heard his voice, that odd New York accent, alien when heard in her own house, her own bedroom. She didn't reply.

Down in the kitchen Elizabeth called a cab and they giggled all the way back into the city, making silly jokes and comments, touching and kissing longingly. They were in love, out of control, and that was the most frightening and the most terrible part for Elizabeth.

When Elizabeth returned to Camden that evening, there was a message on the answering-machine from Martha. Elizabeth didn't call her back straight away. She suddenly felt depressed and couldn't cope with Martha's confusion and upset. She went into the front room and stood with her back to the fireplace, putting a hand on to the cool, white stone, looking at Geoff's painting which was still on the floor. The brooding quality of the Norfolk scene matched her own mood exactly. Elizabeth felt trapped.

Whatever she did would be wrong. She looked around the walls, vaguely wondering where the picture would hang to best effect. Her feet echoed on the shiny floor-boards as she crossed the room and went upstairs to change. She was meeting Howard at the Dorchester for dinner.

Pausing at the bedside Elizabeth dialled Martha's number. Her friend sounded calm and controlled.

'I expect the house seems quiet without James and the boys,' Martha said.

'Yes,' Elizabeth agreed. 'They call every day but I do miss them and they haven't been away a week.'

Martha laughed. 'I'm meeting someone for lunch in London tomorrow, Liz, and then I have some shopping to do. Can I see you at Camden in the evening and stay overnight?'

Elizabeth paused for a moment, her mind racing. How could she refuse without being unkind?

'Of course, Martha,' she said eventually. 'It will be marvellous to see you. Could you meet me at the office?'

'Are you sure?' Martha didn't sound very convinced. 'Won't you be terribly busy?'

'I ought to be, but, what the hell, Martha, it's not every day that you come to London. I'll look forward to seeing you then,' Elizabeth said, bringing their conversation to a close now, anxious to get dressed for her evening with Howard.

Howard was still asleep when Elizabeth left the hotel the next morning. He wanted her to return to America with him at the end of his trip.

'Is this an ultimatum?' she'd asked. 'If it is it's not fair, I can't just leave London at the drop of a hat.'

He'd smiled at her indignation. 'Sure you can, you can

work just as easily from New York. Liz, I have to know where I stand.'

'I should have thought that was obvious.' Elizabeth had glared at him then. 'I won't be pushed into making a decision like this.'

'You always knew that this moment would come.' He'd been infuriatingly calm.

'What happens if I don't come?' She sat up. 'Do you withdraw this offer?'

Howard didn't answer.

'I can't just pull up sticks and leave like that. It's totally impractical.'

'No,' Howard shook his head, 'if you love me, there should be no question.'

'And what about James? What about the boys?'

'No one's kidnapping you, Liz. You make the decision, or not.'

'This is impossible,' Elizabeth grumbled.

'It's not impossible,' he contradicted. 'Nothing's impossible, if you really want to do it.'

'Don't be so bloody sanctimonious.'

'Listen,' he began, 'I'll put my life on hold for as long as it takes, Liz, you know that, but,' he grinned, 'how long *do* I have to wait?'

'For as long as it takes,' Elizabeth told him.

Howard had turned over and gone to sleep. He saw no point in continuing the conversation, it wasn't getting them anywhere.

Elizabeth had tried to get some sleep herself but it had proved impossible.

'I've been sitting outside your house hitting my hooter for the last twenty minutes,' Ruby said, walking unannounced into Elizabeth's office.

155

'Oh, God, I'm sorry. I forgot to tell you I wasn't going to be there.'

'The lovely Howard brought you to work, I suppose.'

'Don't sneer, Ruby, it doesn't suit you at all.'

'So, how are things?'

'Fine,' Elizabeth replied brightly. 'Martha's coming to London today. What are your plans for later on?'

'I'm meeting Ben. Why is Martha coming?'

Elizabeth shrugged. 'I have no idea. She's seeing someone for lunch and then meeting me here later.'

'What a tangled web we do weave,' Ruby said, enigmatically.

'What's that supposed to mean?'

'Well, Liz, are you seriously going to spend the evening counselling Martha about how she should deal with Sammy's affair?'

'God knows.'

'I'll try to be there, if you like. About ten, after I've seen Ben? Just to make sure everything's all right.'

'Of course it'll be all right. What on earth do you think's going to happen?'

Ruby gave Elizabeth a stern look. 'I don't know, but in your present frame of mind I'm not sure if Martha should be left alone with you for too long. And for God's sake don't tell her about Howard.'

'I'm not completely stupid, whatever *you* might think.'

'What's happening with Howard, anyway?'

'He wants me to return with him.'

Ruby raised her eyes in disgust. 'You told him to forget it, of course.'

'Look, I can't talk about this now.' Elizabeth avoided her eyes.

Ruby turned to leave the office. 'By the way, I had a

card from the boys today. They seem to be having a good time. You should have gone with them.'

Ruby closed the office door quietly behind her.

Elizabeth was still at her desk when Martha arrived at five o'clock, ushered in by George. Elizabeth kissed her friend's cheek, and led her to the black, leather sofa by the window.

'So,' Elizabeth smiled when they were settled, 'how are you?'

'Fine. I met a friend of mine for lunch, a lawyer, Sarah Robertson. I want to know what my position is.'

'Are you and Sammy still living together?'

'In a manner of speaking. I let Sammy remain for the sake of the kids, if nothing else. Everything is fine, there aren't any arguments or anything.'

'And the children don't know that anything is wrong?'

'We haven't said anything, but I suppose they've guessed something's up because Mummy and Daddy are sleeping in separate rooms.'

Elizabeth nodded, her mind spinning, wanting to know all the details and not wanting to hear any of it. 'You seem to be bearing up under the strain, anyway.'

'It's a matter of having to,' Martha replied, sighing. 'God, I wouldn't wish the past few weeks on my worst enemy.' She looked at Elizabeth and took her hand. 'Hang onto your marriage, Liz, you don't realize how good it is until something like this happens to you.'

Elizabeth's expression glazed. Had Martha sniffed something out? 'Well,' she began, retrieving her hand, 'why don't we go home. Ruby said she might pop in later on.'

Martha gathered up her things and, within a few minutes, they were stepping out of the office into the heat and bustle of Regent Street.

Ruby called almost as soon as they walked into the

157

house. She'd put Ben off until much later on and had booked the three of them a table at a new restaurant she wanted to try in Camden.

Over dinner, Martha talked quite openly about Sammy's affair.

'Of course, I know who the other woman is, where she comes from, all of those things.'

'Do you?' Ruby stole a glance at Elizabeth.

Martha nodded. 'It didn't take much to find out, it wasn't very hard.'

'Didn't Sammy tell you?' Ruby asked.

'No, he just wanted to forget all about it, he was looking for forgiveness.'

'How did you discover he was having an affair?' Ruby wanted to know.

'She'd dropped a lipstick in the car. He buckled under the first few questions.' Martha smiled. 'I think he wanted to tell me really. He'd probably had enough by that time.'

'It's over, then?'

'As far as I'm aware. God knows how many others there have been in the past twenty years.'

'Probably none,' Elizabeth stated.

'I hope you're right, I can't stand to think of the risks he's taken if there have been a series of these affairs.'

'So, who is she?' Ruby asked impatiently.

'A student.'

'Really?' Ruby sounded amazed. 'She must be very young.'

Martha nodded. 'Eighteen. Can you imagine it? I mean, really, what can she have seen in him? Sammy's a very nice man but he's hardly Robert Redford!'

Ruby giggled. 'What was she like?'

'Pleasant,' Martha began.

'You've met her?' Elizabeth asked.

158

'Oh, yes, of course. I met her for coffee in Cambridge one afternoon . . . It was all extremely civilized, she cried. I felt sorry for her. Anyway,' Martha continued, 'I told her not to expect Sammy to leave me and the kids for her, I just knew he'd never do that.'

'You seem to have managed the situation wonderfully well,' Ruby gushed. 'I'd have hit him over the head with something.'

'Yes,' Elizabeth agreed, 'you would.'

'There were the children to think of, they adore Sammy. If we can pull everything together and move on from here,' she looked from Elizabeth to Ruby, 'who knows . . . perhaps everything will be all right.' It sounded rather a desperate wish.

Later, Ruby and Elizabeth sat on the patio sipping coffee. Martha had gone to bed soon after they'd come back from the restaurant.

'I thought you had a late-night date with lover-boy,' Elizabeth reminded her friend.

Ruby stared at Elizabeth. 'You know what you should do, don't you.'

'No, but I'm sure I won't be able to stop you telling me.'

'You should call Howard Sands now and tell him to get lost.' Ruby touched Elizabeth's arm. 'I mean it, Liz, before things get even more involved.'

'Don't you think they already are involved?'

'So, you're actually leaving with him.'

'Don't be ridiculous.'

'What are you going to do then?'

'I don't know,' Elizabeth admitted. 'I still have to work with him whatever happens.'

'Forget work, Liz, what about James and the boys?'

'I *know* about James and the boys, you don't have to

159

keep reminding me about them as though I've forgotten they exist. They're all I think about. But I'm in love with Howard.'

'I think it's more like Sammy's fling with the student.'

'It's nothing of the sort.' Elizabeth was becoming increasingly irritated.

'Liz, surely it can't be important enough to break up your marriage and family?'

'Oh, Ruby, don't,' Elizabeth said, her eyes filling with tears.

Ruby moved closer to her on the swing-chair, putting an arm around Elizabeth's shoulders. 'You have to end it, Liz, really you do.'

Elizabeth fumbled for a handkerchief and blew her nose. 'James and I have so little in common these days . . .'

'And that's a reason to leave him?'

'I'm not sure if we ever did have anything to talk about . . . I can see the years stretching ahead of us, when the boys have gone and I'm too old to do anything about it.'

'Your memories are very selective, Liz. I remember when you first dated James, you were totally besotted, completely overboard and you had everything in common then . . .'

'I was eighteen years old, a lot of water has travelled under the bridge since those days . . . we're different people.'

'Nonsense.'

'What do you know about it?' Elizabeth said, crossly. 'You were never in a relationship for this length of time, it's almost twenty years, half my life.'

'So, fight for it, Liz, don't just give up.'

'There's nothing to fight for! James writes books, I help to run a business. He's sad because the career he once

160

wanted for himself seems to have evaporated. We've really come to avoid one another through our work, it's convenient and the marriage works and there aren't any rows, but, at what cost ultimately?' She turned to Ruby for an answer.

'Tell Howard Sands to take a running jump,' Ruby insisted. 'Sort everything out here before taking such an irrevocable step.'

'It's easy for you,' Elizabeth complained bitterly.

'It isn't easy for me, Liz, I want to be with Tim.'

'Do you?' Elizabeth was surprised. 'I thought you hated him.'

'I hate what he did. It doesn't stop me wanting to be with him, underneath it all.'

'You've got Benjamin now.'

Ruby laughed sardonically. 'Benjamin's just passing through.'

'Why do you say that?'

'He's *twenty-three*.'

'So?'

'He's good in bed, Liz, he's gorgeous to look at and every girl's dream. Every *girl's* dream, Liz. I'm a generation ahead of him.'

She took Ruby's hand. 'Is that why we haven't met him yet?'

Ruby nodded. 'It's like tempting fate – if we get too involved in one another's social lives it's almost as though we're a permanent item.'

Elizabeth smiled at last. 'Oh, Ruby, you're absolutely hopeless! Why do I always think you're the brave one, the one who doesn't need any help?'

'Because I spend all my time telling you what to do, I suppose.'

The two women looked at one another in the light from

the house and suddenly burst into awful, hysterical laughter. Holding onto each other for support, as though they could never stop.

At the weekend the house in Camden was full of the sounds of Mahalia Jackson as Elizabeth sat at the big kitchen table working through the details of an exhibition they were mounting on behalf of a large sportswear manufacturer. Sunlight streamed through the open patio windows and the day was clear and warm. Elizabeth finished her planning around lunch-time when Ruby turned up with Benjamin complete with a plastic shopping bag.

'We've come to have lunch with you,' Ruby said after introducing Benjamin, dumping the groceries onto the table.

'That's nice.' Elizabeth grinned, noting that everything Ruby had said concerning the young man was true. Benjamin was very tall and extremely good-looking with a mop of unruly blond hair which he tied back into a pony-tail. His tight jeans were paint-splattered as was his white T-shirt.

'I've just finished work,' he explained, smiling charmingly.

'Let's have a drink,' she said, taking three cans of American beer out onto the patio.

'Ruby tells me that you've known each other for about twenty years.'

Ruby laughed, choking on her beer. 'God, don't remind us of that, it makes us sound ancient,' she spluttered.

'We *are* ancient.' Elizabeth turned to Benjamin. 'And Ruby tells *me* that you're studying for a PhD.'

Benjamin nodded, sitting on the steps leading to the scruffy lawn, his back against one of the stone urns. 'Yes, I don't know why, though. Painting and decorating is much more lucrative.'

162

Ruby went inside to prepare a salad for their lunch.

'I'd better give Ruby a hand,' he said, beginning to get up.

'That's okay,' Elizabeth insisted, 'I'll go in, give her a few minutes to get started.'

'I feel at a bit of a disadvantage,' he admitted.

'Why?'

'Because you two have known each other for so long, because you're so close.'

'Don't let that intimidate you, Benjamin, the length of time you know someone isn't always so important.' She smiled. 'I'm sure you know everything about Ruby by now.'

'I doubt that.' He laughed. 'I doubt that very much.'

Elizabeth picked up the empty beer cans and took them inside where Ruby was busy cutting tomatoes into careful slices.

'What do you think?' Ruby asked, looking out of the kitchen window at Benjamin's prone body; he'd moved from the steps onto the swing-seat now.

'He's very good-looking,' Elizabeth admitted.

'Do you like him?'

'I hardly know him.'

'Do you?' Ruby insisted, the sharp little knife in her right hand.

'Yes,' Elizabeth laughed, raising her hands defensively. 'He seems absolutely wonderful.'

'There's no need to go overboard.' She returned to her slicing.

'Does he know that you want his child?'

'Not in so many words.'

'Are you pregnant yet?' Elizabeth asked, rinsing lettuce under running water and dropping the leaves into a shaker.

'I shall know in a week or so, when my next period is due.'

'Fingers crossed then.'

'The end of another beautiful relationship,' Ruby sighed.

'Do you think so? He seems pretty besotted.'

'They're all besotted until something else turns up, a problem or a better offer.'

'Cynic.'

'I was taught well.' Ruby smiled sweetly at her friend.

'I don't even know if you want to get married . . .'

'I don't want to get married,' Ruby interrupted.

'And yet you want me to remain married.'

'That's different.'

'Why?' Elizabeth sounded interested.

'Because it is.'

Elizabeth laughed. 'You sound just like Alexander.'

'There's one of your reasons. The others are Wessley and James.'

'In that order of priority?'

Ruby ignored that and asked instead, 'Have you seen Howard recently?'

'No, Martha didn't leave until yesterday evening. She went mad buying presents for everyone . . . Marisa has been looking after the kids. I bet she wasn't best pleased, Martha was only supposed to be gone for one night.'

'Martha's cracking up! See, that's what happens when someone does the dirty on someone else.'

'Martha's always been on the verge of cracking up, Sammy's antics have just moved her a fraction closer to the edge.'

'So, you didn't see Howard last night?' Ruby finished cutting up the tomatoes and picked up the bunch of spring onions she'd bought in Camden market.

'No, but I'm meeting him tonight.'

'You're going to end it, aren't you?'

'Well, we shall see.' Elizabeth smiled, opening the lid of the salad shaker and tipping out the lettuce.

'You are going to tell him, though, aren't you?' Ruby asked again, sounding more uncertain now.

Elizabeth ignored her, a half-smile still in place. 'Better go out and tell dream-body that lunch is about to be served.'

'We haven't finished in here yet.'

'Tell him anyway,' Elizabeth said. 'He can go upstairs and have a wash . . . you can help him if you want.'

Ruby ran her hands under the cold tap, wiping them dry on a length of kitchen paper. 'If I didn't know better I'd swear you were jealous.'

Elizabeth hooted with laughter. 'You do know better, though,' she replied, popping a piece of tomato into her mouth before reaching for the vinaigrette.

That evening Elizabeth sat for a long time, watching the light fading in the street outside. When Howard's cab pulled up, Elizabeth had been sitting in the dark house for almost half an hour considering what she should do. Howard had pushed the front door bell twice before she let him in.

'Why are you in the dark?' he asked, bemused.

'Come on through.' Elizabeth led the way into the lounge where she poured him a large Scotch. There was a table-lamp on in the room and their reflections were clear in the French windows.

'Aren't you having anything?' Howard asked, taking the offered drink.

'Yes.' She opened a bottle of bitter lemon and poured it into her glass. 'Cheers.'

'Are you all right?'

Elizabeth nodded. 'You're looking very spruce.'

'Thanks.' Howard looked down at his sober suit. 'It's Savile Row, of course.' He grinned.

Elizabeth smiled at last.

'You don't want to go tonight, do you?'

Elizabeth thought for a moment. They were due to dine that evening with some friends of Howard from New York. 'What have you told them about me?'

'That you're a friend?' Howard laughed. 'No, a business associate, they'll have heard your name in that connection.'

Elizabeth finished her drink and pulled herself together. 'Right then,' she said, standing up, 'we can't let them down, can we?'

'Not really. Deborah's probably spent the entire day slaving over the stove.'

'Right then,' Elizabeth said again as they stood facing one another.

Howard came close, kissing her on the lips.

Elizabeth looked into his eyes, her resolve ebbing away as she took him into her arms.

Howard had reached across her a little later and telephoned his friends telling them a pathetic lie about feeling unwell. They were already an hour late anyway and Elizabeth wondered what they must be thinking.

'How did they take it?' Elizabeth asked as he replaced the bedside phone, looking up at him as he balanced himself over her.

'Said they were sorry.'

'I feel terrible,' Elizabeth admitted.

'So you should, tricking me into bed like this.'

She laughed. 'You're just a horny bastard.'

166

'True, true,' he grinned, falling onto his back beside her.

Elizabeth examined his naked body in the soft bedroom light. He was bigger than James, more defined and muscular, thick black hair curling on his chest and stomach, his forearms and legs. Elizabeth rolled against him, moving her hand across his chest and down to his washboard stomach where the muscular development particularly fascinated her. 'I never really fancied men with muscles before I met you,' she admitted.

He turned his head to her. 'No kidding.'

She pushed her hand down into his pubic hair, cupping his balls, resting her head on his chest, watching as his erection grew. 'It's so easy for you, isn't it,' she stated.

'What do you mean?'

'Oh, sex, orgasms . . . everything.' Elizabeth moved down until her lips touched the head of his penis. She took him into her mouth, slowly sliding her lips back and forth along his length. Her tongue circled the base of the glans and Elizabeth felt him tense, only resuming the smooth up and down rhythm when she heard him groan. She felt exhilarated; she was in control and when Howard came it would be because she made him. Elizabeth felt the strong pulsing vein as he climaxed, pumping salty, white semen into her mouth. Suddenly, Howard relaxed and she looked up to find an almost pained expression on his face, his eyes tightly closed as the waves of orgasm gently subsided. They held one another for a long time, stroking and caressing, but neither spoke. It was as if they were afraid to break the spell.

'This isn't going to work out, is it?' Howard said later as they lay together.

'I don't think it's going to be the fairy-tale ending we might have once considered,' Elizabeth replied, her hand resting on his chest.

167

'You know I've been nurturing this insane dream that we'd end up married or something.'

'Can't we reach some kind of compromise?'

'Compromise never works.' Howard was blunt.

'Then, I don't know what will become of us,' Elizabeth sighed, looking into his sad, handsome face.

'I'm not looking for an extended affair, Elizabeth,' he told her, 'you know that. It's all or nothing.'

Elizabeth stared into his eyes. They were both calm, almost dispassionate. 'So, what happens now? Do we just stop sleeping together and pretend that nothing ever happened?'

'Elizabeth, it must be a clean break.'

'I want to keep on seeing you, though.'

'That's unrealistic – it will never do.'

'What are you going to do then, fly back to New York and consult your little black book of suitable brides to be?'

'I go back to New York and lick my wounds, knowing that James has won.'

'James knows nothing about this.'

'He's here though, Liz. He might as well be standing next to the bed.'

'I never mention him.'

'You don't have to. You'll never leave him, I know that now.'

'I thought I would.'

'It gets too complicated, Liz.' He moved towards her, taking the advantage, encompassing Elizabeth in masculinity, leaving her no room to think, no time to consider.

Elizabeth fitted herself to him gratefully, loving him then as never before, hanging onto him as they made love, engulfed and lost in this embrace.

168

Chapter 10

It was the last afternoon of the holiday and James sat under a pine tree, relaxing in the shade. Images of the past two weeks passed through his mind's eye like a series of brilliant photographs, bodies frozen in time against a background of white sand, blue sea and sky. Large breakfast cups of coffee on the terrace, white china on crisp white table cloths, cool glass jugs of freshly-squeezed orange, misty with condensation, droplets of water running down the sides. The boys on the beach, nut brown and carefully oiled, splashing in and out of the Mediterranean, tireless and revelling in their youth. Geoff's back as he painted knee-deep in water, the rolls of fat at his waist pushed up and out by the tight shorts, the deep brown of his skin under the thick hair of his body.

From time to time he looked across the stretch of white sand towards the sea where Wessley was still swimming. Geoff and Alexander were inside the cool villa, taking a siesta, escaping the hot afternoon sun.

Wessley eventually emerged from the water, spreading his beach towel in the sun just a little way from his father.

'Good swim?' James asked, leaning his arms on his knees as he looked at Wessley.

'Great, are you coming in?'

'In a while.'

'What are you doing?'

'Thinking.' James smiled. 'Just thinking.'

'What about?'

169

'Nothing very much, snatches of conversation, that sort of thing. Places we've been to see, people we've met.'

Wessley lay spreadeagled on his back, his eyes shut. 'Do you think that you'll ever return to teaching?' he asked.

'I shouldn't think so. Why? The time I've been at home hasn't been so bad, has it?'

'No.' Wessley turned his head towards James, squinting up at him. 'It's been better actually; you're not as strict as Mum.'

James laughed. 'I'm not sure how to take that.'

'And you're a better cook.'

'Mum's a good cook, Wes. Don't be critical when you can't justify it.'

'She doesn't cook for us, though. I mean, not often.'

'Well,' James began, not wishing to be led down this familiar, grouchy pathway, 'I expect she will when there's more time.'

'There's never any time for *us*.'

'Come on, Wes,' James encouraged, dropping his notebook into a holdall, 'don't spoil our last afternoon. Come and show the old man something about swimming.'

'I've just come in.'

'Please yourself.' James got up and ran across the hot sand towards the blue water, diving under as the sea-floor shelved away beneath his feet. When James surfaced he turned towards the beach, watching as Wessley waded into the water, and soon they were swimming together.

It was a sweltering afternoon and the sun burned on their shoulders as they moved gently through the smooth Mediterranean towards a large, white yacht anchored just beyond the cove. It was flying the Turkish flag, which hung almost lifeless in the still afternoon. They circled the magnificent vessel, admiring its size and line, the play of water reflecting on its smooth hull. It seemed to be deserted, the tender-boat was missing and the large expanse of the wheelhouse was shrouded with a white canvas cover to deflect the sun's rays.

'Who do you think this belongs to?' Wessley asked.

'God knows,' James replied, looking up at the large boat, 'an arms dealer probably.'

They swam further out, leaving the yacht far behind. The water became deeper and the shadows underneath them grew greener and darker until there was blackness. The beach was a long way away now and a cool breeze touched the surface of the sea as they moved beyond the shelter of land. Wessley suddenly ducked under, somersaulting and swimming into the gloom beneath.

James watched as Wessley's limbs vanished. He called out his son's name, peering down and paddling his legs to keep afloat. James waited, his heart pounding, for what seemed an age. Wessley suddenly emerged behind him, breathing hard, his face flushed from the effort of holding his breath. James spun around in the water and saw Wessley several yards away.

'What the hell was that in aid of?' he asked tightly, trying to contain his anger.

'I just wanted to see what was down there.' Wessley smiled innocently.

'I thought you'd drowned!'

'Oh, Dad,' Wessley laughed, 'honestly!'

James felt cold. He started to swim towards the beach and, in a moment, Wessley was at his side. This time it became a competition, unspoken but determined rivalry. It proved to be an even match until they reached the white yacht, when Wessley put on a spurt of speed, striking out hard for the shore, leaving James one length and then two behind. They staggered from the sea and flopped down side by side, their chests heaving as they gasped for breath. Wessley was laughing, enjoying his success, the masculine desire to beat his rival no matter what.

When they reached the villa, Geoff was sitting at the side of the pool watching Alexander propel the airbed up and down, splashing his legs vigorously behind him. James flopped next to Geoff, dropping his legs into the clear water. Wessley dived in, defiantly remaining underwater for an entire length.

'Come on in, you two, don't be lazy,' he called.

'I've had enough swimming for one day,' James replied. 'First you try to drown yourself and then you act like Johnny Weissmuller.'

'Who?' Wessley asked.

'Never mind.' James stared coldly into Wessley's smiling, handsome face.

'What's all this?' Geoff asked, confused.

'Nothing, just one of Wes's little pranks.'

'Dad's just annoyed because I beat him back to the beach.'

'I wasn't aware that it was a race.'

'Why did you try to beat me, then?'

James felt irrational anger overtake him, but suppressed it quickly, before things got out of control. But in his mind's eye he saw Wessley's watery shape disappearing beneath him, felt again the hopelessness. Out there, in the cold, deep water, everything could have been lost and there wasn't a thing he could have done.

'I think you're taking this too seriously,' Geoff told him later, lying on James's double bed watching him dress for their final dinner.

'Wessley is fourteen years old,' James said, 'and yet I

172

sometimes feel like the child. He frightened me to death this afternoon.'

'Wessley *is* the child,' Geoff assured him, 'you're the adult. Besides, you don't like swimming in the sea, deep water has always scared you.'

James looked down as he buttoned his freshly laundered white shirt. 'He takes risks, like Liz, they're the fearless ones. I just feel out of control and aimless.'

'Crap!' Geoff scoffed. 'What's brought this on, one silly schoolboy prank? What on earth's the matter?'

'I don't know.' James pulled on his jeans.

'You were panicked this afternoon. Why did you swim so far out?'

James didn't answer, he sat down on the hard-backed chair and put his shoes on.

'You were trying to prove something, and you don't need to.'

James pulled hard on a shoelace and it snapped. He looked despairingly at Geoff.

Maria and her daughter served them paella on the long terrace in front of the villa. Geoff poured them all full glasses of red Majorcan wine. The evening was warm and the air full of the scent of pine as the sun started to set. The terrace lights were on and candles burned in glass containers on the table.

'This is a very pretty little scene,' Geoff said, picking up his camera and taking flashlight pictures of them all. 'Raise your glasses,' he ordered.

'What are we toasting?' Wessley asked.

'Spain,' Alexander cried. '*España*,' he corrected himself.

'Health and happiness,' James said.

'To us all, and absent friends,' Geoff suggested, camera in one hand, glass in the other.

173

Everyone waited for Wessley to say something. 'To Dad,' he said at last, grinning shyly at his father. 'To James.'

Their laughter filled the air as they clinked glasses and prepared to enjoy the last evening of their holiday together.

Elizabeth met them at Heathrow the following morning. The boys ran to meet her as Geoff and James followed pushing the trolleys.

'Hello,' she smiled, giving James a perfunctory kiss before moving on and out to the car, the boys talking nineteen to the dozen, Geoff cracking boozy jokes. It was raining and they all laughed as though it never rained in Spain.

Geoff fell asleep on the drive to London and James stared out at the crawling traffic as they inched their way along. Elizabeth had a fixed grin on her face as she listened to the boys' holiday stories but James couldn't help noticing how pale and strained she looked.

'So,' Elizabeth began brightly as they undressed for bed that night, 'how was it?'

'Fine,' James replied. 'The villa was fabulous. You'd have liked it.'

Elizabeth watched him undress. 'You've got a good tan.'

He turned to her. 'You look tired.'

'It's been a tough day at the office,' she joked, but her laughter sounded hollow and her smile was jaded. 'The boys look terribly fit, though.'

James nodded. 'They were really good. They enjoyed themselves.'

'What about Geoff? Drunk every night, I bet.'

James laughed. 'He's a pleasant drunk, though.'

'I still haven't done anything about his picture, I think he'd better come around and hang it himself, it's still sitting gathering dust where you left it.'

James yawned and climbed into bed. 'Don't let Mrs Reed hear you say that.'

Elizabeth took a bath and by the time she returned James was already asleep. His tan looked very dark against the bed linen, the sun had lightened his hair, bleaching it almost white at the temples. He looked incredibly young and handsome, but all Elizabeth could think of was Howard Sands and how much she missed him.

Chapter 11

James visited Jenny Grove's office on the first Tuesday back. He sat opposite her in a square armchair which seemed to enclose and hold him tight. He felt comfortable, safe. He attempted to explain his feelings concerning Wessley, the odd experience of being beaten in the race to land, the contradictory emotions he'd experienced then.

Jenny listened carefully before speaking. 'I'm not sure if people ever have mature or adult relationships with their parents. Adult relationships, where they exist, tend to function outside the family.'

James pondered that. 'Well, I always wanted to have a good, honest, relationship with my kids,' he said. 'I expected to have some problems but not like this.'

'Healthy competition isn't necessarily a negative thing,' Jenny suggested.

'Wessley's growing up.' James sighed. 'You notice it and then you forget.'

'It's good that he's growing up,' Jenny smiled.

'Yes, well, it's just a bit of a shock to realize it. In any case, I don't think it was healthy competition, I think he was making a point.'

'What point?'

'That he was better than me . . . something like that. Anyway, it worked because I felt stupid.'

'That's just your masculine vanity, your pride being dented.'

'I admit it, but it still hurt. I felt humiliated.'

James hung his head and tugged at a shirt button.

'Apart from that one incident would you say the holiday was a success?'

'Yes. It was fine.'

'No problems?'

There was a long moment of silence between them. 'Liz seems tense since we returned.'

'Tense?'

'I think it's probably overwork, but it may be just me, I suppose.'

'In what way you?'

'I can't help thinking that we should never have got married. I've thought about it a lot recently. I don't even know what we have in common anymore, apart from the boys, I mean.' He looked down at his shoes. 'Liz is so . . . so different from me.'

Jenny stared at him. 'Have you said anything to her about these feelings?'

'God, no! Well, not really.'

'Which is it?' Jenny smiled.

'I asked what was wrong, but that's as far as it went.'

Jenny nodded encouragingly. 'Do you think there's a real problem?'

'I don't know. As I say, it might just be me.'

'You?' She tilted her head slightly to one side, as though examining a painting or a sculpture.

'Yes, I'm not sure if I want to stay with her.' Having said the words, James felt a sudden sense of unreality.

'You're thinking of leaving Liz?' Jenny wanted clarification.

James was shocked at hearing it so plainly stated. He looked at Jenny. 'Yes,' he admitted for the first time, 'I suppose that I am.'

* * *

James returned to Camden in somewhat of a daze. He wondered if saying such a thing to Jenny meant it was true or whether it was just a deep thought expressed in the safe womb of her office. The boys were out and everything in the house shone in the bright sunlight streaming through the high windows. James sat in the kitchen for a while pondering the events of the past few hours. He felt that things ought to have changed, that they should be different but it all remained the same.

Upstairs in his study the air was fresh and pleasant. A breeze billowed the curtains back as he sat behind his desk, rolling a fresh sheet of paper into the old typewriter and starting work straight away. The words tumbled out of him, long sentences, conversations and paragraphs, everything in order as though preordained. James typed solidly until Geoff turned up around four when James decided to take a tea break. The boys had returned and Alexander had fallen fast asleep on the swing-chair; Wessley was sunbathing on the grass plugged into his Sony Walkman.

James took the tea into the garden and sat down.

'How are you, Geoff?' James asked, grinning. 'It's nice to see you dressed for a change.'

'I'm great. Everyone at the practice tells me I'm looking *very* good.'

'They're right, you do. Positively bursting with health.'

'What have you been doing?'

'Chores, interspersed with a bit of writing.'

'I thought you were seeing your shrink today.'

'I did. And . . . I told her that I was thinking of leaving Liz.' He shook his head in disbelief. 'Can you believe that?'

'Are you?' Geoff asked, seemingly unperturbed.

'I don't know.' James laughed nervously. 'I *think* I am.'

178

'It would seem a pretty fundamental thing to consider doing if one wasn't sure,' Geoff challenged. 'Come on, James, you can do better than that.'

'I don't know . . . I don't think she's happy.' He turned away. 'I don't think she's happy with me.'

'Has she said as much?'

James shook his head.

'Let me get this straight now.' Geoff leant back in his chair, looking up at the blue sky as he considered the proposition. 'You're planning to leave Liz because she's unhappy with you, but she hasn't actually said anything.' He stared at James. 'Doesn't it strike you as a bit daft?'

'It doesn't feel right anymore.'

'After sixteen years it suddenly doesn't feel right?' Geoff grinned. 'I think perhaps you got just a little too much sun on holiday, James.'

'I haven't decided anything yet.'

'It sounds like you've decided a lot in the last two days.'

James shrugged his shoulders.

'What did Jenny have to say about this state of affairs?'

'She helped me to articulate my thoughts.'

'You're paying thirty quid for the fifty-minute hour to have your thoughts articulated?' Geoff snorted derisively. 'Are you serious?'

'It's what happened.'

'So, Jenny brought you to this realization. How did she tell you to proceed?'

'She didn't. They never tell you how to do anything.'

'What are you supposed to do then, consult the stars? Examine the entrails of a dead dog? Jesus, it's money for old rope!'

'She's helping me,' James insisted.

'Yes, to break up your marriage! I warned you about seeing one of these people, I warned you from the start.'

179

'Keep your voice down,' James warned, glancing at Alexander.

'If there's something wrong you have to discuss it with Liz.'

'I don't know what's wrong . . . I ask her and she says there isn't anything the matter.'

'So?'

'I know there is.'

'I think you'd better come in for a medical, James. I'll run some tests, perhaps it's a physical symptom mixing your brain cells up!'

'Very funny.' James sipped some of his tea. 'When did you become the world's leading expert on saving marriages?'

Geoff looked at his watch. 'I have a surgery at five, don't do anything rash until I've spoken to you again.'

'Are you going now?'

'Duty calls,' Geoff insisted, finishing off his drink and standing up.

'But what am I to do?'

'Take stock,' Geoff suggested, 'and stop being so pathetic. Bloody writers,' he grinned, 'you over-dramatize everything.'

'I'll call tomorrow,' James called after him.

Geoff waved without turning back.

Alexander stirred on the swing-seat, opening his eyes for a moment before turning over onto his other side.

'What's to eat?' Wessley asked, switching off his Walkman.

'Make yourself a sandwich or something,' James suggested. 'Mum's coming in early this evening, I thought we could all eat together for a change.'

Wessley climbed the steps to the patio and sat in Geoff's vacated chair. 'Is there any tea left?'

'If you want to pour it.' James closed his eyes and turned his face towards the sun.

'How's the book coming along?' Wessley asked.

'Fine.' James opened his eyes again and smiled at him. 'Order is being created out of chaos.'

'Do you think we'll write?'

'Do you want to?'

Wessley shrugged. 'I don't know . . . I like reading and I get good marks in English.'

'Why don't you try?'

'I might,' Wessley replied, 'one of these days.'

'Maybe you'll be able to keep me in my dotage with a string of international best-sellers.'

Wessley laughed. 'Let's not get carried away.' He looked at his father. 'When did you start?'

'When I was about your age.'

'Did you think you'd end up doing it for a living?'

'End up?' James said, considering the question. 'I suppose I have ended up, haven't I?' He smiled. 'No, not really and I'm not sure how much of a living I make. Nothing like the one your mother makes that's for sure.'

'But that's different, isn't it,' Wessley stated firmly.

'Why?'

'It isn't artistic.'

'Well, perhaps not but it's what provides you and Alexander with all the little luxuries of life. Tennis can be lucrative, Wes, maybe you'd better stick to that.'

'It's hard, though.'

'Not for you.'

'I wonder what we'll all be doing in ten years' time?' Wessley asked after a long pause.

'I shall be nearing fifty! God, what a thought.'

'I shall be twenty-four. Alexander will be eighteen.'

'Don't.' James laughed. 'Let's stick to the immediate

181

future.' He handed Wessley his mug. 'No sugar in mine, please,' he said, watching as the youth went into the house, enjoying the lithe physique and the developing muscular strength, the emerging sexual awareness. James placed his hands behind his head and tried to remember what he'd been like at Wessley's age, but this rumination wasn't allowed to continue for long. Alexander woke up in a whiny mood and crossed the patio from his bed on the chair-swing to his father's lap where he snuggled up to James, resting his head against bare flesh.

'What's wrong with you?' James asked.

'I'm sleepy,' Alexander replied.

James laughed. 'You've been sleeping all afternoon.'

'I've got a headache.'

James placed a hand on the child's forehead, it felt normal. 'Are you sickening for something?'

Alexander started to cry.

'What's the matter?' James asked gently.

'I had a nasty dream,' Alexander wailed.

James reached for a handkerchief, mopping at Alexander's tears. 'Come on, it's over now.'

'Where's Mummy?' he snivelled.

'At work, but she'll be in early this evening. Come on, sunshine,' he encouraged, cuddling the little boy, 'it was only a silly dream.'

Alexander lay still as James drank his tea and talked to Wessley and, in a while, he climbed down from the comfortable lap and went off to find his war toys.

James watched him from the corner of his eye. He wanted his children to be safe. He knew it was an impossibility but he always wanted to protect them, to look out for them, to prevent them from ever being hurt.

* * *

182

'When I was a kid,' James said, 'I always assumed that real writers lived in garrets, drank and smoked themselves to death, slept between dirty, crumpled sheets and never got up before noon.'

'Do you want to live like that?' Elizabeth asked.

James shrugged. He was cleaning his teeth at the bathroom basin, standing in his underpants on the cold tiles as Elizabeth took a shower before bed. He rinsed his mouth and spat the contents onto the shiny white porcelain. 'I don't know,' he replied to his steamy reflection. 'But I always thought artists had to suffer for their art.'

Elizabeth stepped out of the shower, wrapped her long, wet hair into a towel turban and pulled on her robe. 'I don't see why,' she replied. 'For God's sake, James, don't start getting all Bohemian on me.'

'I'm not, I was just making a point.'

'What do you want, a grubby room in Paris, on the Left Bank?'

'No,' he said, following her through to the bedroom, 'I don't want that.'

He lay on top of their bed, watching as she removed the turban and combed out her long black hair. 'I saw Jenny today,' he said.

'Yes, and what did she have to say?' Elizabeth felt tired and didn't really want to know, only making the effort because Ruby insisted she must.

'She said I ought to ask you what was the matter.' He avoided telling her what he'd admitted to Jenny.

Elizabeth stared straight ahead, feeling trapped. 'How extraordinary.'

'You have to admit, Liz, things are a bit strained around here. You turn away from me all the time.'

'I'm exhausted.'

'You should have come to Spain.'

183

'I *couldn't*. Look, we've discussed this a hundred times.'

'Couldn't, or wouldn't?'

'I'm too tired to argue.'

'It seems to me you're too tired for everything these days.'

'I'm sorry, James,' she told him, 'things just aren't easy at the moment.'

'Tell me then.'

'It's to do with work.'

'You were talking about giving it up not so long ago,' he reminded her as she sat on the bed.

'That was a pipe dream. Let's get the boys through school and university first.'

'Liz, there's something going on between us. I don't understand what it is, but something's happening.'

'Nothing is happening, James,' she replied with exaggerated patience. 'Can we continue this some other time, I'm shattered.' Elizabeth reached for her hairdryer on the bedside table and drowned out any further conversation under the powerful drone of its fan.

The following day, Elizabeth stayed behind after work to talk to Ruby.

'So, what's wrong?' Ruby asked.

'Only everything.'

'Oh, well, that's okay, then.'

Elizabeth smiled momentarily before looking serious again. 'I'm behaving badly, I know it . . . and James knows that something is wrong.'

'You're over-tired.'

'No, there's obviously something he wants to say; we're too afraid to discuss anything, though.' She turned to her friend on the sofa. 'Sixteen years together and it's as fragile as that.'

'You're just exhausted, Liz, you need a break. Why don't you go away for a long weekend with James, I'll house-sit for you.'

'That's not the answer. I love James but I can't help wanting Howard and I've given him the big heave-ho and I'm thoroughly miserable.' She started to cry. 'I'm really miserable . . .'

'It'll pass,' Ruby comforted.

'Will it?' Elizabeth blew her nose into a crumpled wad of Kleenex. 'Maybe I should tell James, they say that confession is good for the soul.'

'What good would that do?'

'It might make me feel a bit better.'

'I doubt that. Take a break,' Ruby insisted, 'get away from London for a few days.'

'I promised my mother that we'd visit them before they go cruising in October,' she suggested, clinging at straws now.

'Arrange it, then,' Ruby encouraged.

'I don't know.' Elizabeth reached for her Filofax, skimming through the crowded pages.

'Do it,' Ruby said firmly, 'bugger the work.'

'But what good will a weekend at my parents' house do?'

'Long walks in the countryside, miles away from London, a chance to breathe.'

'I'm not sure if that's such a good idea. My mother usually requires my undivided attention when I'm on her territory, plus we'll have to take the boys or it will look too odd.'

'Right, so do it.' She walked over to Elizabeth's desk and lifted the telephone receiver. 'Here, call them now.'

'I have to consult James first.'

'So, ring him and consult.'

Elizabeth laughed at last. 'I'll talk to him this evening, I promise.'

She got up and put on her suit jacket. 'What are you doing later?'

'Tonight is baby night.' Ruby grinned. 'I should be at my most fertile and I've made Benjamin abstain for the last few days and told him not to wear any tight jeans.'

Elizabeth dropped some papers into her briefcase and snapped it shut. 'Good luck, then,' she said, heading for the door.

'What are you doing?'

'The boys have been invited to a birthday barbecue at a friend's house in Camden Square.'

'James will have prepared a little romantic something, then.' Ruby winked.

'I don't deserve that.'

'*Talk* to him,' Ruby called out as Elizabeth finally left.

They made love in the hot evening, just the way she had with Howard, feeling somewhat illicit as it was still light outside and the streets full of noise. They showered together afterwards, James standing behind her, reaching around to soap her breasts and in between her legs, letting his slippery fingers move inside. He slid a hand up to her breasts again, teasing the hard nipples. Elizabeth could feel the springiness of James's penis as it grew hard and pressed into her buttocks. His breath felt hot against her damp skin as he kissed her neck, his tongue sliding into the sensitive part of her ear. The water drummed hard onto the slippery porcelain and steam billowed, enclosing them in hot clouds that created beads of sweat on their skin. Elizabeth turned to him, kissing his mouth, then his chest, and down until she was on her knees in front of him, taking his engorged organ into her mouth, sucking until he forced her head away and lifted her up again. Elizabeth wrapped herself around him, their limbs entwined as James lifted her onto him, her legs crossed behind his back, her muscles aching with the effort to cling on. She reached up to the shower rail, grabbing it for support as James thrust himself into her and, as her strength began to ebb away, Elizabeth climaxed and called out, her breath coming in short spasms. James came with a yell, shuddered and then lost his footing. Elizabeth grabbed hold of the shower curtain as they collapsed into the bottom of the bath tub, the plastic material falling on top of them like an enveloping, white plastic membrane, fitting itself to their twisted bodies as they attempted to extricate themselves, laughing so hard they could barely move. James managed to free an arm and break through the all-encompassing curtain, freeing them until they lay together in the bottom of the bath, exhausted as the water gushed down onto them, luke-warm now, refreshing, envigorating.

'What a mess,' Elizabeth said, drawing him onto her, her hand firmly placed at the nape of his neck, kissing him.

James held himself away, his arms tense on the smooth porcelain. He smiled as he looked down at her then slowly lowered himself to embrace her, not wanting the moment to escape them, not wishing to let it go.

Afterwards they pulled on some clothes and raided the fridge. Their bare feet slapped over the kitchen tiles as they concocted a meal of leftovers: cold meat and potato salad, half a bottle of wine, pitta bread, cheese and liver pâté. They piled everything onto a tray and carried it out to the patio where they gorged themselves in the evening sunlight, sitting on the swing-chair, the food between them. Elizabeth watched him as they ate. She'd gone home with the intention of talking to James, not that she knew what, exactly, she wanted to say. There was the question of Howard Sands, and Elizabeth wondered if she would ever dare to bring that up. Given that confession was supposedly good for the soul, she would have liked to have told James about him, but it seemed impossible.

James was lost in thought. It had been the first time they'd made love since his return from holiday and his sense of urgency and desire had been immense. It was strange to love a woman still, but not know if he wanted to go on living with her. He looked across at Elizabeth, reaching down onto the warm concrete for the chilled wine and, pouring them each a glassful, grinned and asked what they should toast to.

'Health and happiness?' she suggested.

'No,' he replied, shaking his head, not taking his eyes from her face, 'us, Liz, you and me.'

Elizabeth felt a kick of guilt in her stomach but she smiled and raised her glass whilst, in her heart, it felt like darkest betrayal, deep within the portals of Gethsemane.

Chapter 12

Marisa stayed over with them on Friday night. She'd been in Bloomsbury meeting someone at the University of London to discuss a contribution she was making to a paper on adult education and the need for women in the work-force. Rupert was in Canada sorting out a computer virus in the network of a bank there.

'I'm a computer widow.' Marisa grinned, sitting at the kitchen table and spooning honey into the tea Elizabeth had just poured.

James walked in with a sheaf of proofs in his hand and kissed Marisa on the cheek. He sat opposite her and helped himself to some apple strudel she'd brought for them. James had always found her to be a very attractive woman, intelligent, witty and exuding sexuality.

'How are you, Marisa,' he asked, taking a cup of tea from Elizabeth's hand.

'Fine.' She smiled wide, using her generous mouth to full effect. 'How's work?' she asked, pointing to the new book in its crisply printed proof form.

James pulled a face. 'I always get the heebie-jeebies at this stage when it's really too late to change anything.'

Marisa laughed, turning to Elizabeth. 'It must be hell living with an artist.'

Elizabeth forced a laugh. 'How's Martha?' she asked, immediately changing the subject. 'We haven't heard from her or Sammy for a while. Wasn't he supposed to be having an exhibition down here at some point? I thought we might get an invite.'

'They've split up,' Marisa said, looking slightly askance, 'didn't Martha tell you?'

Elizabeth shook her head. 'The last I heard they were living together but in different rooms.'

'He's living with the girl,' Marisa replied, looking at their faces. 'It's quite a shocker, isn't it?'

'What's Martha going to do?' Elizabeth asked.

Marisa smiled. 'You're not going to believe this. It took us quite a long time to reconcile ourselves to it, but she's met a new man, at her ceramics evening class.' Marisa laughed. 'He's not much older than the girl Sammy dumped Martha for.'

'You're kidding?' Elizabeth hooted. 'Are they living together?'

'Oh, yes,' Marisa nodded, 'and he's an absolute knockout. God alone knows what he sees in Martha, a mother substitute probably!'

'That's cruel,' James said, laughing.

'No, not at all. If I wasn't a happily married woman of certain years I wouldn't mind that kind of a fling.'

'You're terrible, Marisa.' Elizabeth grinned. 'Where is Sammy living, then?'

'In the girl's flat, close to the Polar Research Institute, which somehow seems appropriate, don't you think?'

They both laughed at that even though the story was basically sad and awful. 'A happy ending then?' James asked.

Marisa shrugged. 'Sammy's always been a bit of a philanderer . . . I think this is just mid-life crisis, the male menopause or something.'

'What about Martha?' Elizabeth enquired. 'Is her man just a bit on the side?'

'God, you should see Martha, she looks absolutely great, this boy is absolutely besotted with her. It must do wonders for your ego! Well,' she began, picking up her tea cup, 'Martha deserves a bit of luck. I mean, Sammy's nice enough but he's a bit of a drifter . . .'

'But Martha was always besotted with him,' Elizabeth replied. 'You're not seriously suggesting that she's over him now.'

'I don't know, but she was the one who finally split them up, she asked him to leave, so, who knows?'

'Jesus,' Elizabeth breathed, 'really?'

'I know, talk about the worm turning.'

'Good for Martha then, that's what I say,' James interjected.

'Here, here,' Marisa agreed, raising her cup and chinking it against his, 'good old Martha, eh?' She smiled at them both in turn and then laughed to herself at the whole, improbable story.

After dinner James and the boys went into the lounge to watch television leaving Marisa and Elizabeth still drinking their coffee at the table.

'So, what's new?' Marisa asked.

'Nothing much.' Elizabeth smiled.

'You look tired, Liz. When's the big opening?'

'In three weeks' time. I'm not sure how big it will be, I just hope it isn't a damp squib.'

'I expect it'll be your normal success . . . what do the other two think about it?'

'Nick's excited, Ruby's more concerned with getting herself pregnant.'

'Yes,' Marisa nodded, 'I spoke to her a few days ago. This thing with Benjamin seems much more serious than I'd thought.'

Elizabeth agreed. 'It's like everyone's changing their partners.'

'You're not, are you?' Marisa joked and then, seeing

191

Elizabeth flinch, grabbed her friend's hand. 'You're not, *are* you?'

'No,' Elizabeth attempted to laugh it off, 'of course I'm not. God, Marisa, you and me are in it for the duration, I'm not about to be swept off my feet by some handsome youth.'

'Well, perhaps not, darling, but you could always have an affair.'

'Hardly,' Elizabeth replied.

'Do you think we've changed very much since we were eighteen?' Marisa asked, tugging at her hair.

'Yes, of course. We're considerably older for one thing.'

'What about inside here?' Marisa tapped her head.

'My brains are seriously addled,' Elizabeth remarked. 'My short-term memory is atrocious, I have to make lists for everything these days.'

Marisa laughed at that. 'Yes, yes, but what I mean is, have we changed as people?'

'I expect so,' Elizabeth replied. 'I certainly hope so, marriage and kids and responsibility must have left their marks somewhere along the line.'

'What about Rupert and James?'

'They were sweet boys, weren't they?' Elizabeth smiled at the memory. 'I sometimes think that I might have ruined James,' she admitted.

'Ruined?' Marisa stared. 'What a funny thing to say . . . James was always such an idealist, a dreamer, look what he's achieved with you.'

'A lot of books,' Elizabeth admitted, 'but not the novels he really wanted to write.'

'I think that's crap, Liz. He can write whatever he likes, there's no financial imperative after all.'

192

'The creative process is very delicate, though,' Elizabeth continued. 'I feel that our marriage may just have thwarted all of his early promise.' She sighed. 'Jesus, I remember how brilliant some of his early stuff was . . .'

'It may have been brilliant, Liz, but it was never published, you put some order into his life.'

Elizabeth laughed. 'You make me sound like some old harridan.'

'Well, darling, you have to admit he was a little on the dreamy side.'

'That's his artistic nature.'

'I suppose it might have had something to do with his parents being killed like that . . . I dread to think what might have happened if you hadn't come along.'

'Stop it, Marisa. You make him sound like some kind of emotional cripple. James would have been all right. Besides, his grandmother was awfully kind.'

'James was a little preppy bastard, Liz, he hadn't an idea in the world about life. Now look at him, it's an incredible transformation.'

'It works both ways, Marisa. There aren't that many men who'd do what he does: a lot of men think they're liberated until it comes to the crunch, he gave up his teaching job to be at home.'

'Yes, but only because he could write full-time.'

'Not only that.'

'I bet he wouldn't have even considered it if he'd have been earning your salary.'

'That's not the point. Anyway, we've all done all right, we've all survived so far.'

'Everything intact,' Marisa added.

'Just about everything.'

Marisa grinned and got up to fetch them both more coffee.

When the boys were finally in bed and asleep James joined them, and they sat up late talking over their shared past.

'We should do this more often,' Marisa said as they drank their final nightcap.

'It's finding the time,' Elizabeth replied.

'We should find the time,' James insisted.

'Or you could always move to London,' Elizabeth suggested, laughing at her friend's expression.

'I'd rather die. It took me ten years to drag Rupert away. I couldn't come back, not to live, not now.'

'We were talking about moving out,' James admitted.

'Were you?' Marisa looked surprised.

Elizabeth nodded. 'For about ten whole minutes I thought it might be possible.'

'And why isn't it?' Marisa demanded.

'It's too much of an upheaval, new school for the boys, a place in town for me during the week . . . I don't think it's worth it.'

'Believe me, darling, it's worth it.'

'Liz was contemplating giving up working full-time.'

'That was before Ruby announced her intention to make a bid for motherhood,' Elizabeth added quickly.

'You ought to really consider the advantages, Liz,' Marisa told her.

'Of motherhood?'

'No, not motherhood, of working out of town.'

'It's impracticable,' Elizabeth insisted.

'Why?' Marisa pressed. 'You're opening an office in New York when you won't be there all of the time.'

'That's different.' Elizabeth wished they'd never begun this particular topic of conversation.

'Why?'

'Because we're working with associates.'

'Howard Sands and Associates,' James told Marisa from behind his hand in a stage whisper. 'Very snazzy.'

Elizabeth felt her face growing hot. 'Well, anyway,' she began, as calmly as she could, 'we won't be moving out in the immediate future, let's put it like that.'

'Right,' Marisa nodded, 'it's time for my bed.' She yawned and put her glass down. 'I'll see you tomorrow then.'

'Leave the glasses until the morning,' James said as Elizabeth started to collect them together.

She looked at him and then nodded, following him upstairs to bed.

They made love again that night. Elizabeth found sex with James suddenly dangerous and full of amazing possibilities. She let her hands rove his body, watching his reactions, the facial contortions as she stroked his cock and balls. Eventually, she straddled him, taking his penis into her and achieving another orgasm. Her abandon was complete, as though the thought of letting James go released all inhibitions. Elizabeth wasn't sure if their coupling was an actual expression of love any longer, it could just have been a delicious excuse not to have to talk about anything. She gasped and sucked in air as another climax shook her and, leaning forward, watched as James came. He moved his head slowly from side to side on the pillow, his eyes tightly closed with the delicious pleasure, a cry, almost of remorse, coming from his throat. In another moment it was over, his semi-erect penis sliding out of her, sticky and wet, a droplet of semen still at its tip. They exchanged smiles as she went into the bathroom where she squatted in the tub and, taking the shower head, doused herself down, careful not to splash too much water over the edge now that they had wrecked the shower curtain and fittings. James was asleep when she

195

returned to the bedroom. She sat down in front of the dressing-table mirror combing her hair and staring at her reflection. Elizabeth looked into her dark eyes and wondered which would be the greatest mistake now, staying with James or leaving him.

Elizabeth called Howard from her office when everyone had gone home, when everything was quiet beyond her open office door, apart from the cleaners who were working their way along the corridor towards her. She could hear a vacuum cleaner in Ruby's office.

'So, what are you saying?' Howard asked after a few minutes of conversation. 'That you've changed your mind about us?'

Elizabeth paused. 'I want to be with you all of the time,' she admitted. 'I want to see you all the time.'

'I can understand that,' Howard teased.

'Bastard,' she replied.

'Well, since you threw me out of London I haven't quite known what to think.'

'I didn't throw you out, I said we had to cool it. You were the one making ridiculous conditions.'

'What are you going to do?' Howard asked.

'I shall be in New York soon,' Elizabeth began, 'I want us to sit down and talk this through.'

'You haven't answered my question, Liz. What are you going to do?'

Elizabeth hesitated. 'I'm not sure.' She grimaced, knowing this was the last thing he would want to hear.

'So, we're back to square one,' he stated.

'I don't know where we are,' Elizabeth admitted. 'Stop being so damned dogmatic all of the time.'

'Listen, I've got to run, Liz, I'll call you later in the week.'

'Right.' She didn't want to let him go. 'Say something nice to me.'

Howard laughed. 'I love you . . . there, is that nice enough?'

'It'll do,' she said, hearing the connection go dead in her hand, the dialling tone suddenly in her ear. Elizabeth replaced the receiver and considered what she'd started. For a few moments she felt elated then trapped. One minute she could convince herself that she never wanted to leave James and the next she was craving Howard. After a while she pulled herself together and left the office. The evening had clouded over, there were spots of rain in the air. Elizabeth quickened her pace as she headed for the tube.

Chapter 13

Before New York, before Howard, there was the weekend with Elizabeth's parents in Gloucestershire.

They had all piled into the Volvo and driven down on Friday night, Alexander falling asleep for the last part of the journey. Her parents lived in a seventeenth-century manor house of Cotswold limestone. It sat in its own grounds on the edge of the village and was far too big for the old couple. It was crammed with antiques and paintings and Elizabeth worried that they weren't really safe in such an isolated spot surrounded by so much treasure. It was dark when they arrived although there was a bright light over the front door which helped them to see what they were doing. Her parents came out to greet them and helped to carry some bags inside. James took Alexander straight up to bed whilst everyone else congregated in the big kitchen where Alice had prepared some home-made vegetable soup.

'Oliver grew every one of these vegetables,' she announced as they sat down to eat.

'Did you bake the bread as well?' Elizabeth asked.

Her mother looked at her. 'Of course not. Mr Teal delivers it, just as he has done for the past twenty-five years.'

Elizabeth smiled and then yawned. 'I won't take much rocking tonight,' she said.

Wessley went to bed after supper and his parents followed soon after.

'What's it feel like being back?' James asked as they undressed.

'Oppressive,' Elizabeth replied, pushing down her jeans.

'This is such a lovely house.'

'It smells musty – beeswax polish and mothballs. Isn't it odd how smells can transport you right back into the past?' She pulled on her nightgown. 'I wish they'd sell up and move into something more practical.'

'They love it here,' James said.

'They're not safe here, the stairs alone are too much for them and you can see for yourself that it's falling into wrack and ruin.'

'It's not that bad, Liz, be fair.'

'It all needs decorating, I'll have to speak to them about it.'

'Don't upset them.'

'Upset them? I want to help them.'

'They don't need help.'

'They need money, James, a lot of money to make this barn sound. God,' she said, exasperation obvious in her voice as she looked around the room, 'all of this junk, they never throw anything away.'

James smiled, sliding in between the icy cold sheets. 'Come to bed, Liz, don't get upset. We can have a good look around in the morning, make a list if you want.'

The bed creaked as she climbed in beside him. Elizabeth giggled. 'Imagine screwing in this bed, you'd wake up the entire village.'

James laughed too, the creaking growing louder as they shook with the effort of suppressing their growing hysteria.

Rain battering against the bedroom window finally woke Elizabeth the next morning. James had already

199

dressed and sorted the boys out. She poked her arms above the blankets and felt the dull chill of a country weekend permeating her very being. Elizabeth turned to look at her watch on the bedside table, it was just nine-thirty. She was about to duck under the covers for another twenty minutes when Alexander came into the room carefully balancing a breakfast cup full of strong tea in his hands.

'He insisted upon bringing this up to you.' She heard her mother's voice.

'Here you are, Mummy,' Alexander said, proudly placing the beautiful cup and saucer by her side.

'Thank you, darling,' Elizabeth beamed, 'that's very sweet of you.'

Alexander climbed onto the bouncy, creaking bed and sat next to his mother, propping up James's pillow on the oak bedhead behind his back.

'Where's Daddy?' she asked.

'James, Wessley and Oliver have gone into the village to get some petrol for the Bentley,' her mother said, drawing the curtains and allowing the grey morning light to filter through the dusty panes of glass.

'We're all going to Slimbridge to see the birds,' Alexander informed her.

'Are we?' Elizabeth looked confused.

'You don't have to go if you don't want to, dear,' the old woman said.

'Are you?' Elizabeth asked, thinking of the raw day.

'I think not.' Her mother smiled. 'Oliver wants to take the boys, and James said he'd drive, so,' she shrugged, 'that will keep them occupied for a while, won't it. You go if you want, Elizabeth.'

'No, I'm not really very bothered. I'll stay here with you.'

'Daddy said I could take photographs,' Alexander informed her.

'Good, you can take some of Grandpa.'

'Come on,' Alice said, taking the little boy's hand, 'we'll go and make up some flasks of coffee and let Mummy get dressed.'

Elizabeth watched the door slowly closing and then dragged herself out of bed. Crossing the cold boards, she looked out of the window and down into the garden where an ancient gardener was pushing an equally ancient wheelbarrow along one of the gravel paths in the rain. She found her clothes and dressed quickly, pulling on a thick jumper which would keep her warm through the weekend. Elizabeth splashed cold water on her face in the old bathroom, the water knocking through the pipes and sounding like a London bus, and then went down to see what she could do to help.

Alexander was standing on a kitchen chair holding a giant thermos flask as her mother poured in hot coffee. Elizabeth wondered if this was an entirely safe procedure but, not wishing to upset either of them, moved quietly to their side and took over the pouring.

'We were doing it,' Alexander complained.

'I'm helping as well.' Elizabeth smiled down at him. 'Do you think I should make sandwiches?'

'Oh, no, Mummy, they'll be back for lunch, won't they?'

'I doubt it, Elizabeth, your father's bound to find a pub en route.'

'Then they can have a pub lunch, that'll save you a job.' She screwed the top onto the thermos flask.

Her mother grinned. 'I don't suppose they'll need the flask, then.'

'They can have a drink at Slimbridge,' Elizabeth

encouraged, wishing that she'd left them to their own devices and spent another hour in bed.

After the 'men' had left, Elizabeth felt strangely abandoned. She didn't know what she was to do with her mother for the better part of a day. The kitchen was always the warmest place in the house because of the Aga. The cats always curled up next to it – Mr Pops, a rather splendid ginger tom and Rosie, his rather ancient, supine mate who always fell asleep with her paws in the air. The kitchen seemed to be full of her mother's dried flowers which were stuck into every available container. They had more coffee, the kitchen full of its delicious aroma, whilst her mother chatted about the village and its inhabitants, identifying people Elizabeth barely remembered, their children – who she had lost touch with years before – and the calendar of church events which bored Elizabeth to death.

'And you're in New York soon?'

Elizabeth nodded. 'On Tuesday. We're all going this time. Ruby said we ought to travel in separate planes, like the royal family – in case of disaster.'

Alice laughed. 'Do you know the last time I was in New York?'

'No.' Elizabeth smiled, taking another of the home-made shortbread biscuits. 'A long time ago?'

The old woman nodded. 'Nineteen forty-nine. We stayed at the Waldorf-Astoria and saw the Duke and Duchess of Windsor . . . I bet it's all very different now.'

'You should go back,' Elizabeth suggested.

'Nineteen forty-nine,' Alice mused, 'three years later you were born and you'll be thirty-eight soon, won't you? How the time goes.'

'Thirty-eight, don't remind me.' Elizabeth smiled.

202

'Well, that's nothing, darling, I'm almost eighty.' She hooted with laughter. 'Horrible, isn't it.'

'Why is it horrible?'

'To be eighty,' her mother began, 'is to be discouraged. Fifty was all right and even sixty wasn't too bad, seventy was a bore but eighty!' She pulled a sour face. 'The funny thing is I don't really feel very different inside from when I was a girl . . . it's only when you see yourself in the mirror that you catch your breath.'

'Oh, Mummy.' Elizabeth laughed. 'You look perfectly fine.'

'For eighty.'

'For any age, you're marvellous . . .'

Her mother grinned. 'I'm wonderful, but, darling, who wants to be old?'

Elizabeth had no idea, she certainly didn't, she was half her mother's age and already felt decidedly geriatric at times.

They walked out in the fine drizzle a little later on. Elizabeth slung on a long, green, waxed coat which she kept in the cupboard under the stairs for just such days.

'It feels like October,' her mother said, sticking her hands deep into the warm pockets of her heavy tweed coat.

They wandered around the large garden, her mother pointing out the various flowers and shrubs. 'Jim should be around somewhere,' Alice said.

'I saw him earlier,' Elizabeth told her, 'staggering under the weight of an over-loaded barrow.'

'He's an absolute gem, darling, so hard-working.'

'Isn't he a bit old for heavy lifting?'

Alice chuckled. 'They breed them tough in the country . . . he's a good twenty years younger than us.'

Elizabeth followed her mother inside one of the large

greenhouses at the end of the kitchen garden where Jim was attending to the rows of tomato plants. 'Why do you grow so many?' Elizabeth asked.

'Chutney, darling.' The old woman beamed, bending over a plant and examining the fruit. 'It's always a marvellous fund-raiser for the church and WI.'

Jim tipped his cap as they left and Elizabeth closed the door carefully behind them, following her mother along the pathway between the rows of carefully tended vegetables back to the house. There was some broken guttering on the stable block and rain water was pouring down the side of the building, carrying a dark rust stain onto the stonework. She pointed this out.

'Yes, dear,' Alice nodded, 'someone is coming to repair it. We're having the house painted in the autumn when we're away. The smell of fresh paint always makes your father's sinuses act up, so it's easier to take a cruise and leave them to it.'

They walked across the paved courtyard and entered the dusty, echoing stable. There were three stalls all piled high with junk from the main house, broken chairs, rolls of carpet, an ancient television set in its huge wooden case. 'Why don't you ever throw anything away, Mother?'

'It's your father, Elizabeth, he won't throw a thing away. We just continually shift piles of stuff from one place to another.'

'Why don't you just get someone to clear it?' Elizabeth asked, turning towards the piles of rubbish again.

'He knows where everything is. I suppose, in his mind, he can see a use for it.' She chuckled and set off across the yard to the house.

'You're quite right, of course,' Alice told her, back in the kitchen. 'It's all junk, every bit of it. We should really take it all out to the paddock and have a big bonfire, that's what I'd like to do, what use is any of it?'

'There are some nice things,' Elizabeth replied, filling the kettle with water and putting it onto the stove.

'Well, don't worry, darling, we won't throw the family silver out, you can be sure of that.'

Elizabeth laughed. 'I didn't think you would.'

'You'll have it all to sort out in the end, Elizabeth, you can do what you will with it then.'

Elizabeth didn't answer. She didn't want to entertain thoughts of death.

They left for London after lunch the next day. James insisted upon taking family snap-shots for the album, setting his camera on timer so that he might join the group in front of the house. Alexander cried as they left, wanting to stay with his grandparents, but calming down and cheering up when they were half an hour or so into the journey home. Elizabeth had tried to talk to her father about the house, the collected debris of a lifetime, but he'd laughed and patted her back, telling her not to worry.

'I'll help Grandpa clear the house up,' Alexander volunteered as they drove home.

'That's very sweet of you,' Elizabeth told him, 'but your grandfather has no intention of sorting anything out. I'm afraid the piles of rubbish will just grow higher and higher.' She turned to James. 'You know he's taken to buying job lots of things at local auctions.'

James shook his head and grinned. 'No, really?'

Elizabeth nodded. 'They're having a load of redundant agricultural tools and machinery delivered next week . . . he's just adding to the junk.'

'Don't worry,' James encouraged.

'I can't help it, I'm the one who'll have to sort everything out in the end . . . the attic rooms are full of things from their days in Singapore before the war. I think he's going gaga, I dread to think what he'll transport back from their cruise.' Elizabeth sighed.

'What does gaga mean?' Alexander asked.

'Forgetful,' Elizabeth replied.

'Who's forgetful?' Wessley asked, switching off his Walkman to change tapes.

'Grandpa,' Alexander told him.

'He doesn't seem forgetful to me,' Wessley said, switching the new tape on and closing his eyes.

Elizabeth wished her life were as easy as that, just plug yourself into a little machine, turn it on and remove yourself from the world. It would have made for a much less fraught existence.

'Well,' Elizabeth said with some satisfaction that evening, 'just think of it, a whole weekend with my mother and not one argument.'

'So, what does this tell us?' James asked, standing dripping onto the bathroom floor, having just stepped out of the shower.

'I don't know, what does it tell us?'

'That she's really a sweet old thing.'

Elizabeth wasn't too sure about that. 'I think that old age is finally mellowing her.'

'You've always been too hard on them, Liz, they're okay.'

'They're eccentric. Daddy's a sort of Citizen Kane without the imported castle.'

'*Yet*,' James added, picking up a towel and starting to dry himself.

'Don't,' Elizabeth said, 'don't even think such a thing.'

James laughed and walked into the bedroom. 'At least

206

you have parents to complain about, what about us orphans of the storm?'

'Be grateful, that's what I say.'

'You're a hard woman, Liz.'

'Am I?' she stared at him.

James didn't reply.

Elizabeth walked by him into the bathroom and turned on the bath taps. She looked into the foaming green water and swished it around with her hand, stepping in at last and sitting down. She lay back, allowing the oily water to rise higher and higher until it was up to her neck. She lifted a leg and managed to shut the taps with her foot. From where she lay she could see the bottom half of James's torso and his long, tanned legs. She could hear the rustle of the newspaper as he worked his way through the *Observer*, and the television which was on with the sound turned down low. Elizabeth pictured both James and Howard, comparing their looks. The most obvious difference was that James was fair and Howard dark. They were both tall, Howard probably just having the edge. She tried to see their naked bodies side by side; James smooth, Howard coated in curly black hair. James had what Elizabeth considered to be a perfectly ordinary body whereas Howard took pride in his physique although that wasn't what really attracted her to him. He was something of a kindred spirit, every cliché concerning the new spirit of enterprise.

Elizabeth stared up at the ceiling, watching the curls of steam rising from the bath water. James the husband, Howard the lover, perhaps that was it. Elizabeth had wanted the excitement of an affair after all the safe years with James. She'd wanted to know that she was still alive, that she was an attractive woman. She craved the risk and the secrecy, the quickening heartbeat before they met.

Elizabeth had only to be close to Howard for everything to happen. He would smile in a certain way and she would want him. It was a dangerous liaison but Elizabeth couldn't let go, she had tried, but it was impossible. She looked into his eyes and knew that everything was lost. Howard would do whatever she wished in order to satisfy the savage desires that he unleashed. She felt that he didn't need her in the way that James seemed to and that also was part of the attraction. With Howard there was no shared history, everything was for the moment.

James saw Jenny on Tuesday morning. Elizabeth had left with the others for the New York opening and he nearly hadn't kept his appointment because Alexander had been upset at his mother's departure and made himself sick.

'I feel that something is happening,' James began.

Jenny fixed him with a penetrating stare. 'What is happening?' It was a warm day at the beginning of September and she wore a plain white sleeveless dress which had a high collar and a simple belt of the same material. Her long hair was tied back and coiled into a plait.

'Oh, I don't know,' he sighed, feeling ridiculous. He gripped the arms of his square chair. 'I have no control.'

'What do you want control of?'

'Me? Life? Elizabeth? My children?' James looked away. 'God knows,' he breathed.

'Each of those are major issues,' she answered, a smile playing over her lips.

James relaxed a little. 'I'm attempting to finish this book,' he began, '. . . and I'm trying to cater to my kids' demands, I'm trying to be a good father and a good husband and . . .' He stopped talking, looking down at the office rug. 'There's something really weird happening between Liz and me.'

'What's happening, James?' she asked again.

'Things are changing – sexually,' he said and then was silent for a long moment. 'I'm not sure if it's done out of love anymore. It's as though we're inflicting something on one another.'

Jenny pondered for a second or two. 'Have you spoken to Liz about this?'

'No. It feels like the end of something.'

'Has she said anything?'

James shook his head and remained silent as though lost in thought.

'How are things generally with you both?' 'Good, things are okay. We had a pleasant weekend at her parents, although Liz tends to worry too much about them. But she didn't argue with her mother and it all went really well . . . The boys enjoyed themselves.'

'When did you feel that things began to change?'

'There isn't an actual date . . . Over the last few months, I suppose.'

'Have there been arguments?'

'No. I suppose people just grow apart, there may not be any specific reasons.' He crossed his legs, looking down at the clean blue denim and the new Reebok basketball boots. They looked incredibly white against the muted tones of Jenny's office. 'I think that she is, ultimately, disappointed in me, though.'

'Disappointed?'

'I feel that she wants me to act in a certain way, that she would like me to be a stronger person.'

Jenny considered his words. 'In what way "stronger"?'

'Oh, maybe a better provider.'

'You mean she thinks that you don't earn enough?'

James realized that wasn't it at all. 'No, there's no

209

conflict over that. It's as though she's deciding what to do next. I feel that she's testing me out.'

'In what way?'

'It has to do with sex as much as anything else,' James admitted. 'Liz isn't normally very demonstrative.' He started to feel foolish now. 'For a time sex hadn't seemed to be at the centre of our marriage but just recently it's become much more important . . .'

'And, so, what do you think this means?'

James shrugged.

'Do you intend speaking to her about it?'

'Perhaps our marriage just isn't working anymore,' he suggested after a long silence.

'Is that what you think?'

'I don't know what I think.'

'I think you probably do,' she encouraged with a pleasant smile.

James looked at her. 'I'm just angry with Liz,' he admitted, 'because she's so bloody good and I feel left behind somehow.'

Jenny didn't respond, she just sat there calmly listening, her head bent slightly to one side, a finger pressed against her cheek.

'I think,' James continued, 'that when I gave up my teaching post to work from home there was a certain amount of self-sacrifice involved . . . it was how I coped.'

'But you both agreed that you should give up teaching, it was a mutual thing.'

James agreed. 'Everything was supposed to work out for me then, by writing full-time it was supposed to make things change, but one set of restrictions was simply replaced by others. It isn't marking essays now or tutor groups, instead it's making sure the boys are okay and

210

that there's enough food in the house and that the washing's been done . . .'

'And isn't that what you expected?'

'I don't know what I expected exactly, maybe it was to write a better novel now that I supposedly have the time.' James smiled at last.

'It's only been a matter of months,' Jenny reminded him, 'this is still the transitional stage, surely.'

'I think that it's taking me longer than I imagined to come to terms with the new situation.'

Jenny nodded and, smiling at James, closed her notebook, placing it on the table beside her chair. 'We'll continue next time,' she assured him.

James left feeling tired and a little unsteady. He seemed to have said things to Jenny which were only half-constructed thoughts before he set foot inside her office. He found the Volvo in a side street, and sat behind the wheel for a long time going over the things he'd said. Finally, noticing the time, he started the engine and drove back to Camden.

Geoff called in that evening. James had traced a pattern to these Tuesday visits. They'd begun when he'd started seeing Jenny. Sometimes it was late afternoon, sometimes lunch-time or, as now, after his evening surgery.

'Hello, Doctor, busy day?' James asked.

'Awful, nothing but a load of ill people coming to see me.'

Alexander laughed. 'That's your job, though.'

'Yes, I know,' he bent down to pick the little boy up, 'awful, isn't it?'

'You love it,' James told him.

'Well, I don't know about that,' Geoff replied, examining the faint line of scar tissue where Alexander's head had been cut before putting him down.

'I was sick today,' Alexander told him.

'Were you?' He felt the little boy's forehead. 'Was he?' He turned to James.

'He was upset when Liz left this morning, he made himself sick.'

'But you're okay now?' Geoff asked.

Alexander nodded. 'I'm hungry now.'

'You're always hungry.'

'What are we having for dinner?' Geoff enquired.

'We?' James grinned.

'Baked beans,' Alexander called out, 'fish fingers and chips.'

'Actually we're having a mixed grill. You're welcome to stay, of course.'

'Well, if you insist.'

'I don't insist, we'll just divide our meagre rations between three instead of two.'

'Where's big brother?' Geoff asked.

'Tennis practice. His coach is making him perfect his backhand. I don't know when he'll be in.'

'Come on then,' Geoff encouraged, 'let's get this show on the road. I'll do the steak. I'm good at cooking steak.'

Alexander was already putting the knives and forks on the kitchen table.

James leant back against the sink and folded his arms. 'I'll just watch, shall I?'

Geoff removed the plate of meat from the fridge. 'Dad's sulking,' he said to Alexander. 'Here you are, old son.' Geoff turned to James. 'You can grill the chops if you want.'

'Thanks,' James replied, grinning at his friend, 'thanks for letting me help.'

'My pleasure.' Geoff laughed.

James laughed too, he always felt better when Geoff was around.

'No date tonight?' James asked as they sat in the lounge after their meal.

'No date,' Geoff confirmed, sitting on the sofa with his feet up on the old gun chest, a glass of beer in his hand, 'I'm on call, I have my bleeper.'

'You'd better not drink too much pop then,' James advised, 'we mustn't have you being found drunk in charge of a patient.'

'No, Doctor.'

'Aren't you seeing anyone?' James questioned. 'You know, I'm starting to get a bit worried about you.'

'I'm celibate,' Geoff said with a straight face.

'Yes, and I'm Florence Nightingale.'

'How's the shrink?' Geoff asked, changing the subject abruptly.

'Counsellor,' James corrected, realizing that they were to play their usual game.

'Tell me then,' Geoff insisted, 'before the bleeper drags me away.'

James told him everything he could remember, watching Geoff's pained expression as the details tumbled out. 'I don't know why I'm telling you all this,' he said at last.

'Because you love me?' Geoff suggested.

James shrugged. 'Be that as it may . . .'

'So,' Geoff sighed, taking his legs from the gun chest and sitting up, leaning forward towards James, 'what does it all mean?'

'I don't know.'

'Thirty pounds for the fifty-minute hour and you don't know . . .'

'Here we go again,' James complained.

'I'm only saying what any sane person would say to you,' Geoff insisted.

'Don't start.' James looked out of the open French windows at Alexander who was sitting on the swing-chair reading a book. Sunlight played through the leaves of the lilac bush casting dappled, moving shadows over the child's face.

'I warned you about seeing this woman, didn't I? It's like opening a bloody Pandora's box.'

'I have to talk to someone.'

'Speak to me, or Liz.'

'Someone neutral,' James said quickly, 'someone who doesn't have any axe to grind.'

'What axe do I have?'

'Friendship and history.'

'For God's sake, James,' Geoff said through clenched teeth, 'when are you going to stop all of this shilly-shallying, what is it that you want?'

'I want to be a moderately good writer, and I'm not sure that I'm even that.'

'I wanted to be a great painter,' Geoff laughed, 'so what?'

James smiled too. 'Plus, being at home just means that Liz's perception of me is further reduced.'

'Has Liz said that?'

'She doesn't need to say anything.'

'Oh, so you can read minds now, is that it? It's not a shrink you need, James, it's a clairvoyant.'

'I don't really talk to Liz, it's all superficial stuff, her life is all about big business and deals, image and brand values . . .'

'And what are you all about, James?' Geoff asked very directly. 'You hated teaching, you did it for over ten years, you proved to us all that you could hack it. If you'd

214

murdered someone you'd probably have done less time, you always said it was a prison sentence.'

'I always wrote as well. You make it sound so pathetic.'

'Things may not always work out as we'd like them to,' Geoff said. 'Liz does her best, why are you suddenly so critical of her, you're sounding very superior.'

'Why are you defending Liz?' James felt angry and hurt at such betrayal.

'Because you seem to resent her for allowing you to do what you want! Accept the situation with good grace, accept that you can't generate enough income to keep everyone in this amount of luxury.' Geoff encompassed the room with his arms. 'And stop feeling so sorry for yourself.'

James stared, his face feeling hot but he had no reply, no defence, nothing to say that would help.

Alexander walked in through the open windows and climbed up onto his father's lap, snuggling against James's chest, sleepy and needing reassurance. James placed his arms around the child and held him close, his chin resting gently on Alexander's head, breathing in every childhood scent.

'This is what I'm about,' James said to Geoff in a soft voice, suddenly overwhelmed with a deep sense of melancholy, 'this is everything that matters.' His eyes burned with tears that would never fall.

Geoff nodded. 'But children grow up and leave.'

James smiled at last, looking down at the sleeping boy. 'You're a cynical bastard,' he told Geoff, standing up and carrying Alexander to bed.

Geoff examined his beer and relaxed onto the sofa once more, watching the dappled sunlight moving slowly over the warm patio stones.

Chapter 14

Elizabeth returned to London on Saturday afternoon. The house was quiet as she stepped into the hallway. She put her bag down and walked through into the kitchen from where she could see James and the boys busy at work in the garden, tidying up the flower-beds. It was a task James had been threatening them with for weeks. She stood for a while watching; Alexander wielding an impossibly large hoe, hacking away at the thick carpet of weeds, James busy dead-heading roses whilst Wessley pushed the electric mower across the scruffy lawn. She waited a long time before stepping out onto the patio. Everyone looked up as she spoke, Alexander dropping the hoe and running towards her.

James climbed onto the patio from the rose-bed and kissed her cheek. 'You look a bit shell-shocked,' he said.

'I feel it,' she replied.

James dropped his gardening gloves onto one of the metal chairs, following Elizabeth into the house where they made tea. 'Good trip?' he asked.

She nodded, kicking off her shoes. 'We're up and running, at last.'

'Good,' he turned to look at her, 'it is good, isn't it?'

'Yes,' she smiled weakly.

James waited for the kettle to boil. There was a long silence between them. Alexander came in from the garden carrying a faded bloom from the pile of roses his father had been cutting.

'Here you are,' Alexander said, handing the pink flower to his mother.

'Thank you, darling.' Elizabeth beamed, bending down to kiss him.

'Daddy's been cutting them all off, there aren't any left on the bushes.'

Elizabeth laughed. 'Aren't there? Well, they'll soon grow back again.'

James poured the boiled water into the teapot and started to put out cups and saucers. 'Why don't you go to bed for an hour or so?' he suggested. 'I'll bring your tea up.'

Elizabeth nodded. 'I think I will.'

'Good, I'll keep the monsters at bay so you won't be disturbed.'

She started to leave the room, paused for a second as if to say something and then, smiling, walked on.

'Right,' James said brightly to Alexander, 'cup of tea and then back to work.'

'Where's Mum?' Wessley asked, kicking off his boots before stepping into the kitchen.

'Bed,' Alexander told him, 'it's the jet-lag.'

Wessley looked at his father for verification. 'She's tired out, right?'

James nodded, pouring their tea.

He let Elizabeth sleep through. The boys wanted to wake her at dinner time but James insisted that they leave her alone. She surfaced around eleven o'clock when she had a shower and went downstairs to make herself a sandwich. James, who had been working in his study, found her in the kitchen a little later.

'How are you feeling?' he asked.

'Better,' Elizabeth assured him, 'less brain-damaged.'

James smiled.

217

'There's something we have to discuss,' she said.

'Is there?' James looked confused, aware of the sudden tension in the air between them.

Elizabeth nodded, never taking her eyes off him. 'I don't know how to say this, so I suppose it's better to come right out with it.'

'What is it?'

'There's someone else,' she said after a terrible pause.

'Someone else?' he repeated, looking blank.

'Yes.' Elizabeth was holding a small, white, lacy handkerchief in her hands and she clenched and unclenched her fists around it. 'I've been seeing Howard Sands.'

'As in an affair,' he spoke quietly, as though still uncertain of the truth.

Elizabeth looked down at her hands. 'I didn't know it would come to this,' she began.

'To what?'

'I've fallen in love with him,' she whispered. 'It's inexplicable, but there it is, there's the truth of the matter.'

James suddenly sat down heavily, shaking his head slowly from side to side. 'All those trips to New York,' he said as if to himself.

'There's no easy way to say these things,' Elizabeth continued, 'no simple way.'

'So,' James took a long, shaky breath, 'this is it then. What happens now? Do you pack up and fly to New York?'

'I don't know what happens now,' she said, looking at him again.

'Are you going to live with him?'

'Yes,' she said softly.

'Is he married, too?'

'He's divorced.'

218

James shrugged. 'It's me, isn't it,' and then he laughed bitterly, 'what am I talking about, of course it is.'

'It isn't anything to do with you, James,' she said, 'it's to do with me.'

He looked at her. 'Why?' was all he asked.

'I need more than this,' Elizabeth answered. 'I've tried, James, I've honestly tried not to see him.'

'Obviously not hard enough. In any case, you work with him, I suppose that's part of the attraction.' James thought for a moment, staring blindly at the floor tiles. 'That's why you wouldn't come to Spain with us, isn't it?' he asked. 'It's all very clear now.'

'I had work to do, that's why I didn't come to Spain.'

'I bet,' he muttered under his breath. 'So, what have you decided, you and Howard Sands? What's it to be?'

'We haven't decided anything.'

'Do you want to marry him?'

'You and I could stay together for another twenty years, James, but what use would that be, what good would it do?'

'I suppose,' James continued, 'marriage requires a certain amount of compromise. The odd thing is,' and he smiled as he said it, '. . . the strange thing is that I never cheated on you.' He stared out of the kitchen window and into the garden. 'I never did.' James shook his head as though in disbelief. 'I never wanted to . . . more fool me, eh?'

'There has to be something more than this . . . what is there here, for both of us, James?' she asked him.

'The boys?' he suggested.

'That won't change, whatever happens.'

'Everything will change or are you going to give them up so easily?'

219

'It's not a case of giving them up, James. I don't intend to uproot them either, if that's what you mean.'

'That's easy to say now.'

'Do you seriously think that I'd want them to live in New York?'

'It'll destroy them,' he replied.

'Children are more resilient than you give them credit for, James.'

'Alexander throws up when you're leaving for a few days, what's he going to think if we tell him you're moving to New York?'

'You don't have to tell him anything.'

'Don't be ridiculous.'

'It can be broken to them gently.'

'To save your face you mean.'

'There's no point in upsetting them more than is necessary.'

'Jesus, but you're taking this very calmly.'

'It isn't the end of the world, *really*, it isn't.'

'It feels like it to me,' James's voice broke. 'And what does Howard Sands have to say about this?'

'The decision is my own.'

'He's never said a word on the subject, then?'

'Of course he has, but he hasn't forced me to take any decisions.'

'Is he in love with you?'

Elizabeth nodded.

'How can you be sure that it will last?'

'I can't be sure, just as I couldn't be sure that we would stay together for all these years.'

'I don't know why you bothered to come back,' James said nastily. 'What was the point?'

'Because I wanted to see you, would you have preferred

a letter or a telephone call?' Elizabeth bit into her bottom lip. 'I don't want to argue, James, it serves no purpose.'

'How long has this affair been going on?' he asked quietly.

'A few weeks . . . A month or so . . .'

'A few weeks,' James repeated, 'and that's all it takes to end a marriage?'

Elizabeth didn't reply.

'When are you leaving, then?'

'In a few days, a week or so, there are things to sort out.'

'What about this place?'

'What about it?' Elizabeth looked confused.

'Well, as you know, I don't make enough to pay all the bills, the school fees, car, petrol, food . . .'

'Everything will carry on as before.'

'I should be grateful for that, I suppose.'

'No,' Elizabeth said, fixing him with a steely-eyed stare, 'you have no need to be grateful, I don't see it as a duty or an obligation.'

'What about Nick and Ruby? How have they reacted to this, or did they know about it already?'

'They didn't know.' She looked away. 'Ruby knew.'

'So much for friendship.'

'It isn't Ruby's problem, don't start blaming her now. It's all my fault, I've failed you, I've failed the children, I'm a bad mother, I accept all responsibility for everything that is happening.'

'Don't they mind you leaving so suddenly for America?'

'Someone has to run the New York office, it might just as well be me.'

'Such self-sacrifice, Liz.'

'Look, why don't you just get angry instead of this

221

pathetic sniping? I've told you everything,' she said, her voice rising. 'I've tried to do the decent thing.'

'The decent thing?' James laughed bitterly. 'Just think of yourself, Liz, don't change the habits of a lifetime.'

'That's not fair, I don't deserve that.' She dabbed at her eyes as tears began to fall.

James watched her. 'What have I done wrong, just tell me, Liz?'

'It has nothing to do with you, it's all to do with me, why don't you understand?' She looked at him. 'Listen, listen,' she told him softly, 'I'm going over to Ruby's . . . I think that's best.'

James didn't say anything, he felt numb, almost uncomprehending, and so he just sat and watched her leave.

James let Geoff into the house just before six o'clock. Geoff hadn't had time to shave and, as he'd just woken up, looked even rougher than usual. He'd pulled a pair of grey trousers on over his pyjama bottoms and had dragged a sloppy, green V-neck over his pyjama top.

'Is this how you turn up at your patients' houses?' James asked. 'You look terrible.'

'Shut up, James. If you summon me at the crack of dawn, you take me as you find me.' Geoff put an arm around his friend's shoulders and steered him through the house to the kitchen.

'The universal meeting place,' James said.

'The heart of the house,' Geoff replied, filling the kettle and plugging it in.

'This heart is in pretty bad shape,' James admitted.

Geoff sat next to him, lifting up James's wrist and timing the heartbeats. 'So, you finally blew it,' he said.

'It's not my fault, don't blame me.'

'Isn't this just what you've been talking about?'

'No,' James protested.

Geoff got up again, made instant coffee, popped bread into the toaster, went to the fridge and poured them orange juice. 'Here, drink this,' he commanded, pushing a glass into James's hand. He spread sunflower oil margarine onto the hot toast and returned to the table.

'Are you angry with me?'

'No, why should I be angry with you?' Geoff asked, crunching into a piece of toast. 'You look bloody awful.'

'My marriage is over.'

'It's what you want.'

'It isn't.'

'Then, do something about it.'

'Like what?'

Geoff reached for his orange juice, gulping it down. 'Is she coming back here again?'

James nodded, staring at the drink in his hand. 'She's bringing the car back.'

'Where is she now?'

'Over at Ruby's place . . . the chief conspirator.'

'Oh, come on, James. Ruby's not like that.'

'They're all "like that",' James insisted darkly.

'You've convinced yourself that this would happen, that one of you might leave, you've talked about it in the past and now it's become some kind of self-fulfilling prophecy.'

'Because I knew something was wrong.'

Geoff nodded. 'What's she going to do now?'

'She's going to live in the Big Apple with Howard Sands.'

'Howard Sands?'

'Her business associate, it's the perfect merger.'

'What about the kids?'

'She says that nothing is going to change but, if she

223

wants them in New York she'll have a fight on her hands, those boys don't leave London.'

'Have you asked her to stay?'

'What's the point?'

'What's the point?' Geoff laughed, exasperated. 'This is your marriage, man. Liz, remember, sixteen years together and two boys?'

'She's in love with him, she told me that. I'm not begging her to stay.'

'Then you must really want it to end.'

James didn't answer. 'God knows what I'll tell Wes and Alexander.'

'James,' Geoff said sharply, 'what are you going to do?'

'The problem is,' he replied, looking at Geoff, 'I don't know if I do love her and, what's even worse, I can't help feeling that she's to blame for that.'

'Come off it.' Geoff sounded disgusted. 'That doesn't make any sense.'

'It doesn't have to make any sense,' James argued, 'life doesn't make any sense but we all live it.'

Alexander wandered into the kitchen at that point looking from one man to the other. 'Where's Mummy?'

'Your mum is at Ruby's,' Geoff explained. 'Ruby's not feeling well.'

'Yes,' James agreed, 'she had to go last night.'

Alexander shrugged but seemed to accept the offered explanation. 'When is she coming home?' he asked, sitting down at the table.

'Soon,' James said, smiling as hard as he could, 'very soon.'

'Right,' Geoff said, standing up and stretching, 'who's for more toast?'

Geoff busied himself with breakfast preparations and James remained at the kitchen table in something of a

224

daze thinking that the first hurdle had been jumped, the first lie accomplished.

The boys seemed to accept that their mother had to be with Ruby for most of the time due to her unspecified illness and, when the explanation was changed – that she was staying over with Ruby for a few more days because of pressure of work – they appeared to accept that too.

For James it was, he imagined, like the phony-war period. At times it felt as though he'd imagined Elizabeth's decision to leave and that perhaps, if he didn't think about it too much, everything would be all right, nothing would have to be said, they could go on as before. However, this was not to last for very long. Elizabeth turned up at the end of the week and told the boys that she had to return to New York for a while on business. It was as simple, and as mendacious, as that. The boys groaned and complained but accepted it just as they had accepted all the other times when Elizabeth had had to fly away. They had other things on their mind. School began on the following Monday and they were full of moans because the holiday was finally over but also excited at the prospect of the new academic year.

'You're really going through with it then?' James asked, sitting on their bed, watching her pack a big suitcase.

'I'm really going through with it,' she answered, turning her back to him as she pulled another suit out of her wardrobe.

'And when are you finally going to tell them the truth?'

'Later,' she said, carefully folding the material, 'when it won't come as such a shock.'

'Oh, and when might that be?'

'In a week or so, a month at the most.'

'And I'm supposed to string them along until you decide that the time is right.'

'I shall be back in London in two weeks' time, we'll take it from there.'

'Then you'll tell them?'

Elizabeth didn't answer. 'There's no point in upsetting them.'

'Wes already knows something's wrong.'

'What do you mean?'

'He's hanging around here a lot. I virtually had to force him out to tennis practice this week . . . I suppose he thinks that I might disappear too when he's out.'

'Don't be so melodramatic. Why do you want to be such a martyr?'

'I just want you to understand what you're doing.'

'I know what I'm doing.'

'What about me?'

'You'll be all right. You've got what you want, you've got your work.'

'That you've never valued.'

'I don't think that you've valued it, James.'

'What's that supposed to mean.'

'You write books the way other people make motor cars, you've a collection of components which you assemble over and over again.' She stared at him. 'You were once looking for greatness.'

'How many books do you think I'd have sold looking for greatness?' James sneered, grabbing Elizabeth's wrist and holding it fast.

'Then be satisfied with what you've achieved,' she said, attempting to pull away from him.

'And just what is that, would you say?' he asked.

'You've created a certain body of work,' she answered.

'A certain body of work,' James mimicked. 'And what have you created, Elizabeth?'

'My business,' she replied defiantly.

'P bloody R, what the hell is that? Office blocks and tacky hotels.' He released his grip on her wrist.

Elizabeth held it in her other hand. 'It pays the bills, so don't knock it.' She walked to the dressing-table where she sat down, gathering her things together.

'Do you despise me that much?'

'Don't be so absurd.'

James crossed to her side, standing over her. 'Don't go, Liz,' he said simply.

Elizabeth didn't reply but continued with her packing, picking up a large bottle of Chanel No. 5.

James, suddenly seized with anger at her apparent coolness and composure, her lack of concern, snatched the bottle of perfume from her hand and threw it against the wall above their bed where it shattered. The aroma of the expensive fragrance began to permeate the room. 'You're not to go,' he shouted at her.

Elizabeth stood up and faced him. 'What the hell are you doing?' she asked, shouting back, staring into his angry eyes.

'You're not going,' he repeated.

'Don't be ridiculous.'

James went to the bed where he upended her suitcase, tipping out most of the contents before forcefully slinging it across the room. 'I'm not the ridiculous one here,' he screamed as he let the case fly.

Elizabeth ducked as the suitcase hit the window, smashing a full pane of glass before falling back onto the dressing-table where it scattered the contents and cracked the mirror. 'James,' she yelled, feeling a mixture of furious anger and blind panic, diving towards James as he started to attack the jumbled pile of clothes. Elizabeth tried to grab a silk blouse away from him but they ended up in an absurd tug-of-war, only succeeding in ripping it in half. 'James, for God's sake, stop it.' Elizabeth tried to force him away but he was throwing her things all over the room.

'I won't let you go,' he shouted, splitting open a pack of Body Shop powder and filling the air with a fine white mist which settled over everything.

Elizabeth had never seen him in such a furious state. 'I can't stay here . . . I'll call the police if you don't stop.'

He paused to look at her and laughed nastily, picking up an armful of her clothes and throwing them in all directions.

Elizabeth went to the dressing-table where she retrieved the suitcase.

'Leave it,' James commanded.

'I'm packing my things,' Elizabeth insisted.

James came towards her, pulling the case out of her hands and, with another manic swing, smashed it through the top pane of glass and down into the street where it landed with a hefty bang on the roof of the Volvo. 'There, now go and pack your bloody clothes.'

'Have you gone mad?' Elizabeth demanded.

James stood still now, looking at the heavy curtains hanging from the broken rail. He pushed a hand through his messy hair and turned towards Elizabeth. 'Fuck off, then,' he bellowed, brushing by her, pausing at the door, 'go to your fucking lover but just remember this, you don't get the boys, whatever happens you'll never have them.' He pointed his finger at her as he spoke, stabbing the air and now, red-faced and breathing heavily, he slammed the bedroom door behind him with all of his force. The impact caused the window frames to rattle and a large piece of jagged glass broke away and crashed into the front garden.

Elizabeth stood fixed to the spot. She heard James slam the front door and listened to him driving the Volvo away, the tyres squealing at the corner. She sat down on the bed surrounded by the wreckage of their bedroom and, picking up her shredded blouse, buried her face in the fine material and burst into floods of tears.

The next week passed quickly for James. The old routine they'd established before the summer holiday was soon back in place, the morning and the afternoon shuttle between home and school. The frantic rush in the morning to get there on time. The arguments in the car, the forgotten homework books, the lost training shoes. The next time he saw Jenny, James talked about his scene with Elizabeth.

'Anger is frightening,' James remarked.

'Why should it be?' Jenny pushed. 'It's just another useful emotion.'

'It's destructive,' he said.

'But it's quick, quick as lightning and then it's over and done with.'

James thought for a moment. 'People kill when they're angry, don't they?'

Jenny smiled at his logic. 'Sometimes.'

'Sometimes,' James repeated to himself, thinking of the terrible mess he'd made. 'But what if anger is all there is between people?' he asked. 'What if it's the only thing?'

'Is that what you're saying about you and Liz?'

He looked at her. 'People are very sensitive, we hurt easily. That saying,' he smiled, '"sticks and stones can break my bones but names will never hurt me", that's so much crap.'

229

'You're too controlling, James, you have to let go sometimes, names are meaningless,' Jenny insisted.

'Anyway,' he continued, 'Liz left, and that's that, I suppose.'

'And how do you feel?' Jenny asked gently.

'How do I feel?' he repeated the words to himself. 'I feel as though I'm part of some dreadful dream and keep hoping that I might wake up soon.'

'Are you still working?'

'Oh, God, yes, that never stops.'

'Perhaps you should take a breather, give yourself a chance to recover from the shock.'

James scratched his head and gave a wry smile. 'Men are supposed to be strong, aren't they,' he stated, 'they're not supposed to be like this.'

'Like what?'

'Oh,' James sighed, 'feeble, out of control, powerless, impotent, ineffective . . .' The words broke off as he began to cry silently, reaching forward for a tissue from the box on the table between them. He wiped his eyes and blew his nose. 'There you go,' he laughed, embarrassed now, 'point proven.'

'Tears aren't a sign of weakness, James,' she told him, like a teacher repeating a well-worn lesson. 'Quite the opposite.'

'Someone told me that all of this was a self-fulfilling prophecy.'

'Do you think that?' she asked.

'No,' he shook his head, 'not really.' He looked up at Jenny and grinned like a little boy. 'Not really,' he said again.

Ruby called him that afternoon and asked if they could meet for lunch the next day. Hesitant at first, James finally agreed. She said that she'd read a piece about him in that day's *Guardian*. James was perplexed for a moment, not understanding what Ruby meant.

'That piece by Marilyn Fullar, don't tell me you haven't read it?' Ruby asked.

'No,' James admitted, 'I haven't even looked at a newspaper today.'

'Read it,' she commanded before ringing off.

James had forgotten the interview he'd given to the young reporter a couple of months after giving up teaching. He sat at the kitchen table and turned the pages until he found a picture of himself, accompanied by a long article based upon his conversation with Marilyn conveying his thoughts concerning house-husbandry. It was an extremely positive piece of writing that showed him in a particularly good light. James considered having it copied and sending it to Liz. After reading through it for a third time James went to his room and worked through the afternoon until it was time to pick the boys up.

Geoff turned up in the early evening after surgery. They sat in the lounge for a while, he was going out and couldn't stay long. The boys drifted in and out with questions about homework, or food, or lost clothing.

'Your dad's a star,' Geoff told Alexander. 'Did you see his picture in the paper?'

'Oh, that,' Alexander replied, leaving the room again, 'I've seen that picture lots of times.'

The two men looked at one another and laughed.

'Have you heard any news?' Geoff asked.

'No, I don't expect I will.'

'Has Liz called the boys?'

'Yes, yesterday.'

'And?'

231

'She always calls them when she's away, it's not anything special. They still think she's coming back here in two weeks' time.'

'What about Wes, does he think that?'

'He knows something is up, of course he does. He keeps asking me questions like why has Liz returned to New York, what's she doing there that's so urgent.'

'What do you say?'

'What can I say?' James asked. 'I go along with the story line.'

Geoff nodded. 'Well, anyway, the *Guardian* piece was good.'

James agreed. 'It mentioned my new book at the end, maybe that'll help sales a bit.'

'And now,' Geoff said, 'I have to love you and leave you.'

'What is it, a date?' James asked, showing him out. 'Who's the unlucky woman?'

'Another doctor.' Geoff grinned, from ear to ear. 'Apart from that my lips are sealed.'

'God help her then,' James replied, waving him away.

'Is there something up, Dad?' Wessley asked later that night.

'Shouldn't you be in bed?' James looked up from his pages of typescript.

'I came down to get a drink,' Wessley explained, sitting down next to James on the sofa. 'Is there?' he asked again.

'No,' James assured him, 'what could be wrong?'

'Mum going away like that.'

'What did she tell you on the phone?' James asked.

'That she'd see us in a few days.'

'There you are then.' James grinned. 'Now, go to bed.'

Wessley turned to him. 'You would tell us though, wouldn't you?'

'Yes,' James assured him, 'now skedaddle, you've got school in the morning.'

Wessley grinned at last and, kissing his father on the cheek, left the room and started up the stairs.

'What about your drink?' James called after him.

'I'm not thirsty anymore,' Wessley replied, running up the last few steps.

He met Ruby at their usual restaurant. It was raining and James had worn his long white trench coat which had dripped water all down his black jeans. Ruby was late, dashing into the small room, almost poking out a waiter's eye with her umbrella.

'I'm sorry I've been so long in contacting you,' she began, 'I haven't been avoiding you or anything.'

'I know that.' James smiled.

'We've really had our work cut out rearranging things since Liz decided to front our New York office.'

'Before Liz decided to run off with Howard Sands, you mean,' he said.

'Yes.' Ruby fiddled with the menu. 'So, where have you been?'

'I've just come from my publisher's office, delivering the proofs of my next masterwork.'

'Then we should celebrate,' Ruby smiled, 'I've got some good news as well.'

'I can't think what it might be.' James laughed. 'You're not, are you?'

Ruby nodded. 'It's just been confirmed. Pregnant at last, you're only the . . .' she paused to think for a moment, '. . . third person to know.'

'So, life as you know it is about to change for ever, eh?'

'I hope so.' Ruby laughed. 'Benjamin's pleased, too, thank God!'

James reached across the small table and kissed her cheek. 'It's marvellous news,' he said.

'Yes, I can still hardly believe it.'

'Does Liz know?' he asked.

'She was the second person.' Ruby grinned.

The waiter arrived to take their orders and, after he'd gone, James asked Ruby about Howard Sands. 'You don't have to tell me anything if you don't want, but there's no use pretending that I'm not interested,' he admitted.

'I'm not sure I know much,' Ruby told him. 'Besides, you've met him, don't you remember? That dinner we all had together last year?'

'Oh yes, the spouses were allowed to join the grown-ups.'

'James,' Ruby warned him, 'don't be mean.'

'Did you know about them?' he asked.

'This is embarrassing,' she said, fiddling with a napkin.

'Come on, Ruby,' James coaxed her.

'Liz told me, of course . . . I sometimes wish she hadn't.'

'Were you surprised?'

'Yes.'

'So, tell me, what's he like?'

Ruby took a deep breath. 'Handsome, accomplished, successful, rich . . . extremely rich, divorced, powerful, direct, sophisticated,' she looked at James, 'get the picture?'

James nodded. 'I get the picture.'

'I tried to stop her, James. I tried to make her see sense.'

'They seem to have a great deal in common.'

234

'Oh, James,' Ruby gasped, 'I didn't mean it to sound like that, I wasn't making a direct comparison or anything.'

'That's all right, Ruby, I asked for it.'

'What will you do now?' she asked.

'The boys still don't know the truth,' he replied, 'that's something I still have to face.'

'Isn't Liz going to speak with them?'

James shrugged. 'Who knows what Liz is going to do?' He stopped talking as the waiter brought their first course. 'Well,' he began again, 'it looks as though it's catching, doesn't it?'

Ruby looked confused. 'What?'

'Everyone changing their partners, first you and Tim, then Martha and Sammy, now Liz and me.' He broke a bread roll over his steaming dish of soup. 'How did you cope?'

'I didn't,' she admitted, 'there's no way of dealing with something like this. I was lucky, Benjamin sort of dropped into my lap, but,' she sighed, 'that was nothing short of a miracle.'

James nodded. 'You know, I've never had an affair. In all the time I've been with Liz I've never done that,' he laughed at himself, 'I suppose that sounds pretty unbelievable.'

Ruby shook her head. 'I think that's the way it's supposed to be, isn't it?'

'God knows,' James said softly, 'and it's funny, you know, because my books are full of unfaithfulness, rampant men and predatory women.'

'Yes, but that's fiction, James, it's make-believe.'

'And now it's fact.' He smiled. 'What do they call it?' James asked, thinking to himself for a moment. 'Hoisted with my own petard?'

Ruby grinned. 'It just happens, James, there doesn't necessarily ever have to be an explanation.'

'People just grow tired of the same old routine, you mean.'

'You're going to be all right, James, you're going to be fine, really.'

'You think so?'

'Absolutely,' Ruby insisted, raising her glass. 'Here's to us, to you and me and my baby.' She smiled with delight, reaching across to clink their glasses together.

James grinned back, wondering all the time if Ruby could possibly be correct.

After that the time seemed to fly by. Elizabeth extended her 'working' trip to the States, phoning the boys every few days and sending them various cards which featured dramatic views of the New York skyline.

'Is Mum ever coming back?' Wessley asked him one day early in October.

James looked up from the preparation of a meal, wiping his floury hands on a tea-towel. 'Of course,' he said, 'you know how busy she is . . .'

Wessley fixed his father with a stare. 'Is there something wrong?' he asked. 'Something you're not telling us?'

'No,' James replied immediately.

'She's never been away for this long,' Wessley continued.

'Well . . . there's a lot to do, I suppose.'

'So, when *is* Mum coming home?'

'In a few days.'

'You said that two weeks ago.'

'Listen, Wes, all I know is that she can't leave at the moment, okay?'

Wessley shrugged. 'I suppose it'll have to be.'

'She's calling tomorrow evening, why don't you ask her yourself?'

'I'm always asking her . . . She just tells me it's work.'

'There you are then.'

Wessley still looked unconvinced. 'I know you think I'm still a kid but I'm not brain-damaged, I know what's been going on.'

'What's been going on, Wes?' James challenged.

'You and Mum, there's something up, it's obvious.'

'Not to me, it's not.'

'Normal parents don't spend this much time apart,' Wessley countered. 'Normal parents spend time with their kids and lead a normal life.'

'Wessley,' James warned, 'don't go on.'

'Why won't you tell us?'

'Tell you what?'

'What's wrong?'

'Nothing is wrong, *nothing*.'

'So, Mum's coming home in a few days?' Wessley asked, nodding to himself, a supercilious grin across his face.

'That's right,' he replied, turning back to the task in hand. Wessley stood at his side, unspeaking, making his presence felt however. 'Haven't you got anything better to do?' James asked at last. 'Homework, tennis practice, what about clearing up that room of yours?'

Wessley shrugged and finally slouched away without further comment.

Alexander had begun bed-wetting again and, as the weeks progressed, James noticed that Wessley stayed closer to home, hanging around, something he hadn't done for years. James began to feel guilty at the deceit to which he was party. He hated such mendacity. The signs

237

were all there, it didn't take a genius or a child psychologist to work them out. The boys were concerned, watching him like hawks, watching him for the slightest sign, the merest suggestion that he was about to depart as well.

'I can't stand this for very much longer,' he admitted to Geoff.

'So, tell them.'

'That's your simple solution? What about Liz?'

'What about her?' Geoff looked at him. 'You can't go on and on spinning a yarn . . . They have to know sometime.'

'Wes already knows,' James said quietly. 'Kids always know. If Liz isn't prepared to face the truth . . .' he allowed the sense of his statement to drift into the warm kitchen air as he looked out at the gloomy afternoon.

November the 5th fell on a Sunday that year and so James, deciding not to break with tradition, organized a bonfire party for the Saturday evening. Wessley and Alexander invited their friends and James invited Geoff, Ruby and Benjamin. The boys had had almost a month to come to terms with Elizabeth's departure by then. When he'd finally told them the reason for her move to New York Wessley had shrugged his shoulders and glared at James, as though to say 'I told you so'. There was a gleam in his eye, a certain pleasure in having known the truth all along. There had been a long silence from Elizabeth when James warned her of what he'd done and, for a while, Wessley refused to speak to her when she called. Alexander had spent the first week in floods of tears. Sometimes, as James stripped the little boy's bed each morning, taking the soaking sheets down to the washing machine, he considered that Alexander had

238

become completely water-logged. If it wasn't coming out of one end it was pouring from another. Elizabeth, having accepted the inevitable, called more frequently and tried to reassure them that everything really would be fine. It seemed an empty promise to Alexander, who started to fill his room with pictures of his mother as though frightened that he'd forget her face. James asked her to send some recent photographs of herself in the weekly letters. Elizabeth complied and soon Alexander's wall was plastered with pictures of his mother grinning in front of New York's tourist traps. Gradually life returned to a semblance of normality although, James realized, it didn't take much for tempers to explode and fights to break out. It felt very much like walking on broken glass, picking his way through the dangerous shards, gently moving his boys along, encouraging, cajoling them to live their lives, to carry on as before.

'What do you see your job as now?' Jenny had asked him.

'To provide stability,' James replied without any hesitation, 'and to prove that I'm not about to leave, to make them thoroughly secure in that understanding.'

Jenny had nodded and smiled at him. 'I think that's right.'

James, for once, felt very strong and secure within himself. 'I *know* it's right,' he said.

'What do you think?' Ruby asked Geoff as they tended the barbecue, flipping the sausages and chicken legs over, enjoying the heat from the glowing coals in the clear, frosty air. The light was fading now and the bonfire at the bottom of the garden was just starting to take hold, its flames licking around the outer edges and darting upwards through the diminishing smoke. James and Benjamin were about to supervise the firework display.

'About what?' Geoff asked.

'Don't be dense,' Ruby said, 'the situation, of course.'

'Oh, the situation.' Geoff paused in a moment of phony reflection. 'I think James is coping extremely well in the circumstances.'

Ruby nodded. 'The kids have taken it pretty badly, though.'

'Kids are resilient.' Geoff wondered just how many more clichés he could dredge up. 'They'll manage.'

'My parents divorced when I was about Wes's age and I don't think I ever got over it.'

Geoff looked skyward as the first rocket shot through the air, bursting into a cascade of bright stars above them. He laughed at the excited reaction of the assembled children, watching Alexander's beaming face as he circled around, his head tipped back to watch the splendid sight. 'What else can they do?' he asked, returning to their conversation. 'Kids go on and endure the worst of times, that's part of their wonder.'

Ruby turned the food over again. 'What about James?'

'James?' Geoff started to slice open the bread rolls. 'James is stronger than you think . . . he's stronger than *he* thinks.' Geoff smiled to himself at this and, reaching for their drinks, handed Ruby a half-glass of white wine. 'Here, drink this. Doctor's orders.'

Ruby took a few sips of the cold drink and watched as another rocket rushed into the blackness trailing red sparks as it headed for destruction.

Afterwards, when it was over, James and Wessley were left to damp down the circle of bright, red embers. Alexander had been put to bed by Geoff and Ruby was making coffee with Benjamin. Sparks flew as the final piece of wood fell in on itself. James shovelled another spadeful of earth around the edge of the fire.

'Did you enjoy the firewords, Wes?'

Wessley shrugged. 'Fireworks are for kids.'

James grinned to himself. 'I think you enjoyed yourself.'

'It was all right,' Wessley grudgingly admitted. 'Dad?' he asked after a pause.

'Yes?' James rested on the spade, looking across the crimson circle of fire. 'What is it?'

'What's going to happen?'

'Happen?'

Wessley nodded. 'Yes, to us, Alexander and me.'

'Nothing's going to happen.' James laughed at the suggestion. 'What do you mean?'

'It doesn't matter,' Wessley grumbled.

'Tell me,' James encouraged gently.

'If you and Mum divorce . . . what happens to the house and everything?'

'It's far too early for all of that, besides, nothing's going to change . . . At least not in the way you mean. We're not planning to sell the house, Wes, I'm not planning on moving anywhere either, if that's what you mean.' He finished his task and, pushing the spade into soft earth, walked back towards the house, his arm around Wessley's shoulders. Wessley stopped dead as they approached the patio steps where, above them, framed in the bright kitchen lights, Elizabeth stood watching them through the darkness.

Chapter 15

In the cold, blue light of dawn Elizabeth stepped out of the warm Camden house onto the frosty patio. She wandered across the white grass down to the bottom of the garden where the grey bonfire ashes were still warm, kicking over spent firework cases as she walked around it. Even with jet-lag Elizabeth hadn't been able to sleep much. Her thoughts kept returning to the last few days in New York.

Howard hadn't seemed surprised when she'd told him of her decision to return. They arrived back at his apartment from some awful dinner party on Fifth Avenue, and Elizabeth recalled the rustle of her black taffeta silk dress across the floor. He'd leant over and kissed her bare shoulders, making some comment about another success-ful evening.

'It isn't working,' she said, abruptly.

'What isn't?'

'Us, this situation.'

'We're doing fine,' he replied, starting to undress.

'I'm going home,' she announced.

Howard shrugged and fell onto the bed, watching as she removed the long, black dress. 'Do you mean home as in England or as in your apartment?'

'London, where my children are.'

'Where your husband lies,' he replied with a smirk.

Elizabeth ignored him and went into the bathroom where she removed her make-up and cleaned her teeth.

When she returned, ready to continue the discussion, Howard was already fast asleep.

There had never been an argument. Howard seemed to brood over the problem for a while and then told Elizabeth that she'd miss him. It had taken a day or so.

'I will,' Elizabeth agreed.

'Why leave?' he asked reasonably. 'Your boys could come here, easy as that.' He snapped his fingers.

'I don't want them here.' It must have sounded very ungrateful, Elizabeth thought, extremely ungracious.

'Why did you come to New York?'

'I wanted to be with you . . . And there was a job to be done.'

'You wanted to be with me,' he repeated, almost to himself, 'but not for ever.'

'You knew it wouldn't last for ever, nothing ever does.' She'd examined Howard as he fell across her, stroking a hand over the hard muscles of his shoulders.

'Why don't you love me more?' he asked, his face buried in a pillow.

Elizabeth forced his head around, taking it between her hands, staring at him. 'You're such a brute, Howard,' she told him, grinning all the same, 'you go out there and fight your bloody wars and,' she paused to think, '. . . you have absolutely everything . . .' Elizabeth broke away and moved from the bed to the window, looking out across the sparkling city of lights. 'You have everything,' she repeated.

'Don't you?'

Elizabeth peered across towards the Chrysler Building with its distinctive lights and Art Deco shape, the familiar cresting and jagged casements. 'I have to be near Wessley and Alexander.'

243

'Wessley and Alexander,' Howard breathed, 'what ridiculous names.'

Elizabeth ignored the jibe and turned back to him. 'I suppose you'll hate me for ever now.'

'Don't be ridiculous.' Howard shook his head in disbelief. 'You're so totally married, Liz, you and James, like Siamese twins, unable to part, joined at the heart.'

She walked to the bed and draped herself across him. 'Why didn't we have a courtship?' she asked suddenly.

'Didn't we?'

'Over office desks and in yellow-cabs . . .'

'. . . and London taxis . . .'

Elizabeth was forced to laugh. 'Boardroom to bedroom . . . I know, I know,' her voice trailed away into a husky whisper, 'I know all of that.'

'So, what did you want?'

'I wanted you . . . Jesus, I wanted you and I wanted us to have met twenty years before . . . it's just so impossibe to undo everything, to release the past.'

'You could if you wanted,' he said, rearing up suddenly and looking intently into her eyes. 'What are you going to do in six months' time when you find out that you've made this huge mistake, when you really miss me?'

'Then, I'll miss you,' she said simply. 'I have to go home.'

Elizabeth's eyes filled with tears at these memories, and she crept back into the house, making a cup of tea before returning to bed.

When she woke again it was late morning and the house was quiet. She dressed quickly and walked along the landing, peering tentatively around Wessley's door before stepping inside his room and looking down into the garden. Wessley was slouched on a patio chair, the old one her mother had given them years before, the only one they never stored in the winter. He was muffled up against the cold in a black tracksuit, his tennis racket at his side. She decided to confront him before he had a chance to escape once more and, turning, ran down the staircase.

Wessley looked up as she stepped out of the house, looking distinctly uncomfortable.

'Hello, Wes,' Elizabeth began, hands deep in pockets as she walked across to him. 'Playing today?' She turned away for a moment, surveying the garden.

Wessley nodded. 'Dad's taken Alexander over to Geoff's . . . He's done a painting of us all in Majorca.'

'That's nice.' Elizabeth grinned. 'I'm afraid that I rather surprised everyone last night.'

Wessley shrugged but made no comment, picking up his racket and turning it over and over in his hands.

'I rather surprised myself, too,' she continued, 'if it's any consolation.'

'Why have you come?' He was uncomfortably direct.

'To be with you all, to live here again, to work.'

'Did Dad say it was all right?'

'He didn't say it wasn't.'

'You didn't give him much of a chance,' Wessley snapped, 'just arriving like that.'

'This is my home, Wes,' Elizabeth answered, feeling panicky now, a little unsure of herself.

'You walked out of it and left us,' he reminded her. 'We weren't told anything then, either.'

'You don't understand these things,' Elizabeth began, clutching at straws.

'What things?' Wessley asked, openly hostile now. 'You mean like running off with another man?'

Elizabeth didn't answer. She stared at him, at his angry, handsome face, wondering at the beauty there and the

245

flickering hate. 'I made a mistake, Wes, I'm sorry for that.'

'I don't know why you ever bothered to live here. We never saw anything of you before and Dad doesn't need you, he can manage all right. You only upset everything.' He stood up to leave.

'Wessley!' Elizabeth found her voice at last.

They stood for a moment staring at one another before Wessley broke the awful spell and walked away.

'Wessley,' Elizabeth said to herself, feeling utterly defeated as she slumped down onto the hard chair swallowing back tears that threatened to consume her.

Ruby turned up in the late afternoon. 'What's going on?' she demanded, tossing her long, purple woollen coat over the back of the sofa.

'I'm back,' Elizabeth replied.

'You look awful,' Ruby commented, looking closely at her friend.

'Thanks.'

'What a bloody fool,' Ruby sighed.

'What, for returning?'

'For everything.'

'Aren't you glad? Everything you warned me about came true.'

Ruby looked sternly at her friend. 'How was New York?'

'Oh, Ruby, really.'

'Was it as attractive as you thought once you were living there?'

'New York is fine.'

There was a long silence between them. 'Good,' Ruby said at last. 'You should never have gone, of course.' She looked more closely at Elizabeth. 'What has James said?'

'We've hardly had a chance to say anything yet.'

'God knows you don't deserve him, but he'll forgive you no doubt, that's what he's good at, isn't it?'

'Why are you being so bloody?' Elizabeth demanded. 'You're supposed to be on my side.'

'Don't be ridiculous, Liz, we're not twelve years old, this isn't a game.'

'Well, I don't intend to beg for forgiveness, not from James, not from my kids, certainly not from you.'

Ruby continued to fix Elizabeth with a penetrating stare. 'What happened to Howard Sands? Did he throw you out?'

'No, not like James when I left. He wrecked our bedroom, did you know . . .?'

'Some men might have taken out their anger in other ways,' Ruby said darkly.

'Oh, and I suppose that would have been all right. A broken jaw and a black eye would have been justifiable in the circumstances, I suppose.'

'Of course not, but what did you expect James to do? Drive you to the airport?'

'Don't be ridiculous.'

'Tell me what happened,' Ruby insisted, ignoring Elizabeth's indignation.

'Nothing happened . . . you were right all along, it would never have worked out, and so here I am, home again and waiting for the verdict, to stay or not to stay. James is over at Geoff's, I suppose he'll make a decision there . . . The jury is out . . .'

'And you're here to stay for good?'

'If James doesn't throw me out.'

'There's not much chance of that,' Ruby replied. 'James is too kind, besides, don't you actually own this house?'

247

'God, you can be a bitch at times,' but she smiled all the same.

Ruby smiled too. 'You've put this family through something, Liz.'

'I had to go.'

'So you keep saying.'

'Is my office still vacant or have you and Nick taken it over?'

'It's still there, with your name on the door and everything. What happens about New York now?'

'Nothing, Howard said he'll find my replacement for us.'

'Business as usual then.'

'Business as usual,' Elizabeth agreed.

'And, are you over Howard?'

Elizabeth looked into Ruby's eyes. 'No, not really.'

'So, what's all of this then?'

'I never stopped loving James.'

'You just fell in love with another man.'

'You don't think that's possible?'

'It doesn't matter what I think, Liz, it's what's true that matters.'

'I'm here with my family, now and forever. Once Wes stops hating me things will calm down. They'll never be quite the same, but perhaps that's a good thing.'

'Why didn't you tell me you were coming home?' Ruby asked.

Elizabeth thought for a moment before answering. 'It wasn't something I'd thought about – it just happened. I looked at Howard one day and knew, I just knew, this wasn't to be.' She smiled. 'None of it makes any sense, but you know that, don't you.'

Ruby laughed at last. 'Jesus, but you're a hopeless case, Liz, absolutely hopeless.'

'Don't judge me too harshly, just because your impending motherhood has made you suddenly so awfully worldly-wise, everyone is entitled to make mistakes now and again.'

'Yes, they might dent the car or smash a milk bottle . . . Anyway, Howard Sands wasn't a mistake, was he? I thought he was the love of your life.'

'You're just trying to make me feel worse.'

'Yes,' Ruby agreed, taking Elizabeth's hand in between her own and smiling at such frailty.

Elizabeth was in her room unpacking when Wessley came up to see her.

'Dad says that I should apologize,' he told her, standing just inside the door.

'That's all right.'

'I'm sorry anyway.'

'Thank you.'

'I still don't think you should have left Dad, though.'

Elizabeth nodded. 'I think you made that clear.'

'It was wrong,' he continued.

'Right.' Elizabeth sat down on the bed. 'I don't expect you to understand now, Wes, but perhaps, when you're older, you'll see that life isn't quite as simple as we'd like to think it is.'

Wessley didn't reply.

'I know it's what parents always say to their kids, but in this case it's true.'

'Are you all right?' he asked.

Elizabeth smiled. She looked into his beautiful black eyes. 'I know, I look a fright, Ruby already very kindly informed me of that fact.'

'No, I mean, are you really all right?'

'Yes.' She laughed. 'I'm absolutely fine.'

249

'Good. Well, Dad says that supper will be ready soon, so I'd better wash my hands and stuff.'

Elizabeth watched him leave. Perhaps this was a truce, the place from where they moved on. She hoped with all her heart that it was.

'I suppose if the boys turn into delinquents,' Elizabeth began later that night, 'then it will all be down to me.'

'The boys are fine,' James insisted.

'No thanks to me.'

'I'm pleased you're home,' James said.

'Are you?'

'Of course,' he smiled, 'what a question.'

Elizabeth took his hand as they sat together on the comfortable old sofa, tracing a forefinger along his life-line. 'I wanted to come back, it was all I could think about in the end.'

'Are we to pick up the pieces and go on as before?'

'What do you want?'

'I want you to think about what you're doing,' he told her.

'I have thought,' she assured him. 'Oh, I know you can all manage without me . . . Well, I suppose that's right, I mean, I read that *Guardian* piece about you after all . . .'

James grinned, standing up and pouring them both a nightcap. 'You read Marilyn's piece?' He sounded pleased. 'How did you get hold of that?'

'Ruby sent me a copy,' Elizabeth replied, watching as the golden liquid splashed into the glasses, smelling the aroma of good whisky. 'It was meant to make me feel even more guilty.' She took the offered glass and took a first sip.

James laughed. 'It's not true, we can't manage without

you,' he raised his glass, clinking it against hers, 'you know that.'

'I don't know anything anymore,' she replied hopelessly.

'Yes, you do,' James laughed even harder, 'you know *everything*, Liz.'

Elizabeth laughed too, putting her head back and rocking with laughter until the tears began to fall.

They slept together that night and Elizabeth woke up no longer feeling as though a heavy weight was pressed up against her heart. James reached over and kissed her gently on the lips.

'What are you thinking?' he asked.

'That this bedroom needs redecorating.' She looked up at the large stain on the wallpaper above their bed.

'I think we should leave it as a sign of the times.'

'It's what brought me back, in a way,' she admitted.

'What, a broken bottle of Chanel and a suitcase through the window?' He slipped out of bed and put his robe on.

Elizabeth smiled at this description although she knew how terrified she'd felt at the time. 'It made me think that, perhaps, you really did want me after all.'

James stood at the end of the bed looking at her. 'It was awful, I know, I'm sorry. Jenny says that anger isn't always negative, it's just another useful emotion.'

'So I have Jenny to thank.'

He shrugged. 'Who knows . . . The boys,' he explained, leaving the bedroom, 'time to get them up.'

Elizabeth got up a little later in time to see them off.

'Aren't you going to work anymore, Mummy?' Alexander asked, pulling on his blazer.

Elizabeth straightened his tie. 'I'm having a holiday, a few days off.'

'But you've just had a holiday, haven't you?' Alexander asked, confused.

'Not exactly,' she answered, brushing some fluff from his shoulder.

The little boy shrugged. 'Will you still be here when we get back?'

'Of course.' Elizabeth grinned.

'Good.'

Elizabeth stood at the front door, feeling a little fraudulent as she waved them away. She returned to the warmth of the kitchen where she made fresh coffee ready for James's return and looked through the morning papers. Elizabeth wondered if this was a routine, a way of life, that would be possible for her to bear. It was an idea that soon flickered and died.

When James came back they had breakfast together as Mrs Reed started to vacuum the lounge.

'Were you late?' she asked him.

'No, we got there with a few minutes to spare.' He looked up from the *Guardian*. 'How are you?'

'Tired, otherwise absolutely fine,' she assured him. 'Nothing changes after all, does it?'

'The more things change the more they remain the same,' James replied, 'or words to that effect.'

'Don't you mind?'

'That things don't really change?'

'About me.'

'It's over, isn't it?'

'I'm here to stay,' she replied, not answering his question directly, 'for the duration.' Their eyes met but neither smiled. Mrs Reed bustled through to fetch a floor mop and then disappeared once more.

'Are you going to work today?' he asked.

Elizabeth shook her head.

'That's not like you.'

'Perhaps that's a good sign.'

James shrugged his shoulders. 'What do you want to do now, Liz?'

'You mean today or for the remainder of my life?'

'Whichever,' he replied, not taking his eyes off her face.

'Today, I rest. Right now,' she said, picking up her paper, 'I'm going back to bed for an hour or two.' She touched his shoulder as she passed by. 'And tomorrow,' she grinned to herself, 'to quote that other scarlet woman, "is another day".'

James took her hand. 'You don't get away with it as easily as that.'

'What do you mean?' she asked, laughing.

'Are you going to be happy now?'

'God, don't ask that.'

'Too late.'

'Are you?' She turned the question back on him.

'I was first.'

Elizabeth thought for a moment. 'Everything I have is here, James, everything I want now.'

James nodded and let her go. 'And the future?'

'We're going to be all right,' Elizabeth insisted. 'Let's just take it one day at a time, let's not rush into any decisions about anything.' She left him, smiling at Mrs Reed, who was dusting the hallway, before climbing the familiar steps up to her room.

Elizabeth felt shattered. She was home now and that seemed to be the most important thing. The words of a letter her mother had written from the cruise-liner came into her head: '. . . whatever you've done,' the old woman wrote, 'whatever mistakes you make, you'll find that home is truly where the heart lies . . .' Elizabeth had

253

sneered at such sentiments then, but now she saw things in a different light. She had turned back and found forgiveness. As Elizabeth lay down she could hear James at work in his study overhead, pounding the keys of his old typewriter. There was great relief to be found in such continuity, such certainty, great relief at being home where, perhaps, her heart really lay. As she drifted off to sleep Elizabeth smiled because the circle had closed once again.